People
who have
changed the
World

imagined interviews

People Who Have Changed The World: Imagined Interviews
© 2022 Bernard Marin
All Rights Reserved.

No part of this book may be reproduced in any form or by any electronic or mechanical means including information storage and retrieval systems, without permission in writing from the author.
The only exception is by a reviewer, who may quote short excerpts in a review.

This book is a work of fiction. Names, characters, places, and incidents either are products of the author's imagination or are used fictitiously. Any resemblance to actual persons, living or dead, events, or locales is entirely coincidental.

Printed in Australia

First Printing: April 2022

Shawline Publishing Group Pty Ltd
www.shawlinepublishing.com.au

Paperback ISBN- 9781922701572

Ebook ISBN- 9781922701626

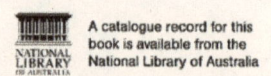

A catalogue record for this book is available from the National Library of Australia

People
who have changed the
World

imagined interviews

Bernard Marin

For my wife, Wendy; daughters, Amy and Rachel; daughter-in-law, Deb, and son-in-law, Joel; and grandchildren, Goldie, Ziggy and Millie.

BY THE AUTHOR
(These titles can be found at bernardmarin.com.au)

My Father, My Father

Good as Gold

Stories of Profit and Loss

Stories and Remembering and Forgetting

Letter to my Father

Contents

Acknowledgements ix
Author's Note xi

Preface 1
Albert Einstein 3
Marie Curie 29
Mahatma Gandhi 49
Mother Teresa 83
Sigmund Freud 99
Simone de Beauvoir 117
John Stuart Mill 141
John Maynard Keynes 169

Source of photographs 191
About the Author 193

Acknowledgements

In writing these interviews, I was fortunate to have the support of many people.

I am grateful for the help of my editors. Nan McNab's extensive work in editing these interviews has been instrumental in making them infinitely better. I have greatly benefited from her insights, counsel and assistance. She has been remarkably patient with me, nothing was too difficult, and she was a pleasure to work with. I owe a huge debt of gratitude to Sharon Lapkin for her incredibly generous support. I am truly grateful to her. She gave willingly of her time and I have benefited from her understanding, acumen and direction. She also has made this book immeasurably better.

My heartfelt thanks to Bob Sessions for his support and guidance in the editorial and publication process. I have also benefited from the endless hours of typing, retyping and researching by Noni Carr-Howard.

Finally, many friends have been there for me along this journey. They are too numerous to name – you know who you are. Thank you for your support and encouragement.

And last but not least, thank you to my family who have helped me keep everything in perspective.

Author's Note

While I have endeavoured to be rigorous in my research, I make no claim as to the factual accuracy of my portrayal of the lives and points of view of these seven historical figures. The actual encounters and conversations that appear in this book are works of the author's imagination, and the characters herein are not intended to bear any resemblance to any person now living. Like all historical fiction, the narratives in this book draw inspiration from the lives of the main characters while retaining sufficient artistic licence to enliven the stories as the author interprets and sees fit.

Preface

Biography and historical fiction have always been my great literary loves. Therefore, it only stands to reason that at some point, I would merge the two genres in a single book.

By so doing, I hope both to enlighten and entertain: enlighten by providing the reader with accurate insights into the personal characteristics, foibles and life stories of the historical figures featured in the book; entertain by delivering this information through a fictional interview format.

When writing this book, I have aimed for *verisimilitude*: the appearance of being true, natural or real. The degree to which I succeeded in each of the interviews can only be judged by you, the reader.

In preparation for writing this book, I spent hundreds of hours researching the life stories of my interview subjects. This included accessing both primary and secondary sources, documents and films – words my characters wrote themselves and words or visuals that were written or produced about them by others. The object was to establish a baseline of facts that would lend credence and plausibility to the fictionalised stories I wanted to tell.

I was equally dedicated to verisimilitude when creating my interviewers. In some cases, I chose actual historical figures who lived and worked in the same place and time. In others, I created purely fictional characters who were crafted to be plausible in terms of the interviewee's era and circumstances.

My choice of characters – both interviewers and interviewees – was personal: prominent figures in history who had long been a source of interest and fascination to me. I can only hope that by the end of this book, my readers will share those sentiments.

Bernard Marin
Melbourne, 2022

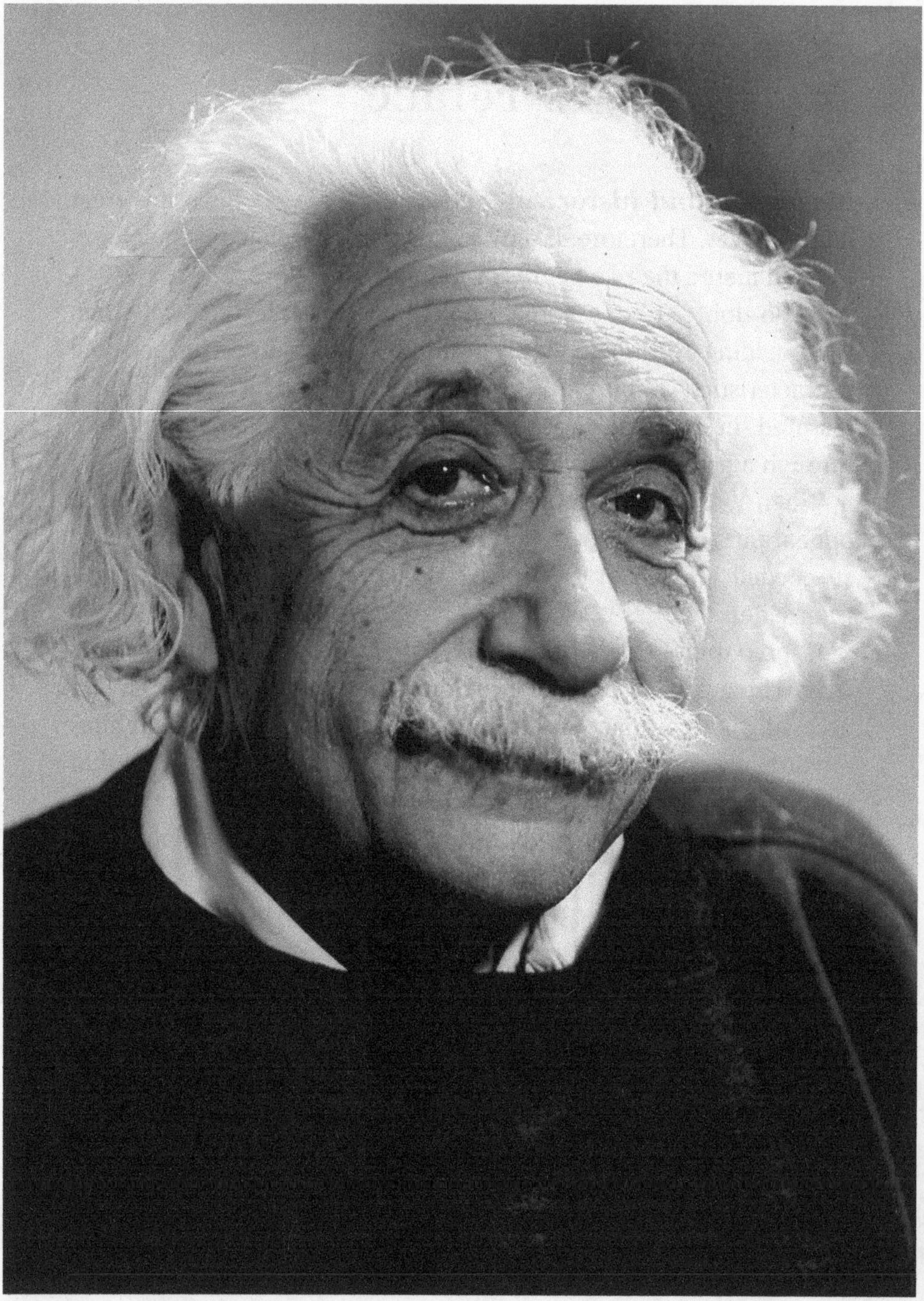

Albert Einstein

Princeton, New Jersey, United States, 15 March 1953.

The door swung open, and I was met by a middle-aged woman whose slate-grey eyes cast an inquisitive gaze through her wire-rimmed glasses.

'I'm Margot Einstein,' she said, extending her hand in greeting. Her schoolmarmish appearance was accentuated by grey-streaked hair pulled into a tight bun at the back of her head. 'Please come through. Father is expecting you.'

I followed her into the office, where I caught my first glimpse of the man I had come to see. Albert Einstein stood facing a large blackboard covered with scrawled mathematical equations. He turned towards me, his trademark bushy eyebrows arched in a quizzical expression.

'You were expecting a man, I suppose?' I said, needled by his expression.

'Well, your first name is Lee.' He brushed off the sleeves of his heavy brown knitted cardigan, sending a cloud of chalk dust into the air.

My nose began to tickle, and I feared I might sneeze.

'Spelled L-e-i-g-h,' I replied.

'My apologies. But welcome, nonetheless. I see you've met my daughter,' he said with a smile.

'Yes, she was very gracious.'

'And brilliant as well,' replied Einstein.

Margot smiled shyly. 'I'll leave you to your business, then,' she said and left the room.

'And what about you?' asked Einstein, his eyes examining the contours of my face. 'Have we met before?'

'I don't think so,' I replied.

He shook his head in puzzlement. 'There's something familiar about you ....'

'Well, be that as it may, I'm grateful that you agreed to be interviewed.'

'Yes, yes,' said Einstein. 'Just remind me where this article will be published?'

'I'm a freelance reporter, who writes primarily about scientific issues,' I replied, 'so I've pitched this interview idea to a few publications. *Time* and *The New Yorker* have shown interest. I'll keep you apprised and will send you a copy when it comes out.'

'Thank you very much,' he replied. 'Now, let's begin. Please sit.'

I pulled back the chair and sat down on the opposite side of the desk, smoothing my skirt while Einstein sat waiting, fiddling with his trademark pipe.

'All right,' I said, extracting a notepad and pen from my bag. 'Much has already been written about your theory of relativity, so, with your permission, I thought we might leave your scientific accomplishments for the time being. I'd like to begin with your family, followed by your involvement with the Hebrew University, your refusal to be president of the state of Israel and, if we have time, maybe your pacifism and the atomic bomb.'

He chuckled. 'I do get tired of speaking about $E = mc2$ over and over. To tell the truth, I'm a bit fed up with relativity. Even something so momentous can lose its lustre over time. So, I am happy not to talk physics.'

I nodded. 'Tell me about your childhood, then. Where were you born?'

'In Germany. Ulm, to be precise.'

'The scene of Napoleon's great victory,' I volunteered.

'Yes, in 1805. I see you know your history,' said Einstein with a smile. 'What year?'

'I was born in 1879. The 14th of March, to be precise.'

'Did you have a happy childhood?'

He shrugged. 'More or less. My father was in business with his brother Jakob. When I was fifteen, they moved their factory from Munich to Italy, but I stayed behind with family to finish my education.'

'Where were you studying?'

'At a gymnasium.' He broke off and said, 'I should explain for the benefit of our American readers that this is not a sports hall, but the German name for a high school with an academic orientation where students are prepared for university studies. Later, I went on to the Zurich Polytechnic, where I graduated in 1900.'

'So, you were living in Switzerland?'

'Yes. I renounced my German citizenship to avoid conscription into the army.'

'And after graduation?'

'I worked at the patent office in Bern while working on my Ph.D. I published my thesis in 1905 – almost fifty years ago – and today, people still insist on talking to me about it. But I've moved on. Now I'm more interested in general relativity, quantum theory and unified field theory. I'm also concerned with promoting nuclear control, world peace and Zionism.'

'I'm happy to leave your doctoral dissertation to others, but before we go any further, may I ask just one general question? I'm interested to know what sparked your fascination with science.'

'My father ignited my passion when he gave me a pocket compass when I was only five years old.'

I raised an eyebrow.

'It aroused my curiosity; I thought that there must be something that caused the needle to move. I suspect this is where my interest in science began.'

'Thank you for that,' I said. And now, if I may, I'd like to broach a topic that you might find a bit awkward. We've all heard the stories about your mediocre academic results. Is there any truth to them?'

He frowned slightly, then said, 'In 1896, at the age of seventeen, I left home to attend school in Zurich, Switzerland.'

I nodded, indicating for him to continue.

He smiled and said, 'I got top marks in algebra, geometry, physics and chemistry ...' He stopped to think for a moment, then continued, 'Over 80 per cent for German, Italian and natural history, and respectable passes in geography and drawing.' He gave me a confident smile.

I noted down his impressive result then said, 'Let's talk about your mother.'

His face softened. 'She was a quiet, intelligent woman ….'

'And an accomplished pianist, I believe?'

Einstein paused for a moment and studied me intently. 'Yes. Because of her, I learnt violin from the age of five. She encouraged my love of music.' He was still watching me closely, his eyes wide and gentle. 'And today, I get endless pleasure from playing Mozart and Bach on the violin.'

'And your father?'

He shifted in his chair. 'Initially, he sold feather beds.'

I scrawled notes as he went on.

'But, as I mentioned before, he later started an electrochemical factory with his brother, Jakob. They manufactured dynamos and electrical meters based on direct current and were instrumental in bringing electricity to Munich.'

'That's a big deal,' I said, impressed.

'Yes, and in 1885, they won the contract to provide direct-current lights to illuminate the Octoberfest for the first time.'

His brown eyes were warm as he remembered his father.

'Eight years later, they lost their bid for the electrification of Munich because alternating current was increasingly replacing direct current. Their fortunes took a downward turn, and they were forced to sell their Munich factory.'

I made an appropriately sympathetic noise as I wrote.

'In 1896, they were forced to abandon their Italian factory. And six years later, having lost most of our family's money, he moved us back to Germany.' Einstein's chin dropped onto his chest, and he sighed ruefully.

'Your IQ of 160 is exceptional,' I said, shifting topics to something I hoped he would find more congenial.

Einstein smiled but remained silent.

I pressed on. 'And Mileva, the mother of your children, was also extremely intelligent. It has been suggested she contributed to some of your work – discussing aspects of it with you in detail.'

Einstein glowered. 'Groundless gossip. My first wife was a smart woman, but my work is my own.'

The indignation in his tone caused me to shift uneasily in my seat.

'And what about your children?'

He was silent a long time as he bent forward and looked down at the floor. Then, with an edge of sadness in his voice, he said, 'Eduard was a promising medical student but developed schizophrenia and has been institutionalised for a large part of his life.' The lines around his eyes deepened, and he slumped in his chair as if he carried the burden of his sick son like a dead weight. 'Unfortunately, the primitive treatments he was subjected to deeply affected his cognitive abilities.'

I nodded, not knowing what to say.

'I wish there were something I could do,' he sighed.

After a long moment, I said, 'And your other son, Hans?'

Einstein's face relaxed into a smile of paternal pride. 'He is a brilliant scientist – a professor of hydraulic engineering at the University of California, Berkeley, and the world's foremost expert on sediment transport.'

'That's impressive,' I said. 'I see he makes you proud.' I flipped a page on my notebook and said, 'Now let's turn to the Hebrew University if you don't mind.'

He nodded. 'It is something very close to my heart.'

'Indeed. You were one of the founders of the university, I believe.'

'That's correct.'

'And you served on the first university board of governors, along with Sigmund Freud and Chaim Weizmann, correct?'

Another nod of confirmation.

'And you were also the honorary chairman of the board of trustees?'

'Correct again,' replied Einstein. 'I commend you for your background research.'

'You were also chairman of its academic committee and very involved in raising funds for the university's development.'

'Yes, in 1923, I visited Mount Scopus, where I gave the first scientific lecture at the university to help raise money.'

'I know. I was there.'

'Ah-ha!' said Einstein, his brown eyes flashing with interest. 'So perhaps we met there?'

'No, I was sitting at the back of the lecture theatre. Back then, I was just an anonymous young science student.'

'Now you're writing for *Newsweek*,' he said with a grin.

'So we hope,' I said, my deadpan tone intended to convey modesty. 'I understand that the campus on Mount Scopus in Jerusalem was opened on 1 April 1925?'

'Yes, there was a gala ceremony attended by the Earl of Balfour and many other dignitaries, distinguished scholars, leaders of the Jewish community, and so on. I published a manifesto – *The Mission of our University*. I stated that the opening of the university was an event that should not only fill us with pride but should also inspire us to serious reflection.'

'In what way?' I asked.

'It is a significant place of higher learning. My hopes for the university were that it would develop into a great spiritual centre and arouse the respect of mankind worldwide.'

His eyes moved to the cluster of papers on his desk, then back to me as he continued. 'I felt we had a responsibility to future generations to build a great centre of learning. A university where the human spirit can manifest itself, where science and investigation recognise truth as their aim, and where Israel can develop economic and political independence.'

I raised my hand and interjected. 'Investigation?'

'Perhaps enquiry would be a better word,' said Einstein. 'Even after all these years in America, I sometimes struggle to find the precise English word.'

'*Forschung*?'

'Precisely,' he affirmed with a grin. 'Your German must be good.'

'Thank you,' I replied. 'But please continue.'

'I am proud of the accomplishments of the university throughout the nearly thirty years of its existence – its achievements have been amazing, and I have great hopes for it and for Israel's progress.'

'I understand you have bequeathed your manuscript archive and the copyright of your works to the university.'

'Yes, I have implicit trust and confidence that the university will safeguard them and make them available to the world.'

Outside, a muffled car horn sounded in the distance, and then another pitched higher.

'You describe yourself as a Jew and a Zionist,' I prompted.

'My parents were Jewish, but they were not practising – they worked on Shabbat and ate *treyf* – even shellfish and pork. They even sent me to a Catholic school!' he said, sounding annoyed.

I was surprised by the vehemence of his response. 'And you didn't care for this?'

Einstein's face flushed. 'I hated it, despised it – I've never reconciled myself to this. For a while, I was a devout Jew. I observed the sabbath, festivals and high holy days. But later in life, even though I no longer practised Judaism, I didn't tolerate people calling me an atheist either.'

'I'm not sure I understand,' I said.

He raised his head and looked directly at me. 'Yes, to answer your question, I'm a proud Jew and a Zionist. I joined the Zionist movement in 1919 and have been a long-time advocate for the establishment of a sanctuary for the Jewish people. But I am not fond of nationalism, so I did not support the notion of a Jewish state.'

He glanced out the window as the car horn sounded again, then turned back to me. 'The bond that has united the Jews for thousands of years and that unites them today is the democratic ideal of social justice, coupled with the ideal of mutual aid and tolerance among all men.'

I nodded. 'But aren't ideals one thing and reality something else entirely?'

'Quite true,' he replied. 'Some might ask how we could displace the Arabs. Some might say that a Jewish homeland where a majority of the population is Arab would be unjust and impractical.'

'And have you reached a conclusion?' I asked.

Einstein sighed. 'It's a devilish problem.'

'I'm also Jewish,' I said, hoping to enhance the rapport between us.

He smiled and asked, 'Are you practising?'

'I would describe my adoptive parents as cultural Jews rather than religious Jews. So, we celebrated Sabbath and the high holy days, but we didn't attend synagogue regularly.'

Einstein adjusted his glasses for a moment. 'Adoptive parents?' he asked finally.

'I was adopted at birth,' I replied, embarrassed to find my throat constricting.

'Are you at peace with that?'

I shrugged. 'I had loving parents. How many people can say that?'

Einstein continued to gaze at me over the top of his glasses, raising his eyebrows in an unspoken question.

I felt my eyes grow moist and looked down at my notebook. 'Sometimes I have a good cry if I need to,' I confessed. 'At other times, I'm angry, even bitter, but that never lasts long. I try to concentrate on all the good things in my life. And I spend many hours a day writing ... I love it.'

Einstein smiled and said, 'The way you bring meaning into your life is by doing something that gives you a purpose. It's the same for me with science.'

I nodded in agreement. 'I bury myself in my work. Writing has been my lifeline, my oxygen; when I see my stories in print, I know that, in at least one way, I am alive. And I like to think readers are nourished by my articles. You never know who will read them, and....'

My voice trailed off, and Einstein's expression shifted to concern.

'What is it?' he asked.

I shook my head and said nothing.

'Say it.' He smiled. 'Have courage!'

I took a breath. 'Even today, I dream that one day they'll realise and come back to fetch me.'

He fell silent, perhaps embarrassed by my confession.

After a few moments, I cleared my throat. 'I'm sorry. We got distracted. We were talking about Zionism.'

Einstein's smile seemed to betray his relief that the conversation was moving to a less personal plane. 'Yes. Well, long before the emergence of Hitler, I made the cause of Zionism mine because I saw it as a means of correcting a blatant wrong.'

'What wrong do you mean?'

'He leaned forward in his seat. 'The Jewish people have for centuries been victimised, denied all the rights and protections that most people enjoy. We know now that millions of Jews perished during the Second World War because there was no place on the globe where they could find sanctuary.'

I was about to speak, but my throat had tightened, and I began to cough. 'I'm sorry. As a young girl, I developed asthma, and it has stayed with me.' My voice sounded hoarse, and my breathing became audibly laboured.

'I know how troubling that can be,' he said, in a tone that bespoke concern for my wellbeing. 'Mileva, my first wife, suffered from asthma.'

I fixed my eyes on the blackboard behind him, which might as well have been in Hebrew for all the sense I could make of the algorithms scrawled on it. After several moments, I began to breathe more easily.

'Can I get you something?' he asked. 'Water?'

I shook my head. 'I'm fine. Please continue.'

Einstein paused, perusing me for several moments before nodding. 'Well, it's my view that Zionism offered the means to end this discrimination and suffering. That Jews would no longer be pariahs if they returned to the land of their ancestors.'

'I see.' I consulted my notes. 'So when President Harry Truman recognised Israel in May 1948, you declared it the fulfilment of the Jewish dream. And you supported unlimited Jewish immigration to Palestine. Can you elaborate?'

'That's right,' he said, peering over the top of his glasses as if to ensure I really was all right. 'I regret the constant state of animosity that exists between Israel and the Arab states. But such tension can hardly be avoided in view of the nationalistic attitude of both sides. It's tragic,' he said, exhaling in a loud sigh.

'And what about the presidency? The first president of Israel, Chaim Weizmann, described you as "the greatest Jew alive" and wanted you to be his successor. You would have been a very popular choice, despite your ... ah ...age.'

He laughed. 'There's no need to dance around the issue of how old I am. But when Chaim Weizmann died in November last year, Abba Eban, Israel's Ambassador to the United States, also wrote to me. He said he was acting under the instructions of Prime Minister David Ben-

Gurion and asked me if I would accept an offer to serve as president of the state of Israel. He added that should I accept the position, I would be required to relocate to Israel and accept Israeli nationality.'

I nodded. 'And?'

'I was moved by the offer and at once saddened and ashamed that I could not accept it. I would have been free to continue my scientific work, but ...'

He fell silent for a time as I consulted my list of questions, but before I could speak, he forged on.

'All my life, I have dealt with scientific matters; hence, I lack both the natural aptitude and the experience to deal properly with people and to perform adequately at official functions.'

'But I find you quite charming,' I said, only half in jest.

He laughed. 'That's because you've never seen me arguing with bureaucrats. That's why I am completely unsuited to high political office.'

'Fair enough,' I said. 'But I'd now like to move on to a more sensitive issue.'

Einstein was silent, gazing quizzically at me as he waited for me to continue.

'I'd like to ask you about your first wife, Mileva. In particular, about your divorce.'

He extended his right palm in a pre-emptive 'stop' gesture.

'I'm prepared to say this, and no more. When Mileva and I were divorced in 1919, I made provision for her financial support. At the time, it had been made reasonably clear that I was in line for the Nobel Prize, something that happened two years later, in 1921. So, I agreed to put the Nobel money into a trust account that would generate interest for Mileva and the boys.'

'And how much was this?' I smiled apologetically. 'My readers will want to know.'

Einstein's grimace betrayed his growing annoyance. 'Just over 120,000 Swedish Kronor.'

'A respectable sum,' I observed in a conciliatory tone.

'Indeed, it was. Until the entire amount was lost during the Depression.'

'That's terrible,' I commiserated.

Einstein shrugged. 'That's all I have to say on that topic.'

I nodded my agreement. 'Very well. You have been a lifelong pacifist –' I began, but just then, there was a knock on the door.

'Come in,' he said.

I turned as a different middle-aged woman in a white blouse, and black skirt entered the room carrying a tray with crackers and cheese, a pot of tea, two cups and a jug of water with two glasses. She smiled. 'I thought you might like some refreshment,' she said, holding out the tray.

'Thank you.' Einstein pushed aside the pile of papers and magazines to make space on the desk.

After the woman left, Einstein busied himself with the tea for a few moments, then said, 'Let me ask you something.'

'Of course,' I replied.

'Will you tell me about your adoptive parents?'

I blanched. 'Forgive me. I don't make a habit of talking about myself or about my parents. Especially with people I've only just met. I apologise for my unprofessional lapse earlier.'

He waved away my apology and urged softly, 'Make an exception.' I looked him in the eye and thought for a long moment. He was easy to talk to, and he seemed interested.

'After all the questions I've asked you, I suppose it would only be fair. I was adopted by a Jewish family. My adoptive father was a tailor, and he and my adoptive mother were very poor, uneducated people. We lived in a small two-bedroom apartment on public assistance much of the time. It was dark and cramped. Sometimes, to make money, my younger brother stood at the corner of the street hawking magazines, turning whatever money he made over to my mother to buy food.'

'That must have been difficult,' Einstein observed with a sage nod.

'Yes, it was. At times, when we sat at the dinner table, there was only bread to eat. My mother would sing to me in Yiddish when she tucked me into bed. She was warm and loving, and I took comfort from her voice.'

He picked up one cup of tea and handed it to me without a word.

'Thank you,' I replied as I took a delicate sip, careful not to burn my mouth. 'Despite our circumstances, my parents would accept nothing but excellence in my schoolwork. Perhaps because they saw education as the only escape from poverty. At night, I sat with my brother by the lamp at the kitchen table, and we studied.'

He examined my face and said, 'Your parents must be very proud of you.'

'Yes, I suppose they were ….' I continued.

'And you came to America when?' he asked.

'So my accent isn't as good as I thought it was,' I said, smiling, then added briskly, 'But that's enough about me. I read that you are a pacifist.'

Einstein shrugged. 'There is nothing that is more important or closer to my heart than pacifism.'

He turned in his swivel chair, took a book from the shelf behind him, and showed me the cover. It was about Gandhi.

'I have been a pacifist all my life and regard Gandhi as the greatest political figure of our age. My views are virtually identical to his.'

He paused to take a sip of tea. 'I do not recognise brute force as a legitimate solution to international conflicts. But before I go on, I'd like to hear how you became a journalist.'

'It was completely contrary to my parents' wishes. I rejected medicine because I didn't like the sight of blood and law because I didn't like lawyers.'

Einstein chuckled and nodded.

'At university, I began to write a regular column for the student newspaper and managed to publish the odd article in various journals. Eventually, I just became a freelance columnist. I enjoyed writing so much that I subsequently did a master's degree in journalism. But let's get back to Gandhi and your pacifism.'

'Fine, fine,' he said, holding up his palms in a signal of surrender. 'Proceed with your questions.'

'Despite your pacifist views, following the rise of Adolf Hitler, you became a vocal advocate for military preparedness. How do you reconcile that?'

Einstein ran a hand through his hair, leaving it more dishevelled than before. He said nothing, so after several seconds I continued to probe.

'What about your Two Percent Plan? According to that, nations would be unable to wage war if one in fifty men refused to serve in the military – is that your belief?' I asked.

Einstein took off his reading glasses and stared across the room for a moment. 'I recognised the dangers of Nazi Germany gaining an advantage over the Allies.'

He paused again before speaking, this time in a sharper tone. 'It was necessary to fight Hitler. He attempted to destroy an entire people.'

I nodded my emphatic agreement. 'You'll get no argument from me.'

'Think of what would have happened had Germany been victorious. You may be sure that the last remnants of the Jewish people would have been destroyed, along with personal freedom throughout Europe.'

Einstein's eyes began to glitter with tears. He pulled a handkerchief from his pocket and wiped his face.

'I'm sorry you find this so upsetting,' I said.

He shook his head. 'No, no. The plain fact was that Germany posed a grave threat to Europe and the survival of its people. That threat could not be combated by moral means alone; it could only be met by organised might. To prevent the greater evil, it was necessary that the lesser evil – the hated military – be accepted for the time being. Had the German army prevailed, life would not have been worth living anywhere in Europe.'

'Is that why you regard yourself as a convinced pacifist rather than an absolute pacifist?' I asked, reaching for my cup of tea.

He nodded. 'Yes, as I said, I am convinced that there are circumstances in which the use of force is appropriate – in the face of an enemy bent on destroying my people and me, or any people.'

Einstein fell silent as the light inside the room dimmed; he looked tired and drawn. I glanced out the window at the slate-grey sky dominated by a building bank of cumulus clouds.

'Are you all right to continue?' I asked.

'For a bit longer,' he replied.

'Thank you. At the end of the Second World War, you once again became a vocal activist for world peace, warning of the dangers of a military mentality.'

'Today, the existence of this mentality is more dangerous than ever because the weapons that are available to aggressor nations have become much more powerful.'

'Because we now have nuclear weapons?' I asked.

He stopped for a moment and, almost as an afterthought, added, 'Also, the insecurity caused by this mentality threatens our civil rights, which are being sacrificed to the alleged cause of national interest.'

I reached for my tea cup, but it had cooled. I sat back and waited for Einstein to continue.

'Governments ... everywhere... take control over teaching, research and the press, and they do not encounter the resistance that ought to otherwise serve to protect the population.'

Einstein pushed the plate of crackers and cheese across the desk towards me. 'Please. the local cheese is quite good.'

I cut a piece of the soft cheese and placed it on my tongue, so I could continue with my notetaking as he spoke.

'We must teach our children to resist military propaganda by educating them about pacifism,' Einstein said, as he nibbled absent-mindedly on a piece of cheese. 'Textbooks and our education system should not perpetuate prejudices but infuse into our children the merits of pacifism. And parents everywhere have a responsibility to sow the seeds of peace into the souls of their children.

Einstein stood up from his seat behind the desk and began to pace back and forth in lecture mode.

'Unfortunately, when those who are bound together by pacifist ideals hold a meeting, they are usually consorting only with their own kind.'

'Preaching to the converted,' I suggested.

'Precisely,' he replied. 'They are like sheep huddled together while wolves wait outside. The sheep's voices do not reach beyond this circle and are, therefore, ineffectual. That is the real weakness of the pacifist movement.'

Einstein leaned forward, picked up another piece of cheese and spread it on a cracker. Before placing it in his mouth, he looked directly into my eyes. 'How old are you?'

Taken aback, I flashed him an uneasy smile. 'Don't you know it's impolite to ask a lady about her age? But for the record, I'm fifty-one. Why do you ask?'

He closed his eyes, nodded slowly and said, 'I'm going to tell you something that nobody else knows. Well, no one except my first wife, Mileva, and her family.'

I flipped to a fresh page in my notebook, but he said, 'This is not for your notebook, my dear. Put it away.'

I did as asked, and he began to speak in a tone heavy with sorrow. 'A year before Mileva and I married, we had a daughter. Her name was Lieserl. Mileva's mother insisted we put the baby up for adoption. She worried what people would say.'

'I'm sorry to hear that,' I said, flattered that he had taken me into his confidence. 'What became of her?' I asked. 'Do you know?'

He pressed his lips together, and I watched as a tear ran down the side of his cheek. 'We never heard from her again,' he said. 'She was born in 1902—' he stopped mid-sentence and turned his face towards the window. I could see he was deep in thought. Then he turned back to me and said, 'the same year you were born.'

He looked me square in the eye, and I saw deep sorrow etched on his face. Disconcerted by the direction the conversation was taking, I was at a loss for words.

After several awkward seconds, I broke the silence. 'I'm very sorry to hear about your daughter. She would be proud to know you, I'm sure.'

Einstein shrugged but said nothing.

I pulled out my notebook and reread my last note to occupy myself. 'We were talking about pacifism,' I said quietly.

With a visible effort, he collected his thoughts and began to speak. 'Indeed. Pacifists must endeavour to act in a manner that is of practical value to the cause. Deeds, not words.'

'Is that why you support conscientious objectors?' I asked.

He cleared his throat noisily. 'Yes, under the present military system, every man is compelled to commit the crime of murder for his country. The aim of all pacifists must be to convince others of the immorality of war and rid the world of military service.'

'Is that feasible?' I asked, eyebrows raised.

Einstein smiled. 'We are hardly justified in assuming that the struggle against armaments and the spirit of militarism can be safely left in the hands of governments. We must refuse to do military service. In countries where conscription exists, the true pacifist must refuse military duty. In countries where compulsory service does not exist, true pacifists must publicly declare, in times of peace, that they will not take up arms under any circumstances.'

'Every man is responsible for what he does because he has a will and, by that will, he directs his life. There is no such thing as a man who can't help it,' I said, reciting a section from the Talmud.

His face creased in a smile of recognition. 'That's right. From the *Ethics of the Fathers* no?'

'Correct,' I replied.

Einstein again fell silent, rubbing his eyes as if his passion had drained him of energy.

'Many people who are pessimistic about the chance of avoiding war say it's human nature,' I ventured. 'Can we change human nature?'

'What do you mean by "human nature"?' he demanded.

I shrugged. 'The hates, fears and prejudices that make for wars.'

He was silent a moment. 'Human nature and war are like a river.'

I looked at him, puzzled.

Einstein smiled the pedagogical smile of an educator on the cusp of a teachable moment. 'When a river continually overflows its banks and destroys our lives and homes, do we sit down and say, "It's too bad, we can't change the river. We can do nothing about it."?' He gave me a straight look. 'No! We build a dam to keep the river in check. So, let me ask you, my dear. What type of material do we use to build this type of dam?'

I glanced up from my notebook and hesitated, not quite knowing how to respond. After a long moment of reflection, I said, 'We use reason, I suppose. Our ability to think.'

He leaned forward with a smile and patted my hand in approbation. 'That is correct. This ability to think is a part of human nature. We must foster the human capacity to reason, the ability to learn from experience and to plan ahead. A person's security and happiness depend on a well-functioning society and that, in turn, depends on the existence and observance of laws to which people must submit in order to have peace.'

'And you believe that thinking people can solve our great problem?'

Einstein pondered in silence for several seconds before speaking in a voice that resonated with a deeply held faith. 'It's our only hope. Just as we use our reason to build a dam to hold a river in check, we must now build institutions to restrain the fears and suspicions and greed that motivate people and their rulers. Such institutions must be based on law and justice. They must have control over atomic bombs and other weapons, and they must have the power to enforce that control.'

I took a deep breath. 'Yet, your name is linked to the atomic bomb.'

'I know,' he said, with a grim, purse-lipped nod. 'In 1938, I learned that three chemists working at a laboratory in Berlin had split the uranium atom and discovered that the energy released was enough to power an atomic bomb.' He looked away at the blackboard before turning back to me. 'I knew numerous technical problems would have to be overcome before such a weapon could be built.'

I nodded. 'So, what did you do?'

'In 1939, a fellow physicist, Leo Szilard, urged me to write a letter to President Roosevelt and helped me draft it. I told the president of my concerns that the Nazis were working on an atomic bomb. And I wrote of the need for America to do so as well.' Einstein stood up and walked towards the window, staring out at the bare trees in the garden. After a long moment, he returned to his desk. 'It seemed probable that the Germans had every prospect of success. If the Nazi regime had been the first to come into possession of the atomic bomb, the results would have been devastating.'

'So, you felt you had no alternative, despite being a pacifist,' I prompted.

'Precisely,' he replied. 'By 1942, this effort had become known as the Manhattan Project. I was denied a security clearance in July 1940 to work on the project, and the hundreds of scientists working on it were forbidden to consult me.'

'You were deemed a potential security risk because of your left-leaning political activism, I suppose.'

Einstein nodded.

'As I understand it, the Austrian-born physicist Lise Meitner was invited to work on that project,' I offered.

He smiled warmly and said, 'She was our Marie Curie. It was she whose discoveries led to splitting the atom and, ultimately, to the atom bomb and nuclear power.'

'But she's not well known,' I observed. 'There's almost nothing written about Lise Meitner. Why do you think that is?'

Einstein shook his head. 'Because she is a woman, I suppose, and that would make the normal scientific jealousy among her colleagues far worse. Also, she is a Jew.'

I smiled ruefully.

'But even the Nazis couldn't deny that she was the first to recognise that the $E = mc^2$ equation explained the conversion of mass into energy. Lise Meitner deserved to share Otto Hahn's 1944 Nobel Prize. It was her discovery that nuclear fission could produce a chain reaction of huge explosive power.'

'Yes,' I said with a nod of confirmation. 'And by mid-1945, the United States had developed operational nuclear weapons and used them on the Japanese cities of Hiroshima and Nagasaki, killing over 200,000 people.'

Einstein grimaced.

'Do you regret your letter to Roosevelt?' I asked in a softer tone.

He shook his head. 'Please understand that I do not consider myself the father of atomic energy. My part in it was quite indirect. Nevertheless, had I known that the Germans would not succeed in developing an atomic bomb, I would have done nothing, like Lise Meitner.'

'So, when she was invited to work on the Manhattan Project ...?' I prompted.

'She declined, saying, "I will have nothing to do with a bomb." But enough about that. Can we move on?'

'Certainly,' I replied. 'Why does science, which is magnificent in so many ways, bring us such little happiness?'

Einstein sighed, shaking his head. 'The simple answer is that we have not yet learned to make proper use of it. In times of war, science has given us the means to poison and mutilate one another. In times of peace, science has made our lives hurried and uncertain.' He picked up his pipe, tamping the tobacco and then hovering a match over it. He puffed mightily until he exhaled a mouthful of smoke that tickled my nose with its spicy scent.

'Instead of liberating us from the monotonous work that has to be done, it has enslaved men to machines. Men now work long hours with the continual fear of losing their income.'

I could hardly argue with that, although my brother might think differently. He was very happy with his new Chrysler.

'Can we shift to the topic of civil liberties?' I said.

Einstein nodded.

'When you arrived in America, you objected to the mistreatment of Negroes, and you worked with a number of leading civil-rights organisations to demand equality and denounce racism and segregation.'

'In 1946, I travelled to Lincoln University in Pennsylvania, the first school in America to grant college degrees to Negroes. At Lincoln, I received an honorary degree and gave a lecture on relativity to the students.' He took another long draw from his pipe. 'Unfortunately, in America today, equality and human dignity are mainly limited to people with white skins.' He thought for a moment. 'When two Negro couples were murdered in Monroe, Georgia, I wrote a letter to President Truman calling for the prosecution of the lynch mob and passage of a federal anti-lynching law ... ' His voice trailed off.

I tried a different tack. 'You thought highly of Vladimir Lenin. I believe you said, "He was a man committed to social justice."'

Einstein looked at me as if trying to discern whether I had an ulterior motive.

'I do not consider his methods practical,' he said, 'but one thing is certain, men of his type are the guardians and restorers of the conscience of humanity.'

'Given your links to Germany, Zionism and your socialist ideals, the US Federal Bureau of Investigation may have kept a file on you. What is your view on that?'

He smiled proudly. 'Unthinking respect for authority is the greatest enemy of truth,' he declared. 'Senator McCarthy is a danger to intellectual freedom. For years he has been making accusations of subversion and treason against government employees, those in the entertainment industry, academics and labour-union activists.'

'Yes, and this is despite questionable evidence,' I agreed.

'Hundreds of Americans have become the subject of aggressive questioning, and many have been called before the House Un-American Activities Committee.'

'Would you go so far as to say that political repression is rife?' I asked.

'Yes,' he said. 'And Paul Robeson, a friend of mine for twenty years, was blacklisted because of his activism against racism. I opened my home to him. I believe every intellectual who is called before the Un-American Activities Committee ought to refuse to testify.'

'But wouldn't that mean a charge of contempt?'

Einstein regarded me soberly. 'People of good conscience must be prepared for jail and economic ruin. They must be ready to sacrifice their personal welfare in the interests of the cultural welfare of their country. If enough people are ready to take this grave step, they will be successful. If not, then the intellectuals of this country deserve nothing better than the slavery that is intended for them.'

'So, you're in favour of a socialist state?' I probed.

'I'm convinced that is the only way to develop in man a sense of responsibility for his fellow man, in place of the glorification of power and success in our present society,' he said, his voice low.

'That's quite a courageous view to voice in 1953, at the very moment Senator McCarthy is conducting his hearings,' I added.

Einstein didn't immediately respond, so I forged on.

'For a scientist, you seem to have had progressive views on a number of subjects. I understand you were one of the thousands of signatories to Magnus Hirschfeld's petition against Paragraph 175 of the German penal code that condemned homosexuality.'

Einstein rolled his eyes. 'That petition ran for more than thirty years. It collected many signatures from the Jewish intellectual elite,' he said.

'And I also understand that you oppose violence against animals?'

'Yes, we should embrace all living creatures,' he said, tamping down the tobacco in his pipe and applying a match to the bowl once more.

'Does that mean you are a vegetarian?'

He was silent a moment until the tobacco caught, then he said, 'Yes, I have been a vegetarian for these last years. I have always eaten animal flesh with a somewhat guilty conscience.'

He drew on his pipe, the tobacco glowing and crackling. 'But now,' he continued, 'I am feeling quite good about vegetarian food. We were not born to be carnivores.'

I glanced at my watch and realised we had been together for over two hours, although it seemed like twenty minutes. I pondered what else I could ask before our conversation ended. I could tell he was growing weary. Outside, the sky was bleak with clouds.

'Before we finish, can I ask you how you have enjoyed your time at the Institute of Advanced Studies?'

He smiled as if to himself. 'My time at Princeton has been quiet and enjoyable. I remember I wrote to my friend, the physicist Max Born, that I had settled down splendidly, and I hibernate like a bear in its cave. I really feel more at home here than ever before in all my varied existence.'

'And what do you do for relaxation?' I asked.

'My recreations are playing Mozart and Bach on the violin at musical evenings with friends, sailing in a little second-hand sailboat on Lake Carnegie and walking in the countryside near the institute.' He stood up and plucked a framed photograph from a shelf and handed it to me. It was a photograph of him in a little sailboat looking relaxed and happy.

'No pressure is exerted on me to do research. I like the working conditions at the institute. I can continue my studies in general relativity, my work on quantum theory and my investigation into a unified field theory. At the same time, I can advocate for nuclear control, world peace and Zionism.'

He was quiet for a moment then continued, 'In the morning, I am at the institute, and in the afternoon, I like being at home, meeting friends and eminent people from science and politics.'

Looking at my watch again, I said, 'It's lunchtime. With your permission, I think we might finish here – I'll leave you in peace.'

He smiled at me as I stood and extended my hand.

'Thank you for your time, Professor Einstein. I'll make sure to keep you informed about when and where the interview will be published.'

His handshake was warm, and I felt myself once more a little overwhelmed by his presence. And when I tried to withdraw my hand, I found him unwilling to let go.

'You remind me of Mileva,' he said suddenly. 'You have the same wide mouth and square brow. But your eyes are more like my son's.'

I retrieved my hand and turned towards the door to leave. But he continued to speak rapidly as if desperate to say his piece before I could leave.

'Your smile is very like Mileva's. She died, you know, five years ago.'

'I'm so sorry for your loss,' I responded, not quite knowing what else to say.

He gently took my hand once again. 'Lieserl had a small brown birthmark on her forearm,' he said, pointing to the centre of his own forearm, 'like a crescent moon.'

I froze. Suddenly I couldn't speak. I stared at him and began to lift my sleeve; my eyes flooded with tears.

He glanced at the brown crescent moon on my forearm. A moment of silence ensued, and then he pulled me into a paternal embrace.

I felt his heartbeat and the sinewy strength of his arms. 'Leigh … Lieserl,' he murmured. 'Liebling.'

Endnote

This imaginary conversation with Albert Einstein is set in 1953, the day after his seventy-fourth birthday. It uses translations of Einstein's own remarks or close interpretations of them (many taken from letters he wrote while on lecture tours) to remain faithful to what he actually said.

When Einstein was away from home on his many lecture tours in Europe and the United States, he wrote hundreds of letters to his family, destroying the myth that he was cold towards them. Many of them suggested his marriage to Mileva Maric was miserable. And even though his marriage to Elsa was best described as a marriage of convenience, he wrote to her almost every day, describing his experiences and openly discussing his extra-marital affairs with her. He also discussed his affairs with his stepdaughter and confidante, Margot. Einstein had ten lovers, in addition to the two women he married. He sailed, read books and attended concerts with each of them. He described many women with whom he spent time and told his wife they showered him with 'unwanted' affection. During his marriage, he had an affair with his secretary, Betty Neumann, as well as Estella, Ethel, Toni and his 'Russian spy lover', Margarita. Others are referred to only by initials like M and L.

M was Berlin socialite Ethel Michanowski, with whom Einstein was involved in the late 1920s and early 30s. She was about fifteen years younger than him and was friendly with his stepdaughter. Einstein told Margot in 1931 that, 'It is true that M followed me to England and her chasing after me is getting out of control.' In respect of L, he said, 'Out of all the dames, I am, in fact, attached only to Mrs L, who is absolutely harmless and decent.'

After his death, these letters were kept in the Einstein Archive at the Hebrew University in Jerusalem. Under the terms of his stepdaughter's will, more than 1300 of these letters were made public in 2006, twenty years after her death. One surprising discovery was the birth of a daughter a year before his marriage to his first wife, Mileva Maric. He and Maric named the baby Lieserl. Historians did not know of her existence until 1986 when they found a letter between Einstein and Maric that mentioned her name. After 1903, no one ever heard of her again. It is not known if she was adopted or died of scarlet fever.

The FBI started to keep a dossier on Einstein in December 1932. He and his wife Elsa had just moved to the United States from Germany, and Einstein had been very vocal against racism. By the time of his death, the dossier had grown to 1427 pages. Agency director J. Edgar Hoover thought Einstein was quite possibly a Communist, certainly, 'an extreme radical'.

In the quiet New Jersey town, Einstein intended to lead a life of research and reflection, but once again, his international fame required him to travel widely, attending conferences and giving lectures.

Einstein retired from the Institute for Advanced Studies in 1945 but continued to live and work in Princeton until his death.

At the beginning of the 1950s, despite worsening health, Einstein continued to work on his field theory.

After a short illness, he died on 18 April 1955, at the age of seventy-six. He had been politically active until his last days.

He hated personality cults and prohibited any funeral service. Only his closest relatives and friends bade him farewell at the cemetery.

The Daily Princetonian devoted an entire issue to Einstein on his death, with tributes from friends and colleagues. Physics Department chairman, Allen G. Shenstone, said his character was 'the most beautiful' that he had ever known. Henry D. Smyth, chairman of the university's Research Board and a former member of the Atomic Energy Commission, spoke of 'the informality and simplicity which characterised his relations with lesser scientists of all ages.' He declared that the physics of Princeton had 'immensely benefited by his presence at the Institute of Advanced Study'.

A statement from the institute proclaimed that 'one of the great figures of mankind's struggle for intellectual insight and moral improvement' had passed 'into the indelible record of history where his lofty place has long been assured.'

✢ ✢ ✢

Physicist and mathematician Mileva Maric, who married Einstein in 1903, faced almost insurmountable odds in her quest to work in her chosen field. Physicist Lise Meitner, born in 1878, three years after Maric, faced similar difficulties, but perhaps because Meitner chose not to marry or have children, her career followed a different path. In 1912, she and her lifelong friend, chemist Otto Hahn, moved to the Kaiser Wilhelm Institute in Berlin. Together, they discovered several new isotopes. Initially, Meitner worked unpaid in Hahn's department of radiochemistry but was given a paid position at the institute in 1913 after being offered an assistant professorship in Prague. In 1917, she was given her own physics section at the Kaiser Wilhelm Institute.

In 1925, French physicist Pierre Auger was credited with a discovery Meitner had made two years earlier. The phenomenon was called the Auger effect, and Meitner was not acknowledged.

Meitner, Hahn and others experimented with uranium and other elements, bombarding the nucleus with neutrons. Most assumed that this would produce heavier elements; only one chemist, Ida Noddack, suggested that it might produce lighter elements. Hahn's results were puzzling until Meitner and her nephew, Otto Frisch, while walking in the snow one day, proposed that the nucleus might have split in two.

Meitner and Frisch sent a paper to Nature, naming the process 'nuclear fission'. Hahn and Strassmann sent a separate paper without acknowledging Meitner in the paper or when he was awarded the Nobel Prize in chemistry in 1944.

When the Nazis came to power in 1933, annexing Austria in 1938, Meitner, who had been acting director of the Institute of Chemistry, escaped to Holland, where she worked with Niels Bohr and continued to correspond with Otto Hahn.

Meitner became a Swedish citizen in 1949 and continued to work on nuclear reactions. Although she had wanted nothing to do with the development of a nuclear bomb, she was involved in Sweden's first nuclear reactor. She died in 1968, weeks before her ninetieth birthday. Had Maric had similar opportunities, who knows what she might have achieved. The loss of women's contributions is incalculable.

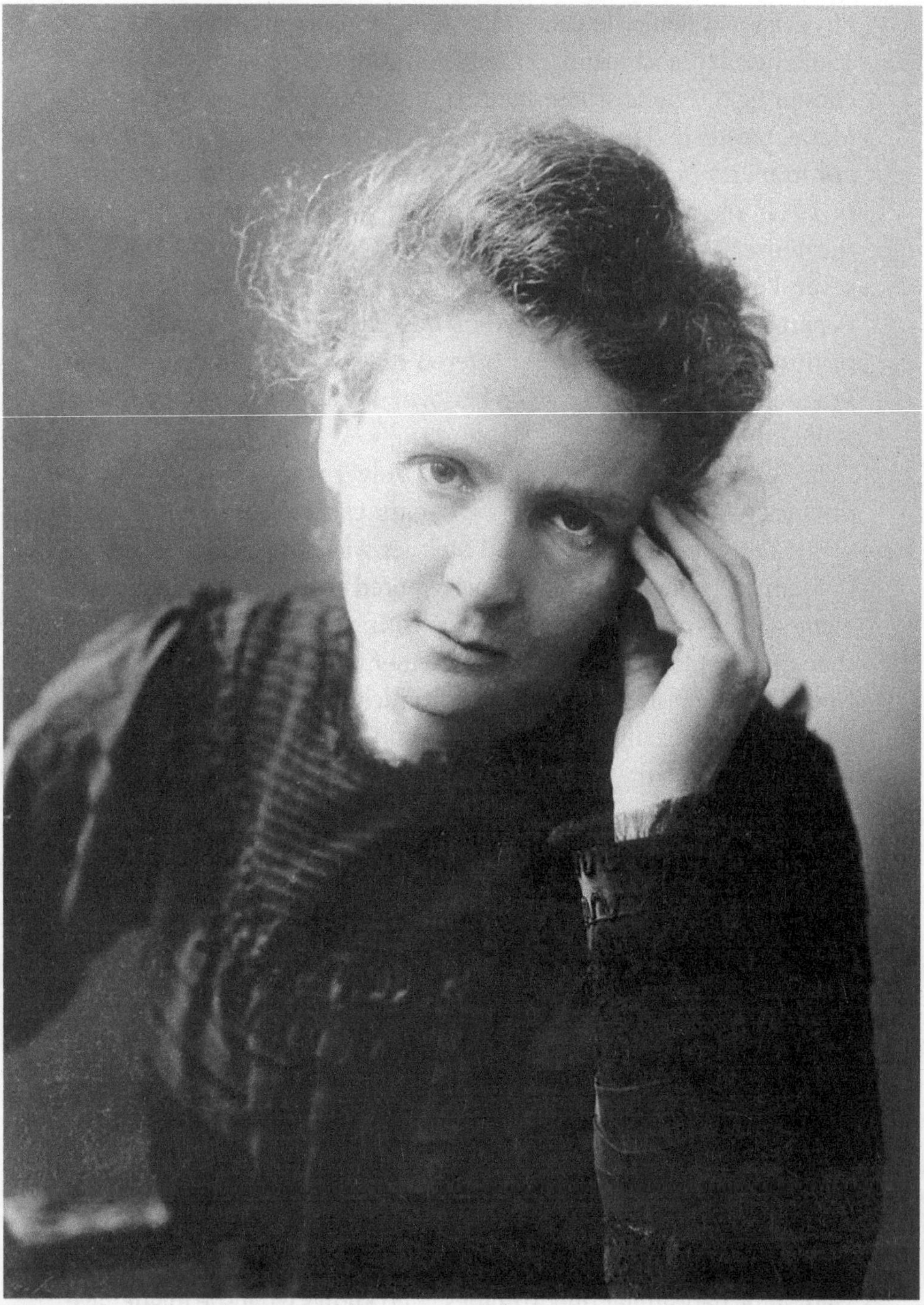

Marie Curie

Paris, France, 1927.

'Good morning,' I said as I walked up the steps to the private entry of the Radium Institute, an imposing building under the auspices of the Université de Paris.

A man in a lab coat stood near the door. Plucking a cigarette from the corner of his mouth, he said, 'Can I help you?'

'I have an appointment with Madame Curie.'

'*La patronne* is on the ground floor,' he said, turning to point down a hall. 'Her office is to the right.'

'Thank you,' I replied. My heart began to race. I was about to meet the first woman to win a Nobel Prize, the only woman to win it twice and the only person to win the prize in two different scientific fields.

The door was open. Standing at the entrance, I scanned the room. It was narrow, small and austere. Totally inadequate for a scientist of such eminence. In the centre of the room, an oak desk with deep drawers held a leather-bordered blotter almost covered with papers, scientific magazines and folders. The top of the desk was cluttered with a telephone, typewriter, writing pad, pencils and pens, an ink bottle and a brass desk lamp with a green glass shade.

Behind it was an armchair and a bookcase with glass doors full of books, journals and folders arranged in an orderly fashion. To the left of the bookcase were filing cabinets, and to the right a door leading to an adjoining room, which appeared to be Mme Curie's own laboratory. I could see a sink, the usual lab paraphernalia, as well as some devices I couldn't identify.

Sunlight poured into the office through the high windows to the right, which looked onto a courtyard. I could see a well-tended garden with a large, leafy basswood tree. It was early November, and the flowerbeds were past their best. In doing research for this interview, I'd read that Curie often met informally for drinks with doctors, chemists and biologists after a thesis defence. When the weather was fine, they would all congregate after work for a casual discussion about their day.

'Hello,' said Marie Curie in accented English that betrayed her Polish origins. She walked through the laboratory door into the office. 'You must be Monsieur Hoffman from the *Delineator*.'

I nodded and extended my hand.

'I'm very good friends with your editor, Missy Meloney. Some years ago, she did a story about me and my work for your magazine. She was also instrumental in creating the Marie Curie Radium Fund to raise money to purchase radium for my research.'

'She's the reason I'm here,' I said. 'She suggested I write a human-interest story about you.'

Curie sat down at her desk, gesturing for me to take a seat on the other side. She examined me with penetrating blue eyes beneath a high forehead marked with frown lines. Her face was small and oval, her chin pointed, with features neat and regular, and it was clear she had been a pretty woman in her youth. Her dark curly hair was greying now, pulled into a loose bun from which a few curling strands escaped, and age had etched deep lines beside her nose and mouth. Her expression was at once exhausted, determined and slightly amused, but her eyes were sad. She wore a long-sleeved dark dress that reached to her ankles, belted loosely at the waist, although she was still slender.

'Thank you for taking the time to speak with me. I know you must be busy.'

'A pleasure,' she said in a businesslike manner. 'Now, where would you like to start?'

Glancing at her, I saw her watching me with eyebrows raised, waiting for me to say something.

'At the beginning?' I suggested, flipping open my notebook. 'You were born Marya Sklodowska …'

'*Skwodovska*,' she corrected. 'It's pronounced *Skwodovska*. In Polish, the "w" is pronounced as a "v".'

'Excuse me,' I replied, feeling embarrassed. 'In Warsaw on 7 November 1867…'

'Yes, I was the fifth and youngest child,' she said, pushing at a lock of hair that had slipped from behind her ear.

'And Warsaw was at that time in Congress Poland, which was part of the Russian Empire ….'

'The people of Poland were subjected to a brutal repression by the Romanovs,' she interjected, leaning forward for emphasis. 'They simply absorbed Poland into Russia. Both sides of my family were involved in efforts to restore Polish independence.'

'I see. Your father taught mathematics and physics and was the director of two Warsaw gymnasia for boys, correct?'

'It seems that you hardly need my contributions to write your article, Monsieur Hoffman,' she said with a small smile.

'I try to be thorough in my research,' I replied. 'I read that you had some initial scientific training from your father?'

There was a short silence, then she said, 'After the Russian authorities stopped laboratory instruction in Polish schools, Papa brought a lot of the laboratory equipment home and instructed us children on its use. But he was fired by his Russian supervisors for expressing pro-Polish nationalist sentiments. He lost his directorships and was forced to take lower-paying jobs.'

'How did your family cope? With his loss of income and status?'

Curie sighed. 'Our situation was worsened by a series of bad investments that Papa made. We were forced to supplement the family income by taking in boys as lodgers.'

I followed her gaze out the window, admiring the basswood tree that was displaying its full golden autumnal glory.

'And what about your mother?'

Curie shifted in her chair and pursed her lips. 'She ran a prestigious private boarding school for girls located on Freta Street in Warsaw but resigned after I was born. She died of tuberculosis when I was ten. Less than three years after my eldest sister, Zofia, died of typhus.'

'Can you tell me how those deaths affected you?' I asked as delicately as I could.

Curie's eyes glistened, and she pulled out her handkerchief and blew her nose. 'They were the first great sorrows of my life. My mother and I were devout Catholics. My father was an atheist, but after my mother's death, I gave up religion and became agnostic.'

'Even at such a young age? You were only ten.'

Curie simply nodded affirmation.

I glanced down at my notes. 'Can we talk for a moment about your education?'

Curie nodded. 'My parents placed a high value on learning and insisted their children receive a good education both at home and at school. They were imaginative parents and employed playful, educational techniques, such as creating a collage of historical events or a giant paper map of the world. This instilled a love of education in all of us.'

'I've read that you have a prodigious memory, which must have made schoolwork easier.'

Curie's eyebrows arched. 'Perhaps, but that is not what I was trying to convey. When I was ten, I was sent off to boarding school, and after that, I went to a government-run gymnasium for girls in Warsaw. I found it unbearable. I lost all joy in life.'

Curie paused, and I waited in the hope she might wish to elaborate. After a few moments of silence, I thought it best to press on. 'You graduated in 1883, at age sixteen, and you received a gold medal for academic excellence.'

Curie nodded.

'And then what?'

'I spent the following year in the countryside with relatives.'

'Why is that?'

'I needed the rest. I was suffering from depression. Once I finished school, the impact of my mother's death came crashing down on my soul.'

'I'm very sorry.'

Curie smiled. 'Thank you. It was a difficult time. Then I returned to live with my father in Warsaw.'

'And to attend university, I presume?'

She half-laughed, half-snorted. 'At that time, women were not allowed to enrol in a regular institution of higher learning. So my sister Bronisława and I became involved with the clandestine Flying University.'

'I've heard of the Flying University. Can you elaborate?'

Curie smiled. 'Certainly. At the time, the Tsarist government imposed policies of Russification on the Polish education system. And the opportunities for women to be educated were almost non-existent. The Flying University was a response to both of these issues. It was a Polish patriotic institution of higher learning for women. Prominent Warsaw scientists, historians and philosophers were invited to teach in quite a broad curriculum.'

'Very impressive,' I said.

'At the same time, I went to work as a governess for relatives of my father.'

I consulted my notes. 'That would be the Żorawski family, correct?'

Curie nodded. 'It was convenient. I could read and study in my spare time. And I had some tutoring.'

'I've been told that there were also ... personal complications?'

Curie smiled. 'I assume that is a discreet reference to my feelings for Kazimierz?'

I nodded in embarrassed silence.

She shrugged. 'It's a common story. I was penniless, while the Żorawskis were quite affluent. There was no way his parents would allow a ne'er-do-well like me to marry their son. My heart was broken many times during the four years that I worked for the family. Kazimierz went back and forth between defying and obeying his parents. We felt it was a tragedy at the time. But these things pass.'

'Do you know what became of him?'

'Oh yes. He did his doctorate, pursued an academic career as a mathematician and became a professor and rector at the Jagiellonian University in Kraków.'

I nodded, looked down at my notes and said, 'In 1890, aged twenty-three, you began your practical scientific training?'

'I worked in a chemical laboratory run by my cousin, Józef Boguski, at the Museum of Industry and Agriculture, near Warsaw's old town,' Mme Curie said.

'And in late 1891, you left Poland?'

Curie grimaced. 'Excuse me, but are we to work our way through every year of my life? If so, we will be here until Christmas.'

I smiled in apology. 'Sorry. I'll try to move along more quickly. After Poland …?'

'I went to Paris. At first, I stayed for a short time with my sister and brother-in-law. Then I enrolled at the University of Paris to study physics, chemistry and mathematics.'

'Under the name Marie, not Maria. Is that because you wanted to seem more French, perhaps?'

'Monsieur Hoffman!' she exclaimed, her exasperation obvious in both tone and volume. 'You seem to be engaged in … what's the English word … 'muckraking. Why would you want to focus on such an unimportant detail?'

'I thought my readers might find it interesting,' I replied a tad defensively. 'You know, when in Rome?'

'But I was in Paris.'

I bowed my head. 'Touché. Please continue.'

'Within a few months, I moved to an attic in the Latin Quarter, so I could be closer to the Sorbonne. I lived on bread and butter and tea and kept myself warm in winter by wearing all the clothes I possessed. The attic was damp and sparsely furnished. I did my own housekeeping, which kept the rent low and carried my own coal up six flights of stairs to heat my small stove. During the winter, it was not unusual for the water in the basin to freeze overnight.'

'That sounds … hard. But it's the sort of human-interest detail my American readers will love.'

'Of course, it was hard. And unpleasant. But strangely, it was one of the happiest periods of my life. I was one of twenty-three women in a class of nearly two thousand students enrolled that year in the science faculty of the Sorbonne.'

'And you graduated in …?'

'Eighteen ninety-three.'

'What was your next move?'

'Well, I continued studying at the university with the help of a fellowship. I earned my second degree in 1894.'

I nodded. 'Isn't that the same year you met your husband?'

Curie smiled, and her eyes came alive, shining like sapphires. Just then, the sun broke through the clouds, and crisp, beautiful autumn sunlight filled the room. 'Pierre was an instructor at the School of Physics and Chemistry. Professor Wierusz-Kowalski arranged a research grant for me to study the magnetic properties and chemical composition of steel. I was looking for a larger laboratory, and Professor Lippman thought Pierre might be able to provide additional space and approached him.'

'Do you remember the first time you saw Pierre?'

'Of course!' She smiled warmly. 'He was standing at a porte-fenêtre opening onto a balcony. He seemed to me very young, though, at that time, he was thirty-five years old. I liked the open expression on his face and the slight suggestion of detachment in his whole attitude. His speech – rather slow and deliberate – his simplicity, and his smile, at once grave and youthful ... all these things made him interesting.'

'Sounds like love at first sight,' I suggested.

She hesitated a moment. 'Pierre was an accomplished researcher and, although he didn't have access to extra space, he was able to locate premises where I could begin work. We had much in common – our upbringings, our financial troubles, our views on religion and politics and our mutual passion for science. All these drew us together, and we quickly developed an affection for one another.'

'So you were married?'

Curie shook her head. 'Not immediately. He was eager, but I wanted to go back to Poland to visit my family and for further study. So that's what I did during the summer of 1894. I applied for a place at the Jagiellonian in Kraków, but my application was rejected because I was a woman. Pierre then convinced me to return to Paris to do a PhD. And on 26 July 1895, we were married in Sceaux.'

She smiled. 'Neither of us wanted a religious wedding. It was a simple ceremony at Sceaux Town Hall. My father and sisters, Helena and Bronia, came, and we had the reception at our home.'

I returned her smile. 'Sounds like a lovely occasion. With Pierre, you were able to share your work as well as your leisure time?'

'Oh yes. In Pierre, I found not only a new love but also a scientific collaborator on whom I could depend. We enjoyed going into our workroom at night and watching the luminous capsules containing our research material. The glowing tubes looked like faint fairy lights.'

'The way you describe it sounds quite romantic,' I said.

'Oh yes, for a pair of scientists.' She laughed, and I joined in.

'But we enjoyed ourselves outside of work, as well. We loved cycling and travelling abroad. Our daughter, Irene, was born in 1897. And when Eve was born in 1904, we hired a Polish governess to teach the girls Polish and take them back to Poland so that we could continue our research.'

'I see,' I said, making a conscious effort to convey journalistic neutrality. 'Let's talk about your research.'

'Very well,' she said.

Looking down at my notes, I saw my usual shorthand abbreviations for 'where, what, when'. 'First of all, where did you work?'

'Most of it was carried out in a converted shed next to the School of Physics and Chemistry. It was formerly a medical-school dissecting room. It was a hothouse in summer and freezing in winter, with a glass roof that didn't fully protect us from the rain. It was also poorly ventilated – there was no hood to carry away poisonous gasses resulting from my chemical experiments.'

'Sounds ... less than ideal,' I murmured.

Curie shrugged. 'We made do. Pierre became increasingly interested in my work, and halfway through 1898, he decided to drop his research on crystals and join me.'

'That was a big year for you both,' I said, once more consulting my notes. 'In July, you and Pierre published a joint paper announcing the existence of an element that you called polonium. And in December, you announced the existence of a second element that you named radium.'

She smiled. 'We also coined the word "radioactivity". Between 1898 and 1902, we published, jointly or separately, a total of thirty-two scientific papers, including the one describing how, when exposed to radium, tumour-forming cells are destroyed faster than healthy cells.'

I nodded. 'That was a tremendous breakthrough. But you and Pierre didn't patent your discoveries. Why?'

Curie shrugged as if the answer was self-evident. 'Science should belong to the world and not to the individual.'

'A noble sentiment,' I replied. 'So it doesn't bother you that other scientists and chemical companies are now selling radium for cancer treatments and military research at $100,000 per gram?'

'Obviously not,' she replied, her voice curt.

'Very well. Let's move on. In 1903 you, Pierre and Henri Becquerel won a Nobel Prize in physics in recognition of your joint research on the radiation phenomena discovered by Professor Henri Becquerel.'

Curie's face softened. 'Professors Henri Becquerel and Gabriel Lippman served as mentors to me. Almost as father figures, in a way.'

'And you were the first woman to win a Nobel.'

Curie smiled. 'You may not be aware of the background story. At first, the committee had intended to honour only Pierre and Henri, but a female member of the committee alerted Pierre to the situation and, after his complaint, my name was added to the nomination.'

'Wow,' I said. 'My readers will certainly be interested in that. Is that why you and your husband declined to go to Stockholm for the award ceremony?'

'I had health problems at the time, and we were busy with our research. Pierre was also ill. And he hated public ceremonies.'

'It is said the Nobel Committee took your non-appearance as an affront.'

Curie shrugged. 'That was not our intention. And as Nobel laureates, we were required to deliver a lecture. So, in 1905, we travelled to Sweden. We used the prize money to hire our first laboratory assistant. We also made donations to various worthy enterprises, including a scholarship for Polish students and a sanatorium run by my sister, Bronia, in Zakopane.'

'Following the award, the University of Paris gave your husband a professorship and the chair of physics, I believe.'

'That's correct,' she said. 'It was a very welcome development because up to that time, we didn't have a proper laboratory. After Pierre's promotion, the university finally agreed to furnish us with a new laboratory, but it was not ready until 1906.'

'That was also a year of tragedy,' I said sympathetically.

Curie sighed and blinked rapidly. 'In April, Pierre was struck by a carriage while crossing the Rue Dauphine. He lost his footing in the rain and fell under its wheels.'

'I'm so very sorry,' I said, well aware of the inadequacy of my words.

'His death was devastating ... devasting,' she said, her voice mournful. 'I lost all hope for a time. I was in despair.'

'Despite your suffering, you were offered his academic post the following month by the physics department of the University of Paris,' I noted.

Curie looked out towards the garden for a moment before turning to face me. 'I decided to accept the position as Professor of General Physics in the Faculty of Science in the hope of creating a world-class laboratory as a tribute to Pierre.'

'You were the first woman to become a professor at the University of Paris.'

'That did not really concern me.'

'I see. In 1910, your treatise on radioactivity was published, and in the following year, you were awarded a second Nobel Prize for chemistry in recognition of your discovery of the elements radium and polonium.'

Mme Curie nodded, took out a handkerchief and wiped her nose.

'You were the first woman to win the award twice.'

'Again, those questions do not really concern me.'

'But you are the only person to receive Nobel Prizes for two different sciences.'

At last, she smiled. 'That is a relevant issue. And yes, I was very pleased.'

I looked at my watch and was surprised to see we had been talking for almost two hours.

'My readers would also be interested in your relationship with Paul Langevin,' I said quietly.

'What is there to say?' she sighed. 'He was a student of Pierre's, a long-time family friend and Pierre's chosen successor at ESPCI.'

'ESPCI?'

Curie smiled. 'Sorry. École Superieur de Physique et de Chimie Industrielles. The Higher Education Institute for Physics and Industrial Chemistry.'

'One of the elite Grands Écoles, correct?'

She nodded.

'And Monsieur Langevin?'

'Paul was tall and had a glorious handlebar moustache. He was five years younger than me, and his marriage was very unhappy.'

I said nothing, taking shorthand notes and hoping she would continue to be so forthcoming about her personal life. It was just the sort of information that *Delineator* readers would love.

'He was très gentil ... very nice. And a brilliant physicist and mathematician. I admired his wonderful intelligence. He was a friend with whom I could share the depth of my grief, a confidante, a soulmate, even perhaps, one day, a partner. I was also able to give him the ... tenderness he missed at home.'

She paused for a moment, as if in remembrance, before emitting a sad sigh. 'Paul rented an apartment in Paris near the Sorbonne where we were able to meet. He had previously separated from his wife, but they had four children ... So they ultimately reconciled.'

'That must have been difficult,' I said, hoping that an expression of sympathy would spur her on to further revelation.

'His wife threatened to kill me. Paul believed her capable of murder and wanted me to leave France. I refused, but we decided to stop seeing each other.' She smiled. 'But our separation didn't last. It couldn't last. Even so, ours was a difficult relationship.'

'In what way?' I asked.

'Let's just say that it was a distraction from my work. But people must understand their own weaknesses in order to overcome them.'

'What weaknesses do you mean?'

'By this stage of my life, I was worn down and emotionally volatile. My girls were suffering, so I sent them back to Poland. In 1911, Paul and then I went to Brussels for the International Congress of Radiology and Electricity. We travelled separately, but his wife believed the trip was only a ploy to conceal our affair.'

'Was she right?' I asked.

'It was there that I received a telegram from the Nobel Committee telling me that I was the sole winner of a second Nobel Prize,' Curie said, ignoring my question. 'This time, it was for chemistry.'

'You must have been very pleased.'

Curie sat upright in her chair. I noticed dark circles under her eyes. 'I was ... until a second telegram arrived. It informed me that Paul's wife had released our personal letters to the press. She was demanding money and custody of the children.'

'I read about this,' I said in a neutral voice.

Curie took a deep breath. 'I returned to France to venomous publicity. People threw stones at my windows. The far-right *Action Française* newspaper accused me of being a homewrecker, a dissolute woman, a Polish temptress and a Jew – even though I'm not Jewish.'

'Did you receive any support from your colleagues?' I asked.

She smiled faintly and nodded. 'Yes, at that time, I received a letter from Albert Einstein. He said that he admired my intellect, my drive and my honesty and that I should not read the sensational hogwash of the rabble.' She tucked a stray lock of hair behind her ear. 'It gave me strength.'

'Did the scandal have any repercussions for your Nobel award?' I asked.

'Shortly after the scandal broke, I received a letter from the Nobel Committee asking me not to come to Sweden to accept the prize. It also said that, if the Academy had known about the letters, in all probability, they would not have given me the prize.'

'That's very harsh,' I said.

She snorted in obvious contempt. 'When you are angry, you must watch what you say. I waited until I could calmly respond. Then, I wrote back that the prize has been awarded to me for the discovery of radium and polonium, and I believed there is no connection between my scientific work and my private life.'

'So you attended the Nobel ceremony in December of that year, in 1911?'

'Of course, and King Gustaf bestowed the prize.'

'And your Nobel lecture?'

'I mentioned colleagues who had assisted my research but also made a point of speaking in the first person, making it clear that the discovery of radium furnished proof of my hypothesis and that the isolation of radium was accomplished by me alone.'

'You rose above prejudice by virtue of your achievements.'

Curie snorted again. 'My sin above all was that I was not just a mistress, but an emancipated woman when such women are regarded by both sexes as a threat.'

'Can you tell me what happened in the end with you and Paul?'

She shrugged. 'In the end, we separated. He and his wife signed a separation agreement, but three years later, they reconciled. And that was that.'

'Did you stay in touch?'

'Our romantic attachment was over, but we regularly talked about scientific matters.' She laughed suddenly. 'And other matters as well. Some years later, he had an illegitimate child with one of his former students and asked me to find a position for her in my laboratory. Which, of course, I did.'

'Nonetheless, all of this criticism must have taken its toll,' I suggested.

'It did. Nineteen days after my return to Paris, I was rushed to hospital with a kidney ailment and … well, what you might call a nervous breakdown.'

'Because of the scandal?'

'That didn't help,' sighed Curie. 'In any event, I fell into a deep depression. It was darker and lasted longer than all the episodes that had come before. I believe my mother's death produced this lifelong battle with melancholia or depression.'

'I'm very sorry to hear this.'

'I wanted to kill myself,' Curie continued, her voice sombre. 'I refused to eat, I lost a lot of weight and was transferred from the hospital to be cared for by the Sisters of the Family of Saint Marie. Then, at the end of 1911, I underwent an operation to remove lesions from my uterus and kidney.'

Outside, the sun was still bright, and I could hear leaves tumbling across the courtyard in a fresh breeze.

'In 1913, after a long recovery, I began to travel again and returned to science.'

'Is this when you negotiated to build a radioactivity research lab?'

Mme Curie smiled and nodded. 'By July 1914, the first Radium Institute was almost complete. There were two laboratories, one for the study of radioactivity under my direction, and the other for biological research into the treatment of cancer.'

'Which brings us to the outbreak of war.'

'Yes. In 1914, I suspended my research and organised a fleet of small mobile X-ray machines for doctors on the front line. I would wake in the middle of the night shaking, thinking of those wounded soldiers. I knew their best chance would be if they were operated on as soon as possible. So, it was obvious, there was a need for field radiological centres near the front lines to assist battlefield surgeons.'

'Is it true that you toured Paris asking for money and X-ray equipment, generators and vehicles that you could convert and develop into mobile radiology units?'

'Yes, it is.'

'They became known as les Petites Curies,' I believe.

'Correct again. I was appointed the director of the Red Cross Radiology Service and set up France's first military radiology centre. It was ready by October 1914, and I worked with my daughter Irene – she was just seventeen then – at casualty clearing stations X-raying wounded soldiers to locate fractures, bullets and shrapnel.'

'That must have been horrible for someone so young.'

Another shrug. 'It was required. We directed the installation of twenty mobile radiological vehicles and another two hundred radiological units at field hospitals in the first year of the war. We later began training other women as aides.'

I nodded and glanced at my watch. We still had a little time. 'I read that over a million wounded soldiers were treated with your X ray units, is that so?'

Curie nodded, her sense of satisfaction apparent from her smile.

'Yet, despite all you did for the French war effort, there was never any formal recognition from the government.'

'That is so,' she said, then added dryly, 'but unimportant. To me, the Allied victory was proof that science could benefit humanity in unexpected ways. Also, following the Treaty of Versailles, Poland became a sovereign nation for the first time in one hundred and twenty-three years.'

'I think you are too modest, madame,' I said.

She simply smiled briefly by way of response.

'Before we finish, can I ask you about your post-war years?'

'There is not much to say,' she replied. 'I worked as a researcher, teacher and head of the laboratory.'

'You won many awards ... many prizes. And you were appointed to many boards.'

'That is so. And in 1920, on the twenty-fifth anniversary of the discovery of radium, the French government gave me a stipend, something that previously had only been given to Louis Pasteur.'

'Our American readers will be interested in your visit to the United States.'

'In 1921, I sailed to the United States with my two daughters, Irene, then twenty-three, and Eve, sixteen. Within hours of disembarking in New York, we set out on a rather exhausting tour.'

I flipped to another page of my notebook and consulted my notes. 'President Harding received you at the White House and presented you with one gram of radium. The First Lady praised you as ... and I quote ... "a professional achiever and a supportive wife."'

'Supportive wife indeed,' she snorted. 'In 1922, I travelled to Belgium, Brazil, Spain and Czechoslovakia where I lectured and made public appearances.'

'A tour of triumph, so to speak.'

She stared at me for a long moment across the desk as if unclear as to what I meant. 'I've never been particularly comfortable appearing in public. I did it because it provided me with the resources for my work. These tours also weren't easy because I was experiencing health problems. As they wore on, I became more and more exhausted. In the end, I had to cancel events, or at least ask to be excused from speaking at them.'

Signs of weariness were now etched across her face. It was time for me to go.

BERNARD MARIN

'I think I have all I need. But before I go, allow me to say that I think you are remarkable.'

She smiled then. It was a hesitant smile at first, then it broadened. 'Thank you,' she said. 'You are most kind.'

Endnote

This imaginary conversation with Marie Curie is set in 1927, on her sixtieth birthday. It relies on Curie's own remarks or faithful interpretations thereof.

In early 1934, Curie visited Poland for the last time. Just a few months later, on 4 July 1934, she died from aplastic anaemia at the Sancellemoz sanatorium in Passy, Haute-Savoie. She was sixty-six. Her long-term exposure to radiation was likely the cause.

The health dangers of radiation were not known at the time Curie was researching and conducting experiments on radioactive materials. No routine safety measures were employed, and Curie was known to carry test tubes with radioactive isotopes around in her pockets. She even commented on the faint light emitted from radioactive chemicals that she stored in the drawers of her desk.

During the First World War, Curie also didn't wear protective equipment when she conducted X-rays on soldiers in field hospitals. No doubt the many decades of radiation exposure affected her health and caused her untimely death, but she never publicly acknowledged its effects on her body.

More than 100 years later, her 1890 papers are still considered too dangerous to hold, as are her books. Today they're preserved in lead-lined boxes.

When Curie died, the *New York Times* called her a 'martyr to science'. It noted that 'few people 'contributed more to the general welfare of mankind than [this] modest, self-effacing woman'. The physicist Robert Millikan, president of the Californian Institute of Technology, issued a public statement: 'In spite of her continuous absorption in her scientific work, she has devoted much time to the cause of peace.' Cornell University Professor L. Pearce Williams said, 'The result of the Curies' work was epoch-making ... it forced a reconsideration of the foundations of physics.'

With the advent of feminism in the 1960s, Curie's reputation as a remarkable scientist again came to the fore. Physicist Rosalyn Yalow wrote, on the occasion of her own Nobel Prize award in 1977 for research into radioactive compounds, that Curie was her inspiration.

A 2009 poll conducted by the *New Scientist* declared Curie to be the 'most inspirational woman in science'.

Curie battled sexism her whole life. In June 1903, she was awarded her doctorate from the University of Paris. That month she and Pierre were invited to the Royal Institute in London to give a speech on radioactivity. But as a woman, she was not entitled to speak, and Pierre, alone, delivered their presentation. Curie offered herself as a candidate for a seat in the Academy of Sciences in France in 1911. Its members, all male, said they would never allow a woman to be a member, not even Marie Curie. When rumours surfaced of her affair with Paul Langevin, Curie was nearly run out of France – but Langevin was not treated nearly as harshly.

Curie left two daughters, Irene and Eve. She encouraged their academic development by mailing them maths problems every day when she was away on business. Her own father had done the same with her when she was a little girl. Irene and Eve were very different people. Irene was a communist sympathiser who refused to leave France during the war, while Eve left for England and joined the Free French cause. She travelled to the US, where she lectured about the war.

Like her mother, Irene entered the field of scientific research. She studied at her mother's institute in Paris and married her mother's assistant. With her husband, Frederic Joliot, she worked on the nucleus of the atom. Together, they were awarded a Nobel Prize and credited with the discovery of artificial radiation. It was the first time both a parent and a child had won individual Nobel Prizes. Irene, too, died of a radiation-related illness – leukaemia – in 1956. Irene's daughter (and granddaughter of Marie Curie), Hélène Langevin-Joliot, also pursued a career in nuclear physics and became Emeritus Director of Research at the National Centre for Scientific Research in Paris.

Eve became a journalist and wrote the definitive biography of her mother, which was published in 1937 and made into a film. Eve married Henry Labouisse, an ambassador and director of UNICEF. In that role, he accepted the Nobel Prize for Peace on behalf of UNICEF in 1956.

This brought the family's total number of Nobel Prizes to five: Marie was awarded two, Pierre was awarded one, their daughter Irene Joliot-Curie and her husband Frederic Joliot were awarded one for chemistry in 1935, and Eve's husband accepted one on behalf of UNICEF.

Marie Curie headed the Radium Institute (now the Curie Institute), becoming one of the world's four major laboratories researching radioactivity. She had the satisfaction of seeing the development of the Curie Foundation in Paris, which was to fund the Radium Institute and develop and apply radiation therapy. A second Radium Institute was inaugurated in Warsaw in 1932, with Marie Curie's sister, Bronisława, as director. In her final year of life, Curie worked on a book, *Radioactivity*, which was published posthumously in 1935.

Curie was interred at the cemetery in Sceaux alongside her husband, Pierre. Sixty years later, in honour of their achievements in science, their physical remains were transferred to the Pantheon. Curie was the first woman to be buried there on her own merits.

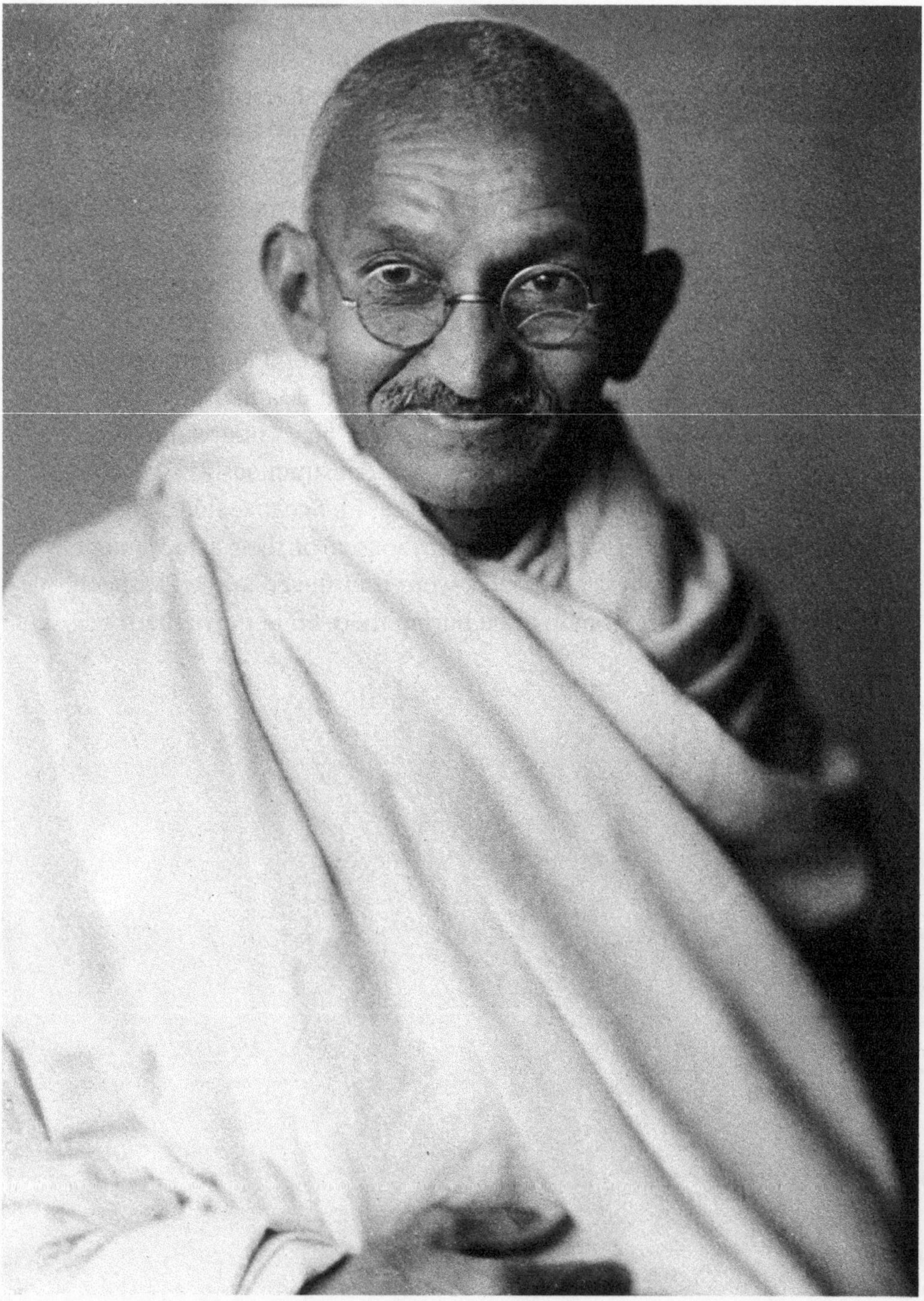

Mahatma Gandhi

Wardha, India, April 1937.

By the time the bullock cart pulled up at the entrance to Shegaon Ashram, I was lathered in sweat, my shirt clinging to my torso as if with glue. The sun beat down mercilessly, my only shade provided by the wide straw brim of my planter's hat.

I dismounted and walked towards my destination, passing a group of people sitting in the lotus position, meditating in an open area surrounded by a bamboo boundary fence. As I drew closer, I saw a slight, bald figure standing on the verandah. Dressed in his trademark white dhoti, he stood about five foot four inches, his feet in handmade, brown leather sandals. I looked at my watch and saw it was one o'clock, right on time.

As I stepped onto the verandah of his one-room hut, Gandhi approached, beaming the trademark smile I had seen in so many newsreels. He was dark-skinned and completely bald with dark brown eyes and a prominent nose on which were perched round metal-framed glasses. His brow was etched with wrinkles, and a thick greying moustache sloped downwards at the corners of his mouth.

Gandhi extended his hand. 'Good afternoon,' he said with a smile.

I swallowed, trying to maintain my composure in the presence of this living legend. 'Good afternoon, sir. My name is Simpson Campbell, and I'm a correspondent for the *New York Herald Tribune*.'

'I see you came by oxen.'

I laughed. 'Well, you do live off the beaten track. It's not as though there was an abundance of travel options. There is only one dirt path leading here.'

'I'm pleased there is no paved road,' said Gandhi. 'Our tiny village has a population of six hundred and is four miles from Wardhi. I want our colonial overlords and native Indian elites to understand the problems of those who live in villages.'

'Isn't it difficult,' I asked, 'with no post office or shops?'

'Aha, but we're well supplied with snakes and scorpions,' laughed Gandhi. 'Not to mention stagnant pools of water and much malaria.' Then he crossed his legs and sat down in the lotus pose atop a palm leaf on the verandah. 'Please,' he said, pointing to the palm leaf opposite.

As I lowered myself clumsily, I noticed a wet curtain hanging at the entrance to the hut. Through the window, I could see the walls were neatly plastered with white earth and decorated with mystic Hindu symbols. The windows and doors were made of bamboo and decorated with symbols.

'Now, where would you like to begin?' Gandhi asked when I'd settled myself stiffly on my palm leaf.

'Let's start with your parents. I understand your father, Kaba Gandhi, married four times?'

'Yes,' said Gandhi. 'My father's first three wives died. He had a daughter by each of his first and second marriages, and his last wife, my mother Putlibai, bore him a daughter and three sons. I was the youngest.'

He went on without prompting. 'I was born in Porbandar, India on the 2nd of October 1869 and given the name Mohandas Karamchand Gandhi.'

'Where did the name Mahatma come from?' I asked.

He gazed at me for a moment. 'That came much later; it was given to me by the Bengali poet, Rabindranath Tagore. 'It means great soul.'

'Your father was the chief minister of Porbandar?'

'Yes. Porbandar was the capital of a small princely state in western India that was under British rule. I believe he was a very able administrator who knew how to balance the often frivolous demands of princes, the needs of their long-suffering subjects, and the mandates of British political officers who were the ones wielding power.' Gandhi smiled and shook his head happily. 'My father had no formal education. But he was incorruptible and strictly impartial. His loyalty to the State was well known, and he loved his clan – he was truthful, brave and generous, but short-tempered. He never had ambitions to accumulate riches and left us very little property.'

'Did he have any religious training?'

Gandhi shook his head. 'Very little, but he often visited temples and listened to religious discourses about Hinduism.'

'Yet your mother, Putlibai, was quite devout.'

Gandhi nodded. 'Very true. She did not care much for finery or jewellery but divided her time between home and the temple and fasted frequently. I would even go so far as to describe my mother as saintly.'

'That's a very powerful word,' I observed.

'Think of it this way: she would never eat without her daily prayers.'

'Impressive,' I said, 'but there are many Christians who also say grace before each meal. I wouldn't describe them necessarily as saintly.'

Gandhi glanced at me with a frown as if unaccustomed to being challenged on this sensitive topic.

'I mean no offence,' I said quickly.

His frown softened into a smile. 'My mother felt that going to Haveli, the Vaishnava temple, was one of her daily duties. She would undertake the most rigorous vows and adhere to them without flinching. Keeping two or three consecutive fasts meant little to her. But she also had considerable common sense. She was well informed about all matters of State, and the ladies at court thought highly of her intelligence.'

'Your own religious quest can be traced to your childhood, to the influence of your mother?'

'That is true. My home was steeped in Vaishnavism. We also worshipped the Hindu God, Vishnu, and adhered to the tenets of Jainism.'

'I am not familiar with them; please enlighten me.'

He beamed with evangelistic pleasure. 'Jainism is a rigorous faith whose chief tenets are nonviolence, reincarnation, and the belief that all living things have souls. Are you familiar with ahimsa?'

I shook my head.

'Ahimsa is the teaching that it is wrong to hurt any living being.

'Right,' I nodded. 'I remember reading about Indian monks so dedicated to this belief that they tried to avoid stepping on insects.'

'Precisely,' affirmed Gandhi. 'We practised vegetarianism, fasted for purposes of self-purification and believed in mutual tolerance of different religious traditions and belief systems.'

'And your interest in Jainism increased after your move to South Africa, did it not?'

'The Christian religious philosophy of Tolstoy also fascinated me, as did Hindu scriptures and philosophy. My studies of comparative religion have brought me to the conclusion that there is truth in all religions. Yet every one of them is also imperfect because they are all interpreted by fallible human intellects that are swayed by passion and bias.'

'So there's no such thing as objective truth,' I pressed.

Gandhi pondered a moment. 'The challenge is not in the existence of objective truth, but in our flawed ability as humans to discern it.'

I heard the sudden patter of rain hitting the thatched roof. I looked out at the courtyard in surprise as members of the meditation circle remained in place, continuing their devotions, seemingly oblivious to the downpour.

My amazement must have registered on my face because Gandhi smiled and said, 'Rain is the tears of the gods.'

I could feel my cheeks flushing with embarrassment. 'Back to Hindu theology. I'm told that you derive particular inspiration from the *Bhagavad Gita*.'

'Ah yes,' he replied. 'I first read it in earnest while in London, and since then, it has become a spiritual dictionary of sorts. It is a work of tremendous wisdom and has greatly influenced my interactions with the world.'

'Influenced how?'

'There are two Sanskrit words in the *Gita* that have been a particular source of fascination for me. *Aparigraha* can be translated as "non-possession". It means the abandonment of material possessions to focus on the spiritual qualities of life. And *samabhava* is the principle of accepting with good grace whatever fate and life have in store for you.'

'Very similar to the Benedictine monastic practice in Catholicism,' I observed.

'Quite true,' affirmed Gandhi, 'which relates to what we previously discussed about the common elements of truth in all religions.' He paused and cocked his head. 'Your name indicates Scottish heritage. Are you a Catholic, Mr Campbell?'

I laughed. 'Hardly. My people were lowland Scots who fought for King George at the Battle of Culloden. Dour Presbyterian Covenanters, the lot of them.'

'Who later emigrated to America?'

I nodded. 'Like hundreds of thousands of others who followed their dreams to the land of boundless opportunity. But back to your religious beliefs ....'

'Yes, of course. As a child, I disliked the arrogance of Christian missionaries who stood near my high school, heaping abuse on Hindus and their gods. Perhaps that is why I have always been tolerant of other religions.'

'And your own religious beliefs?'

'The principles of non-possession and equality require a change of heart to embrace nonviolence and celibacy.'

'Have you found celibacy to be a challenge?'

Gandhi merely smiled in response.

After an awkward pause, I moved on. 'I understand the educational facilities at Porbandar were best described as rudimentary?'

'Yes,' he confirmed. 'At our primary school, we wrote the alphabet in the dust with our fingers.'

I grimaced. 'That sounds terrible.'

Another enigmatic smile from Gandhi. 'Truth be told, I was far from a stellar pupil. I was fine at English, fair in arithmetic but weak in geography. My teachers reported that my conduct was very good, but my penmanship left much to be desired. I was quite surprised to win scholarships in my fifth and sixth years.'

'Perhaps your teachers had a higher regard for your abilities than you did.'

'Quite possibly,' Gandhi smiled. 'I tried to win the affection of my teachers and was gravely upset when chastised. When I once received corporal punishment, I remember being more upset by the humiliation than by any physical pain.'

A sudden gust blew a burst of rain onto the veranda, and I savoured the cool moistness on my face. 'Were you happy at school?' I asked.

Gandhi paused as if to recollect. 'I was quiet and very shy. My books and my lessons were my primary companions. I always ran home from school as soon as it closed. I could not bear to talk to anybody. I was afraid lest anyone should poke fun at me.'

Sensing his discomfort, I switched topics. 'You were married very young.'

'Yes, at age thirteen. Like me, Kasturba was born in 1869 in Porbandar in Gujarat. Her parents were affluent. Our families were friends. They wanted to cement their friendship, so at age seven, we were engaged to be married.'

'In America, that would be regarded as very … premature.'

Gandhi nodded. 'I agree. These days I can see no argument in support of such a ridiculously early marriage. I can still picture how we sat on our wedding dais, how we put the sweet kansar into each other's mouths. And that first night. Two innocent children unwittingly hurled headfirst into premature adulthood.'

The rain stopped, and Gandhi glanced towards the area where people were still meditating. 'We gradually learned to know each other and to speak freely together. But I wasted no time in assuming the authority of a husband. I had no reason to suspect my wife's fidelity, but jealousy does not require reasons. So, I was forever on the lookout regarding her movements. This sowed the seeds of bitter quarrels between us. Kasturba felt she was suffering from a form of imprisonment. She was not the sort of girl to accept any such thing without protest.'

'At the age of eighteen, you went to study in England. This meant a long separation.'

'Yes, but we managed. Kasturba and I are the best of friends. Today, ours is a life of contentment, happiness and progress. She has been a faithful nurse throughout my illness. Certainly, without her patience, endurance and self-effacement, I could not have devoted myself to public causes. Had it not been for her unfailing cooperation, I might have fallen into the abyss.'

'So she was ... at peace with your abstinence?'

Gandhi nodded. 'More than at peace. In fact, it is she who helped me remain true to my vows. She stood by me throughout all my political struggles. She fasted when I was in prison, gave up things she liked – good food, her jewellery and even her religious beliefs. Most importantly, she did not object to my vow of *brahmacharya*. But many of my doings have not met with her approval. Despite her dedication, she is far from a submissive wife.'

'Not a shrinking violet,' I smiled.

'Far from it,' Gandhi chuckled.

'And your children?'

Gandhi sighed. 'Kasturba gave me four handsome boys. But I regret that I did not prove to be an ideal father. While in South Africa, I introduced as much simplicity as possible into my home and brought my children under that discipline. Instead of buying baker's bread, we prepared unleavened wholemeal bread. We engaged a servant to look after the house, and the children willingly helped him in his work. There was hardly any illness in the home, but whenever there was, the nursing was happily done by them.'

'What about their formal education?' I asked. 'There has been some public controversy about your children's schooling.'

'I wouldn't say that I was indifferent to their literary education, but I certainly did not hesitate to subordinate formal schooling to my moral principles. Each day they would walk with me to the office and back home – about five miles in all. This not only gave us exercise, but it also gave me an opportunity to teach them through conversation. My eldest son, Harilal, has often expressed his grievance privately to me and publicly in the press. My other sons have generously forgiven this apparent failing. But at the time, I believed, perhaps wrongly, that this would yield benefits both for them as individuals and for the community. I don't think I was negligent in building their character. I never resorted to corporal punishment as a form of discipline.'

The patter of rain on the roof resumed. There were puddles beneath the gutter pipes and small pools collecting on the gravel path. The rain dripped onto the verandah railings and front steps. I noticed a delicate strip of clouds high overhead, which looked like a thin layer of cotton wool.

'Can we talk for a moment about what you have described as your adolescent rebellion?'

Gandhi sat silently for a moment. 'It was marked by secret atheism, petty thefts, clandestine smoking, and – most shocking of all for a boy born in a Vaishnava family – meat-eating. I convinced myself that meat-eating would make me strong and that, if the whole country took to meat-eating, the English could be overcome.'

'So, it was a political decision to eat meat?'

Gandhi shrugged. 'I don't really know. I can't quantify how much of it came from principle and how much was simple rebelliousness.'

'Did your parents know?' I asked.

Gandhi shook his head. 'Thankfully, they never found out. My meat-eating phase lasted about a year. I was very devoted to my parents and knew that if they came to know of my having become a meat-eater, they would be deeply shocked. There was strong opposition to meat-eating in Gujarat among the Jains and Vaishnavas. These were the traditions into which I was born and bred. After about a year, I realised that deceiving one's parents is worse than abstaining from meat. So, I stopped and never ate meat again.'

'What about girls?' I asked. 'You were married very young. Did you ever think about straying?'

Gandhi hesitated as if weighing the merits of forthrightness against secrecy. He grimaced briefly. 'I'm embarrassed to say that a friend once took me to a brothel. I sat near the woman on her bed, but I was tongue-tied. After ten minutes or so, she lost patience and showed me the door. I felt as though my manhood was inadequate. But I have ever since given thanks to God for having saved me.' He arched both eyebrows and smiled. 'I am pleased it turned out that way.'

'Was there any particular incident that ended your rebellious phase?'

He pursed his lips and shrugged. 'I suppose my adolescence was no different from that of most children of my age and class. But after each escapade, I would vow to never do it again. Eventually, I kept those promises.'

'So, you're saying that you went through a cycle of sin and vows until there were no more transgressions left to commit?'

'Partly,' he said. 'There were other factors at play as well. When I was sixteen, my father was bedridden, suffering from a fistula. I was his nurse. I dressed the wound and gave him his medicine. Every night I massaged his legs and retired only after he had fallen asleep. I loved to do this service.'

'That must have been very hard,' I said.

Gandhi smiled. 'He was getting weaker and weaker. One night I was giving him a massage when my uncle offered to relieve me. I was glad because I could go to the bedroom and be with my wife. But, within five minutes, the servant knocked on the door and summoned me. I sprang out of bed and ran to my father's room, but it was too late.'

Suddenly, he stopped speaking and swallowed hard. 'I felt deeply ashamed. If animal passion had not blinded me, I should have been spared the torture of separation from my father during his last moments.'

'Would you like to stop for a bit?' I asked.

Gandhi dismissed my suggestion with a wave. 'I'm fine. Let us proceed.'

'Can we talk now about England where you studied? You passed your matriculation examination in 1887 at the University of Bombay and went to Samaldas College, correct?'

'That's right,' Gandhi said. 'My original goal was to become a doctor. But an old friend and adviser to the family suggested to my mother and elder brother that if I were to keep up the family tradition of holding high office in one of the states in Gujarat, I would have to qualify as a barrister. He advised that I should go to England to study law. I was not happy at college and imagined England as a land of philosophers. So I jumped at the proposal.'

'How did your mother react?' I said.

Gandhi lifted his chin and squinted as a beam of sunlight hit his face. 'My mother had been told that young men got lost in England. Someone else had said that they took to meat and yet another that they could not live there without liquor. So only when I took an oath not to touch wine, women, and meat were my mother's doubts allayed and her permission granted.'

'Then you set sail?'

Gandhi laughed and shook his head. 'Hardly. My mother was not the only obstacle. The elders of the Vaishya caste issued a decree that forbade me to travel to England, arguing that to leave India was a violation of the Hindu religion. I was summoned to a hearing of sorts where they said, "We have heard that it is not possible to live in England without compromising our religion." I explained that I had vowed to my mother and elder brother that I would abstain from the three things they feared most.'

'Sounds like you were determined to proceed, regardless.'

'Precisely,' nodded Gandhi. 'Which, of course, incensed the elders, who berated me in the harshest possible terms. I was unmoved, so they excommunicated me. I was pronounced an outcast.'

'And what did you do then?'

'I asked a friend to loan me money for my passage and sundries and to recover the loan from my brother. Then, with my mother's blessing, I left my wife and baby of a few months and sailed for England in September 1888.'

'And when you arrived?'

'Ten days after my arrival, I joined the Inner Temple, one of the four London law colleges. I took my studies very seriously. But I also focused on personal and moral development.'

'How did you find the transition from the rural atmosphere of Rajkot to cosmopolitan life in the heart of the British empire?'

Gandhi frowned. 'It wasn't easy. I missed my family. I would often weep, and memories of home sometimes made sleep elusive.'

'It all must have been very alien,' I suggested.

He sighed. 'Everything was very strange. The people and their ways and even their dwellings. I was a complete novice in the matter of English dress, social etiquette and western food. I tried to adapt, taking on the task of becoming an English gentleman. I purchased a chimney-pot hat and evening suit. I even had my brother send me a double watch chain of gold. I was urged to take lessons in dancing, French and elocution. But I soon realised this was a fool's errand. I could spend a lifetime in England but would always be seen as nothing more than an Indian poseur. It was a false idea, so I decided to get on with my studies.'

'Were you a vegetarian?'

Gandhi groaned. 'Yes. It was terrible. The only dishes I could eat were tasteless. I had oatmeal porridge for breakfast, and for lunch and dinner, I had spinach and bread and jam. My friends warned me that such a diet was not good for my health. Fortunately, while living in West Kensington, I came across a vegetarian restaurant in Farrington Street. It provided me with my first hearty meal since my arrival in England. God came to my aid.'

'Rather like the Israelites in the desert receiving manna from heaven,' I joked.

Gandhi smiled. 'An apt metaphor. Before entering the restaurant, I noticed a stall on the footpath with books for sale. Among them was Salt's *Plea for Vegetarianism*. It provided a reasoned defence of vegetarianism as a matter of conviction. I found that its arguments complemented the spiritual teachings of my Vaishnava background. Health was my principal consideration at first, but later on, religion became the dominant motive for avoiding meat.'

'*Plea for Vegetarianism*, you say? I'll have to put it on my to-read list,' I said.

Gandhi smiled his approval. 'Towards the end of my second year in England, I came across a pair of Theosophists who were brothers. They talked to me about the most popular expression of Hinduism, the Gita. They were reading Sir Edwin Arnold's translation, *The Song Celestial*. It provides great insights into the search for truth. They also recommended *The Light of Asia* by the same author. I read both works with even greater interest than I did the *Bhagavad Gita*. Once I began reading, I couldn't put them down.'

'Did you read any other English vegetarians, such as Edward Carpenter or George Bernard Shaw?' I said.

'Gandhi nodded and said. 'Yes. They were socialists who rejected the prevailing values of the late-Victorian establishment and denounced the evils of industrial society. They believed in simplicity and stressed the superiority of the moral over material values and in cooperation over conflict. These ideas helped shape my personality and my politics.

I flipped through my notebook. 'You passed your exams and were called to the bar on the 10th of June 1891. You enrolled in the High Court the next day, I believe.'

'And on the day after that, I sailed home. I was pining to see my mother. My brother had not told me she had died. It was a severe shock to me. My grief was even greater than at my father's death.'

For a moment, Gandhi's chin trembled as if he were waging an internal battle against the onset of tears. Then he recovered his composure.

'What did you hope to do on your return to India?' I asked to change the topic.

'I wanted to teach,' he replied. 'I came across an advertisement in the papers: "Wanted, English teacher to teach one hour daily." I went to Bombay for the interview in high spirits, but when the principal found that I was not a graduate, he refused me. My brother and I concluded that I should settle in Rajkot where he, a petty legal pleader, could give me work in drafting applications for litigants. So I set up my own legal office in Rajkot. I got along moderately well – thanks more to influence, rather than any great ability on my part.'

'What made you decide to go to South Africa? How did that come about?'

'My brother had introduced me to a partner of a large legal firm who had a big case in South Africa. He told my brother I would be useful to them in their Natal office. It was a one-year contract, and they would pay a first-class return fare and a sum of £105. By now, another baby had been born to us, and our love was not yet free from lust. Nevertheless, in April 1893, I accepted the offer. I spent more than two decades there, returning to India only briefly during 1896–97.'

'You became politically and socially active. What prompted your activism?'

Gandhi glanced towards the forest before looking directly at me, his face set in a grim frown. 'I first encountered racial discrimination in 1896, when travelling from Durban to Pretoria. My future employer had booked me a first-class seat. When a passenger saw I was coloured, he went and got two uniformed railroad officials. One of them said to me, "Come along, you must go to the van compartment."

'"But I have a first-class ticket," I protested.

'"That does not matter," they said.

'"I was permitted to travel in this compartment at Durban, and I insist on doing so," I replied.

'"No, you won't," said one of the officials. "You must leave this compartment, or else I shall have to call a police constable to push you out."

"Go ahead and call the constable," I challenged. "I refuse to leave voluntarily."

'A constable arrived and forcibly removed me from the train. I was left shivering on the platform of the railway station in Pietermaritzburg.'

'Outrageous,' I said.

Gandhi shrugged. 'Such humiliations were the daily lot of Indians in Natal. They learned to bear them with the same resignation with which they ignored their meagre earnings.'

'Not an auspicious beginning.'

'Indeed not. But it set the stage for what was to come. At about 8 o'clock that night, my train finally reached Pretoria. As arranged, I went straight to Johnston's Family Hotel. Mr Johnston agreed to accommodate me for the night on the condition that I should have my dinner served in my room.'

'How did you respond?'

'I said, "Thank you, I understand your difficulty. I do not mind eating in my room."'

'You were very gracious.'

'Later that evening, Mr Johnston came to my room and apologised. He said: "I was ashamed of having asked you to have your dinner here. So, I asked the other guests if they would mind you having your dinner in the dining room. They had no objection and did not mind your staying here."'

'What was your reaction to this prejudice?'

'Until that time, I had not been particularly outspoken on such matters. While in England, I simply ignored the social slights I often suffered. But this was different. I suppose, in retrospect, the journey from Durban to Pretoria can be seen as one of the most important experiences of my life. It was my moment of truth, in a sense. From that moment on, I have refused to accept injustice as the natural order of things. Ever since, I have defended my dignity as an Indian and as a man.'

I nodded. 'I know you took on and fought many battles while you were in South Africa.'

'South Africa very quickly drew me into the turmoil of its racial problem. It provided me with the opportunity to hone my leadership skills. I was previously uncomfortable about speaking in public or even arguing on behalf of a client in court. But, by July 1894, in my twenty-fifth year, I seemed to blossom into a proficient political campaigner.'

I smiled. 'A late bloomer, then.'

Gandhi laughed. 'I suppose. But I came to realise the importance of education, representation and nonviolent resistance as a political tool.'

'Is it fair to say that a good portion of your initial activity was focused on informing the Indian community about its rights under the law?'

'Certainly!' he affirmed. 'I called a meeting. It was the first time I had ever spoken publicly. I stressed the importance of unity. I stressed that we were all Indians first and foremost and that we must put aside differences of faith. That Hindus, Muslims, and Christians must all stand together. And I suggested the formation of an association to make representations to the authorities in respect of the hardships of the Indian settlers.'

'What was the response? Were they enthusiastic?'

Gandhi smiled. 'They agreed. So we decided to hold weekly meetings. At their request, I spoke with the railway authorities. I told them that the disabilities the Indians were forced to travel under were unjustified. I got a letter in reply to the effect that first and second-class tickets would be issued to Indians who were properly dressed.'

'But this didn't go far enough?'

He shook his head. 'Hardly. It was a marginal improvement but far from adequate relief. It empowered individual station masters to decide who met the required standard of dress. That wasn't nearly the worst of it.'

'What do you mean?' I pressed.

'In the Orange Free State, the Indians were required to pay a poll tax for entry into the Transvaal. They were prohibited from owning land, except in locations set apart for them. They could not walk on public footpaths and could not go outdoors after nine o'clock at night without a permit. Once I went for a walk through President Street to an open plain. A man, without even asking me to leave the footpath, pushed and kicked me into the street. The incident deepened my empathy for the Indian community.'

'That's outrageous!'

Gandhi simply shrugged. 'By now, I had negotiated an out-of-court settlement in the Natal legal matter, and my year's contract had come to an end. So, in June 1894, I returned to Durban and began to prepare for my voyage home. But before my departure, I saw an item in the *Natal Mercury* about pending legislation in the Provincial Council that would deprive the Indians of the vote. "If this Bill becomes law," I warned, "it will be a fatal blow to our rights."'

'How did the local Indian community respond?'

'They begged me to take up the fight. I was asked to cancel my passage.'

'So you stayed?'

'Of course,' affirmed Gandhi. 'We organised a committee just as the Bill was about to pass its second reading. We immediately lodged a request to delay the discussion of the Bill and obtained a two-day postponement. We used that time to draft a petition to the Provincial Council.'

'Did your efforts succeed?'

Gandhi grimaced. 'No. Despite all our efforts, the Bill was passed into law. But our agitation breathed new life into the Indian community. It fostered unity and the conviction that it was a duty to fight for political rights. Our next move was another petition to the Secretary of State for the Colonies, Lord Ripon. We gathered ten thousand signatures and sent a copy to *The Times of India*. The *London Times* also supported our claim, and we began to entertain hopes that the Bill might be vetoed.'

So that dark cloud of discrimination had a silver lining of sorts?' I asked.

'In a manner of speaking, I suppose,' Gandhi conceded. 'Although we were unable to prevent the passage of the Bill, we were able to draw world attention to the grievances of the Natal Indians. And we thought that sustained agitation was an essential element of our struggle. To that end, we established the Natal Indian Congress on the 22nd of May, 1894. The Congress served to acquaint the English, South Africans and Indians here at home with the terrible state of affairs in Natal.'

'And what were your plans at this time?'

'It was about this time that I was asked to remain in Natal permanently. I said that I would be able to stay if the community could guarantee legal work of £300 a year. As a result, some twenty local merchants gave me retainers for one year of legal work. My previous employer, Dada Abdulla, purchased the necessary office furniture in lieu of a purse he intended to give me on my departure. So, I set up my practice.'

'Did you prosper?'

'I made a living,' replied Gandhi. 'But a large part of my practice was devoted to public-interest work, for which I charged nothing beyond out-of-pocket expenses. In fact, in some cases, I even met those expenses myself.'

'So you were settling into South Africa,' I said.

'Yes, it was mid-1896, and I decided to go home, fetch my wife and children and return. I landed in Calcutta, and on the way to Bombay, the train stopped at Allahabad. While there, I did an interview with the editor of *The Pioneer*. I took the opportunity to write a pamphlet outlining Indian grievances in South Africa. It became known as the Green Pamphlet.'

'So the editor of *The Pioneer* published it?'

'Oh, yes,' said Gandhi. 'I also met with prominent community leaders and persuaded them to address public meetings in Bombay, Poona, Madras and Calcutta on Indian grievances in Natal. I gave long interviews to the editors of *The Statesman* and *The Englishman*, which were published in full. I also tried to expose discrimination against the Indian subjects of Queen Victoria in Africa.'

'You must have been very pleased.'

He frowned and shook his head sadly. 'Initially yes, but garbled versions of my activities reached Natal and inflamed its European population. On landing at Durban in January 1897, I was assaulted and nearly lynched by a white mob.'

'Why were they so up in arms?'

'There was a rumour that I was bringing a shipload of Indian immigrants to Natal. Whites had also heard that I had denounced them while in India. That was enough to trigger a riot.'

'How did you escape?'

'I first made sure my wife and children were taken off the ship separately. When I later disembarked with my escort, Mr Laughton, I was recognised, and people started shouting, "Gandhi! Gandhi!" A crowd gathered, and I was pelted by a barrage of stones, brickbats and rotten eggs. Someone snatched away my turban, while others began to batter and kick me. Luckily, an Indian youth witnessed the incident and ran to get the police, who escorted me to my destination. But a lynch mob of Whites surrounded the house and began shouting, "We must have Gandhi!"'

'That sounds terrifying. What did you do?'

'I resorted to subterfuge. I put on an Indian constable's uniform and wrapped a Madrasi scarf around my head to serve as a helmet. Two South African detectives escorted me, one of them disguised as an Indian merchant, complete with face paint. We threaded our way through the crowd to a carriage and drove off to the police station.'

'Were there any repercussions over this disgraceful incident?'

Gandhi shrugged again. 'Joseph Chamberlain, the colonial secretary in the British Cabinet, wanted to prosecute my assailants. But I refused. For me, it was a matter of principle not to seek redress of a personal wrong in a court of law. Later that day, a journalist from the *Natal Advertiser* came to interview me. My refusal to press criminal charges generated considerable public support and sympathy.'

'So would this be an example of *ahimsa*?'

Gandhi shook his head. 'No, *ahimsa* is the principle of nonviolence. My refusal to press criminal charges was more a case of *samabhava*: accepting one's fate with good grace.

I nodded and consulted my notes. I sensed Gandhi waiting patiently for my next question and swallowed while trying to work up the courage to broach the explosive issue of his bigotry towards Africans.

My nerve failed, something I rationalised by thinking my editor would probably spike any negative reflections on the living legend seated before me. No feet of clay allowed.

My inner dilemma must have registered outwardly through my facial expression, for Gandhi leaned forward and asked, 'Is everything all right?'

Receiving no response, he seized the initiative. 'It was about this time I decided that I did not want more children. I began to focus on bodily self-control and thought about taking the *brahmacharya* vow.'

'The vow of sexual abstinence?' I said, inwardly relieved that the interview had changed direction.

Gandhi nodded. 'It was my attachment to my wife that was the real obstacle. We began to sleep in separate beds, and I finally took the pledge in 1906.'

It intrigued me that Gandhi had taken a vow of sexual abstinence. 'What prompted you to take the vow?' I asked.

'Every day since then, I have experienced freedom, joy and self-realisation,' he said. 'I have stepped closer to conduct consistent with Brahman and the protection of the body, mind and soul.'

I nodded but could think of no suitable question to follow that comment. Instead, I said, 'On the outbreak of the South African, or Boer War in 1899, you advocated for Indians to come to the defence of British rule.'

Gandhi nodded. 'I raised an ambulance corps of 1100 volunteers. I felt it was my duty to instil a spirit of service even though we all viewed British rule over India as oppressive.'

Lifting a collection of clippings from my bag, I said, 'The editor of the *Pretoria News* described your actions on the battlefield thus: "After a night's work, which had shattered men with much bigger frames, I came across Gandhi in the early morning sitting by the roadside eating a regulation army biscuit. Every man in Buller's force was dull and depressed, and damnation was heartily invoked on everything. But Gandhi was stoical in his bearing, cheerful and confident in his conversation and had a kindly eye.'" I folded the newspaper and returned it to my bag. 'That's quite a positive portrayal.'

Gandhi flashed a smile of self-deprecation. 'Our war work earned its share of plaudits. We all hoped this would help to have our grievances redressed. Still, the British victory in the war brought little relief to the Indians in South Africa.'

'Was this the reason you returned to India?'

Another shrug from Gandhi. 'Partly. But to a large extent, I felt my work was no longer in South Africa but rather in India. Farewell meetings were arranged, and gifts of gold and silver were presented to me. One such gift was a diamond and gold necklace worth fifty guineas for my wife. I decided that I could not keep these things. I drafted a deed establishing a trust for the benefit of the community. I appointed independent trustees, deposited those items in the bank and sailed for home.'

I looked at the dappled sunlight on the ground adjacent to where we were sitting, then turned towards Gandhi. 'Would this be an example of *aparigraha*?' I said.

Gandhi smiled as if I were a promising pupil. 'Indeed so. Shortly after I reached India, I attended the 1901 annual Indian National Congress in Calcutta. I prepared a resolution outlining the grievances of the Indian settlers in South Africa that I wanted to put to Congress. The chairman called me to the podium. When I read my resolution, everyone raised their hands, and it was passed unanimously.' He smiled.

'From there, you went to Bombay and took chambers, I think.'

'Yes, and much to my surprise, I prospered. Then just when I seemed to be settling down, I received a cable from South Africa: 'Chamberlain expected here. Please return immediately.' I gave up the chambers and started for Durban. The date for the deputation to Mr Chamberlain had been fixed. It was my task to draft the memorandum that would be submitted and to accompany the deputation.'

'How did Mr Chamberlain respond to your memorandum?'

'With a great deal of condescension, sadly enough. He said to me, "Your grievances seem to be genuine," in that typically English upper-class tone of condescension. "But the Imperial Government has little day-to-day control over its self-governing colonies. I shall do what I can, but you must try your best to placate the Europeans if you wish to live among them.'"

'That must have been a huge disappointment,' I said. 'Particularly in light of the fact that you had travelled all the way from India.'

Gandhi sighed. 'At least I set the ball rolling. But to push it along further, I decided to set up an office in Johannesburg. You see, the Transvaal government published a disgraceful ordinance for the registration of its Indian population.'

'What year was this?'

'Nineteen hundred and six.'

I nodded. 'Uhuh, the same year you organised a mass protest meeting in Johannesburg in September. I believe participants pledged to defy the ordinance through nonviolent disobedience if it became law. In other words, *ahimsa*.'

'*Ahimsa*,' echoed Gandhi. 'The struggle lasted more than seven years. It had its ups and downs, but by its final phase in 1913, hundreds of Indians, including women, were in jail. Thousands more were threatened with imprisonment, flogging and even shooting.'

'That's disgraceful,' I gasped.

'Indeed,' he said, 'It was a terrible ordeal. But it was also the worst possible advertisement for the South African government. The governments of Britain and India exerted political pressure for compromise, which I negotiated with Jan Smuts, a South African government minister at the time.'

'I read that during one of your many stays in jail, you prepared a pair of sandals for Smuts. Afterwards, he said there was no hatred or personal ill-will between the two of you, and when the fight was over, there was the atmosphere in which a decent peace could be concluded.'

'A man and his deeds are two distinct things,' Gandhi said, his gaze sober. 'Whereas a good deed should call forth approval and a wicked deed disapproval, the doer of the deed, whether good or wicked, always deserves respect. Hate the sin and not the sinner.'

I nodded. 'Christianity preaches a similar message.'

Gandhi nodded his agreement. 'I helped to found a journal named *Indian Opinion* in 1904. I bore the brunt of the work and sank practically all my savings into the venture. I remember a time when

I had to remit £75 each month. *Indian Opinion* became a platform for me to expound upon the principles and practice of *satyagraha*. Readers were interested in our campaign of nonviolent resistance and the real condition of Indians in South Africa. Until 1914, excepting the intervals of my enforced rest in prison, there was hardly an issue of *Indian Opinion* without an article from me. Later the publishing operation of the magazine moved to the countryside...'

I glanced up from my notetaking. 'How did that come about?'

'Ah,' said Gandhi, 'in 1904, I read a book by John Ruskin that transformed my life. I found that *Unto This Last* reflected some of my deepest convictions, and I felt an irresistible attraction to a life of simplicity, manual labour and austerity. I proposed that we buy a farm, and everyone on it should live a life of labour, draw the same wage and attend to the press work in their spare time.'

'Rather like the Owenite communities in my country.'

'I'm not familiar,' Gandhi confessed.

'Robert Owen was a Welsh textile magnate who founded a series of communal settlements based on socialist principles. They all failed within a few years.'

Gandhi smiled. 'I'm pleased to report that our story has a happier ending. I talked to all ten of the workers. Some argued that such a move would ruin the journal, while others agreed to the idea. Twenty acres of land were purchased in Phoenix. It had a nice little spring and a few orange and mango trees. Adjoining it were eighty acres that had many more fruit trees and a dilapidated cottage. The cost was a thousand pounds. And so, the Phoenix Settlement was started in 1904, and *Indian Opinion* continues to be published.'

'So you have succeeded where Robert Owen failed?'

'It would appear so,' replied Gandhi.

'And what of Tolstoy Farm?' I asked.

'Six years later, another colony grew up under our care twenty-one miles from Johannesburg. It was named Tolstoy Farm after the Russian writer whom I admired and corresponded with.'

'Is it fair to say that those two settlements were the precursor to the Shegaon Ashram?'

Gandhi nodded but did not add anything.

I studied my notes. 'You've attracted your fair share of criticism, and not only because of your political activity. I would like to read something that British classicist Gilbert Murray wrote about you in the *Hibbert Journal*:

"'Be very careful how they deal with a man who cares nothing for sensual pleasure, nothing for riches, nothing for comfort or praise, or promotion, but is simply determined to do what he believes to be right. He is a dangerous and uncomfortable enemy because his body which you can always conquer gives you so little purchase upon his soul."

Gandhi responded with an enigmatic smile, saying nothing until I filled the void by changing the subject. 'For the benefit of my readers, can you please give me a working definition of *satyagraha*?'

'Of course,' he responded. '*Satyagraha* rejects all forms of violence in all circumstances. This is in contrast to some practitioners of passive resistance in the West. They have resorted to violence in self-defence. English suffragettes, for example, studied jiu-jitsu as a means of protecting themselves against physical attack. But *satyagraha* is a categorical doctrine of absolute nonviolence. Instead, we rely on the moral strength of our convictions alone.'

'Thank you for that. Can we now move on to your final departure from South Africa?'

'I decided to leave during the summer of 1914. We were still at sea on the 4th of August when we received news of the outbreak of war. We reached London two days later.'

'And you returned to India the following year, correct?'

'Yes, in 1915.'

'At that time, I believe you supported the Allied war effort.'

'True. I encouraged enlistment in the British Indian Army. But at the same time, I criticised instances in which British officials abused Indian rail passengers. I met with the Viceroy, Lord Chelmsford, about this problem. But it was the indenture system that drew me back into full-fledged political activism.'

'You are referring to the abolition bill of 1916?'

Gandhi nodded. 'In March of that year, a resolution was moved in the Imperial Legislative Council for the abolition of the indenture system that, in reality, was a form of semi-slavery. These were workers who left India to labour under an indenture for a period of up to five years. In accepting the motion, Lord Hardinge claimed that His Majesty's government had promised to abolish the system... in due course.'

'And this failed to satisfy you?'

Gandhi shook his head. 'Absolutely not! I was determined to press for immediate abolition. In February 1917, I visited Karachi, Calcutta and other places. We held meetings, and there was much enthusiasm. Many Englishmen attended the meetings. Before the 31st of July 1917, the government announced that indentured emigration from India would be stopped. This was the culmination of an advocacy campaign that began with a petition I had drafted in 1894.'

I raised my eyebrows in surprise.

'Yes! It took me twenty-three years to get the indenture system abolished,' Gandhi said. He pointed over my shoulder, and I looked around to see the corner of a glass cabinet inside Gandhi's hut.

'I keep three china clay monkeys in that cabinet side by side. One has his hands over his eyes, the second over his mouth and the third covering his ears. They remind me neither to hear untruth nor speak it.'

'A useful reminder,' I said. 'So, next ...'

'The next major issue came along in February 1919, when the Imperial Legislative Council enacted the Rowlatt Act that legalised the imprisonment without trial of anyone suspected of sedition.'

'And ...?'

Gandhi tapped his lower lip and furrowed his brow. 'The law was unwarranted. The war was over. There was no reason for it. I pleaded with the Viceroy but to no avail. So, we called upon the country to take strike action.

'When was this?' I asked, my pen poised above my notebook.

'The strike commenced on 6 April 1919, and it triggered a political earthquake that shook the subcontinent. In Delhi, the police opened fire on protesters as they peaceably marched towards the railway station. This event signalled the adoption of cruel repressive policies by the British authorities in Delhi. Violent outbreaks followed elsewhere, with similar incidents of unwarranted brutality happening in Lahore, Amritsar and Bombay.'

'Did you suffer any personal harm?'

'I was summoned to Delhi. Before the train reached Palwal Railway Station, I was served with a written order prohibiting me from entering Punjab. As we approached Pydhuni Station, I could see that a huge crowd had gathered. A friend later told me that people were incensed by a rumour that I had been arrested. When I stepped down from the rail carriage, people went mad with joy. A procession was about to proceed towards the Crawford Market when a body of mounted police appeared.'

Gandhi removed his glasses and wiped the lenses with the fringe of his white dhoti.

'The densely packed crowd surged against the police cordon. Then the officer in charge of the mounted police gave the order to disperse the crowd. The mounted police charged through the crowd brandishing their lances. People fled in panicked confusion as the horses battered their way through the crowd. I proceeded directly to the Commissioner's office to complain about the conduct of the police.'

'It sounds like a nightmare,' I said.

'This was only a minor incident by comparison to what occurred in Amritsar. There a British general ordered his soldiers to open fire on protesters. Almost four hundred people were slaughtered.'

'Terrible,' I said. 'I believe the Viceroy seized upon these events as an excuse to impose martial law?'

Before Gandhi could reply, a tall, balding man bearing a teapot and glasses on a tray appeared.

'Can I offer you refreshment?' asked Gandhi, as the tray-bearer stepped onto the verandah.'

'Thank you so much.'

'Meet Mahadev,' Gandhi said as the man placed the tray with a pot of tea and two cups on the ground between us. 'He joined the Ashram in 1917 and has been with me for more than twenty years, serving as my personal secretary and much more.'

'Pleased to meet you, Mahadev,' I smiled.

'He takes care of my schedule and is equally at home in the office and the kitchen. He is also an accomplished author, having written several biographies, translated many short stories and contributed many articles to numerous newspapers.'

'You are too kind,' Mahadev said, bowing his head. 'Will that be all?'

Gandhi nodded, and Mahadev bowed and withdrew down the steps.

'Far more than a mere factotum, I see.'

'Oh yes,' replied Gandhi. 'Mahadev is a vital friend and partner.'

Leaning forward, Gandhi poured the tea into two cups and handed me one. He raised his cup and sipped before continuing. 'Soon after the massacre in Amritsar, I heard that mill workers in Ahmedabad had staged a violent protest and that a sergeant had been murdered. I immediately made my way to Ahmedabad, where a police officer was waiting to escort me to meet the commissioner. I declared my readiness to help restore peace and asked for permission to hold a public meeting. Addressing the crowd, I tried to explain that violence was wrong, regardless of provocation. I then declared that I would be embarking on a penitent fast of three days. After three weeks, a settlement was reached.'

'It's amazing that a simple hunger strike could generate such tangible political pressure,' I said.

'Unfortunately, things weren't quite so simple. Despite the Ahmedabad settlement, the government continued with its policy of political repression in other parts of India, particularly Punjab. Leaders were put under arrest, martial law was declared, and special tribunals were created. These were not true courts of justice but blunt instruments for carrying out the arbitrary will of British autocrats. Innocent men and women were sent to prison on the flimsiest of evidence. It was an outrageous affront to human dignity and Britain's claim to be a beacon of democracy.'

'Were you directly involved?'

'Not in Punjab, for I had been banned there,' replied Gandhi. 'But I was asked to come to Champaran and help the ryots – the peasant farmers. They were being horribly exploited by local plantation owners. Mahadev came with me, and the lieutenant governor invited me to join a committee formed to address this issue. Representatives of peasants made statements, and the planters' association put their point of view. The committee found unanimously in favour of the ryots. Their report resulted in the abolition of the Tinkathia system and the introduction of the Agrarian Act.'

'I'm not familiar with ... what was it, the Tinkathia system?'

Gandhi smiled. 'This was a regime that forced Bihari peasants ....'

'The ryots?' I interjected.

'Yes, the ryots ... to grow indigo on a portion of their land for the benefit of the British plantation owners.'

'I see,' I said with a nod. 'Sorry about the interruption. Please go on.'

Gandhi sighed. 'There was so much injustice and exploitation. In Gujarat, there was crop failure and famine. Thousands were living hand-to-mouth and were unable to pay their annual revenue assessment. Under the Land Revenue Rules, if a farmer's crop was valued at four annas or under, he could claim full suspension of the revenue assessment for that year. But government assessors arbitrarily valued crops at four annas, when in reality, they were worth far less. I advised the farmers to resort to *satyagraha* and request that the government suspend the collection of taxes.'

'I read that you regard the Kheda *satyagraha* as the trigger for a political awakening among the peasants of Gujarat.'

'I think that is a fair assessment,' Gandhi said. 'But at that time, I felt that the Indian National Congress was in dire need of reform if we were to take our struggle to the next level. It was far too unwieldy for any useful discussion of public affairs. So, I agreed to chair the committee that was charged with drafting a constitution. Next, I was asked to write a resolution of non-cooperation for the All-India Congress in September 1920. The revised constitution and resolution of non-cooperation were presented at a special session of the Congress in Calcutta and passed unanimously.'

'By the autumn of 1920, you were the dominant figure on the Indian political stage. Almost singlehandedly, you refashioned the thirty-five-year-old Indian National Congress into an effective political instrument of Indian nationalism.'

Gandhi lowered his head. 'My message was simple. It was not British guns that kept India in bondage. Rather it was disunity among Indians themselves. We began to boycott British products and institutions such as the courts, offices and schools. Thousands of *satyagrahis* peacefully defied British authority and went to prison with smiles on their faces.'

'And you among them. You were tried for sedition in March 1922, were you not? And sentenced to six years imprisonment?'

'Yes. Two years after that, I was released on compassionate grounds after undergoing surgery for appendicitis.'

'How had the political landscape changed in your absence?'

Gandhi frowned in bitter reminiscence. 'The Congress Party had split into two factions. One faction favoured the entry of the party into the legislature, and the other faction opposed it. Worst of all, the unity between Hindus and Muslims that had developed during the non-cooperation movement had dissolved.'

The sudden rattle of a cloudburst hitting the roof distracted my attention. Gandhi paused, and we both sat in silence until the downpour passed.

'I tried to convince these groups to put aside their mutual suspicion. I told them that the unity of all Indians was an essential element in our struggle for freedom. But my logic could not prevail against sectarian bitterness and fanaticism. And in the autumn of 1924, I began a three-week fast to promote the path of nonviolence. In December of that year, I was named president of the Congress Party, a position that I held for one year.'

'What sort of progress did you make during your term in office?'

'Only marginal,' sighed Gandhi. 'In 1927, the British government appointed a constitutional reform commission led by Sir John Simon. It consisted of six members of the House of Commons but failed to include even a single Indian member. This was clearly unacceptable.'

I looked at my watch and saw we had been together for almost two hours. I pressed on, hoping he would afford me extra time as we had not yet canvassed all my issues.

'So we boycotted the Simon Commission. At the annual congress in December 1928, I presented a resolution demanding that India be granted self-governing dominion status within one year, or else we would press for complete independence from Britain.'

'Tell me about the famous Salt March.'

'In March 1930, I launched the Salt March, a *satyagraha* protest against the British tax on salt. More than 60,000 people were imprisoned, but, nonetheless, it was one of my most successful campaigns against the British Raj.'

I knew most of this but took notes nonetheless.

'The following year, I entered into talks with Viceroy Lord Irwin. Our agreement, which came to be known as the Gandhi–Irwin Pact, ended our campaign of civil disobedience. I agreed to attend the Round Table Conference in London as the sole representative of the Indian National Congress.'

I thumbed through my notes, but before I could ask another question, Gandhi continued. 'The conference proceedings focused on the problem of the Indian minorities, rather than on the transfer of power from the British.'

'That must have been a great disappointment to you.'

Gandhi smiled. 'I had long since lost any illusions about Britain's willingness to relinquish control of the jewel in the crown of its global empire. When I returned to India in December 1931, I discovered that Congress was facing an all-out offensive from Lord Irwin's successor, Lord Willingdon.'

'At this point, you were again imprisoned, I believe.'

'This time, the government tried to destroy my influence by insulating me from the outside world.' He smiled. 'I quickly reclaimed the initiative. While still in prison, I began a fast to protest against the British government's decision to segregate the Dalits, the untouchables, who were at the lowest rung of the Hindu caste system. Under the new constitution, these untouchables were to be allotted separate electorates in the new constitution. I viewed this as unjust.'

'Did your fast yield the result you wanted?'

Gandhi nodded. 'A fairer electoral arrangement was negotiated by the leaders of the higher castes and the Dalits. It was then endorsed by the British government.'

'But in 1934, you resigned as the leader and member of the Congress Party. Why was that?'

Gandhi hesitated before speaking. 'I came to believe that the leading members of Congress adopted nonviolence as a political

PEOPLE WHO HAVE CHANGED THE WORLD

means to an end rather than as a fundamental creed. That sort of cynicism I could not countenance.'

'So what then?'

Gandhi smiled. 'I returned to the people. To a program of building the nation from the bottom up. This means education in rural India, where eighty-five per cent of our population is found. It means continuing the struggle against untouchability. Promoting hand spinning, weaving and other cottage industries as a method of supplementing the earnings of our underemployed peasantry. This is why we came to Shegaon, which I have made the central hub.'

Just then, Mahadev appeared at the foot of the stairs. 'It's time for you to spin, Mahatma.'

'I spin every day,' Gandhi explained. 'It gives me time to think. I am also seeking better, cheaper and easily available tools that can be repaired locally. Anything that will promote self-sufficiency.' He turned to Mahadev and said, 'Give us twenty minutes.'

'I will come back,' Mahadev bowed and descended the steps.

'Thank you,' I said. 'I still have a few questions, but I hope they won't take long.'

'My pleasure,' replied Gandhi. 'I am enjoying our conversation. What is next?' he asked in a soft voice.

'Well, let me see. The British authorities portray you as a utopian visionary at best; at worst as a hypocrite whose pacifism masks subversion against the Raj.'

Gandhi again removed his glasses and polished them on his dhoti. 'I am aware of those criticisms. I strive every day through *satyagraha* to prove them wrong.'

'And you have your share of critics here at home.'

Gandhi shrugged. 'It is true there is no shortage of naysayers. Some say that I am going too fast. Others, the more radical faction, complain that I am not going fast enough. Communists argue that I am not serious about evicting the British or confiscating the wealth of Indian princes and landlords. Some of the Dalits doubt my good faith as a social reformer, and Muslim leaders accuse me of partiality to my own community.'

I suddenly found the courage to take the difficult plunge into awkward waters. 'There are also those who have accused you of being a racist. They argue that in South Africa, you kept the Indian struggle separate from that of the Africans even though the latter were also denied political rights. I've heard that you call the Africans by the derogatory term "kaffir" and objected to them mixing with the Indians. That you worked with the British to promote racial segregation in the hopes of gaining benefits for the Indian community.'

'I am aware,' Gandhi said, his voice flat. 'In my view, those arguments are simplistic. Not only was equality for all premature when I was in South Africa, but my struggle for Indian rights paved the way for Black rights.'

'Another criticism levelled at you is your attitude to women. In December 1935, Margaret Sanger, the American birth-control activist, came to visit you. You agreed that women should be emancipated. I understand that Sanger insisted that contraception is essential for women to gain control over their own bodies, enabling them to be the arbiter of their own destinies.'

Gandhi shook his head. 'I believe women should resist their husbands and men should control their animal passion. That is the safest route to emancipation.'

'But Sanger explained that women have feelings as deep and as amorous as men's, and there are times when wives desire physical union as much as their husbands.'

'All sex is lust!' Gandhi said, his words razor sharp. 'But I believe in the rights of women and that women are to be equal to men. I appointed a woman to lead the Congress party. Women joined us as we marched to protest the British salt monopoly and salt tax.'

'It's now time,' said a voice behind my shoulder.

I looked around and saw Mahadev climbing the steps.

'Good timing,' I said, hiding my sense of relief. 'I think we are done.'

'I hope I've answered all your questions,' said Gandhi as he rose to his feet.

'Thank you. I appreciate you giving me so much of your valuable time,' I said as I stood and moved towards the steps.

'Nice to meet you,' Gandhi said politely, then turning towards Mahadev, he said, 'Please take our guest to the gate. I will go to my spinning.'

Endnote

This imagined conversation with Mahatma Gandhi is set in 1937 when he was almost sixty-eight years of age. It uses translations of Gandhi's own remarks or close interpretations of them (many taken from his autobiography) to convey his worldview faithfully. Prior to the date of this conversation, Gandhi had not been nominated for the Nobel Peace Prize. He was nominated in 1937, 1938, 1939, 1947 and 1948. It was generally held that he would be awarded the prize in 1948, but he was assassinated prior to the announcement, and the Prize is not awarded posthumously.

The nationalist struggle in India entered its last crucial phase with the outbreak of the Second World War. The Indian National Congress was prepared to support the British war effort if Indian self-government was assured once victory was achieved. A British cabinet minister went to India in March 1942 with an offer that Gandhi found unacceptable. British equivocation on the transfer of power to Indian hands and the promotion of discord between Muslims and Hindus impelled Gandhi to demand an immediate British withdrawal from India. This became known as the Quit India Movement.

At this time, India was under threat of invasion from the Japanese in neighbouring Burma. The British reacted to the Quit India Movement with ruthless brutality. They imprisoned the entire Congress leadership and set out to finally crush the party. Gandhi, his wife, and several other top party leaders were confined in the Aga Khan Palace in Poona. Kasturba died there in early 1944, shortly before Gandhi and the others were released.

During the two years after the election of Britain's Labour Atlee government in 1945, negotiations were conducted between leaders of the Congress, the Muslim League and the British government. These culminated in the Mountbatten Plan, which led to the partition of the Raj into the two newly independent nations of India and Pakistan on 15 September 1947.

It was a great disappointment to Gandhi that independence was realised without Indian unity. As final constitutional arrangements were negotiated in 1946 and 1947, communal riots between

Hindus and Muslims created a climate in which Gandhi's appeal for tolerance stood little chance. After the Indian partition, Gandhi threw himself into the task of healing the scars of the conflict. He toured the riot-torn areas of Bengal and Bihar, rebuking sectarian bigotry and working to rehabilitate the refugees. It proved to be an impossible task.

In the end, Gandhi was subject to blame from both communities. So he began a fast. By September 1947, his fast had stopped the rioting in Calcutta; by January 1948, the city of Delhi had been shamed into a communal truce. A few days later, on 30 January, while he was on his way to his evening prayer meeting in Delhi, he was assassinated by a young Hindu extremist named Nathuram Godse.

The mainspring of Gandhi's life lay in religion, not in politics. Religion, for him, did not mean dogma, ritual or sectarianism. 'What I have been striving and pining to achieve these thirty years,' he wrote in his autobiography, 'is to see God face-to-face.' Gandhi's deepest aspirations were spiritual. But unlike many of his fellow Indians with a similar outlook, he did not retire to a remote cave to meditate in solitude. As he once said, he carried his cave within him. For Gandhi, the truth was not something to be discovered in the privacy of one's personal life; it had to be upheld in the challenging context of social and political life.

Gandhi's ideas on sex may now sound backward. But it is worth noting that total sublimation, according to the best tradition of Hindu thought, is indispensable for those who seek self-realisation. For Gandhi, *brahmacharya* was part of a larger philosophy of restraint in food, sleep, thought, and prayer, all designed to equip him for service to the causes to which he was totally committed. What he failed to see was that his own unique experience could never be a guide for the average person.

To this day, scholars debate Gandhi's place in history. He was the catalyst for anti colonialist movements that dominated the latter half of the twentieth century. He wrote profusely, with the collected edition of his writings totalling in excess of one hundred volumes. Much of what he wrote was in response to the needs of his followers and a particular political situation. But in principle, he maintained a remarkable philosophical consistency. His opposition to Western colonialism, his reservations about industrialism and urbanisation, his distrust of modern nationalism and his total rejection of violence may all seem overly romantic to those who experienced the trauma of Adolf Hitler and later the atomic bomb.

It must also be remembered that Gandhi's racist attitudes were not limited solely to Black South Africans. In response to a question in 1938 about Nazi antisemitism, Gandhi expressed the bizarre opinion that the German Jews should commit collective suicide in order to arouse public consciousness about Hitler's criminality. His moral tone-deafness continued even after the horrors of the Holocaust were revealed at the war's end when he argued that the Jews had been killed anyway and might as well have died to make a larger point.

In the years since Gandhi's death, his name has been invoked by many political and social movements. Yet, with a few outstanding exceptions, such as Martin Luther King, these have too often made a mockery of Gandhi's contribution.

But he will never lack for champions. Erik H. Erikson, the distinguished American psychoanalyst, wrote that he senses 'an affinity between Gandhi's truth and the insights of modern psychology'. Another great Gandhi admirer was Albert Einstein, who saw nonviolence as a possible antidote to the dangers posed by the atomic bomb.

It remains to be seen whether Gandhi's concept of *satyagraha* will be increasingly relevant as the twenty-first century progresses.

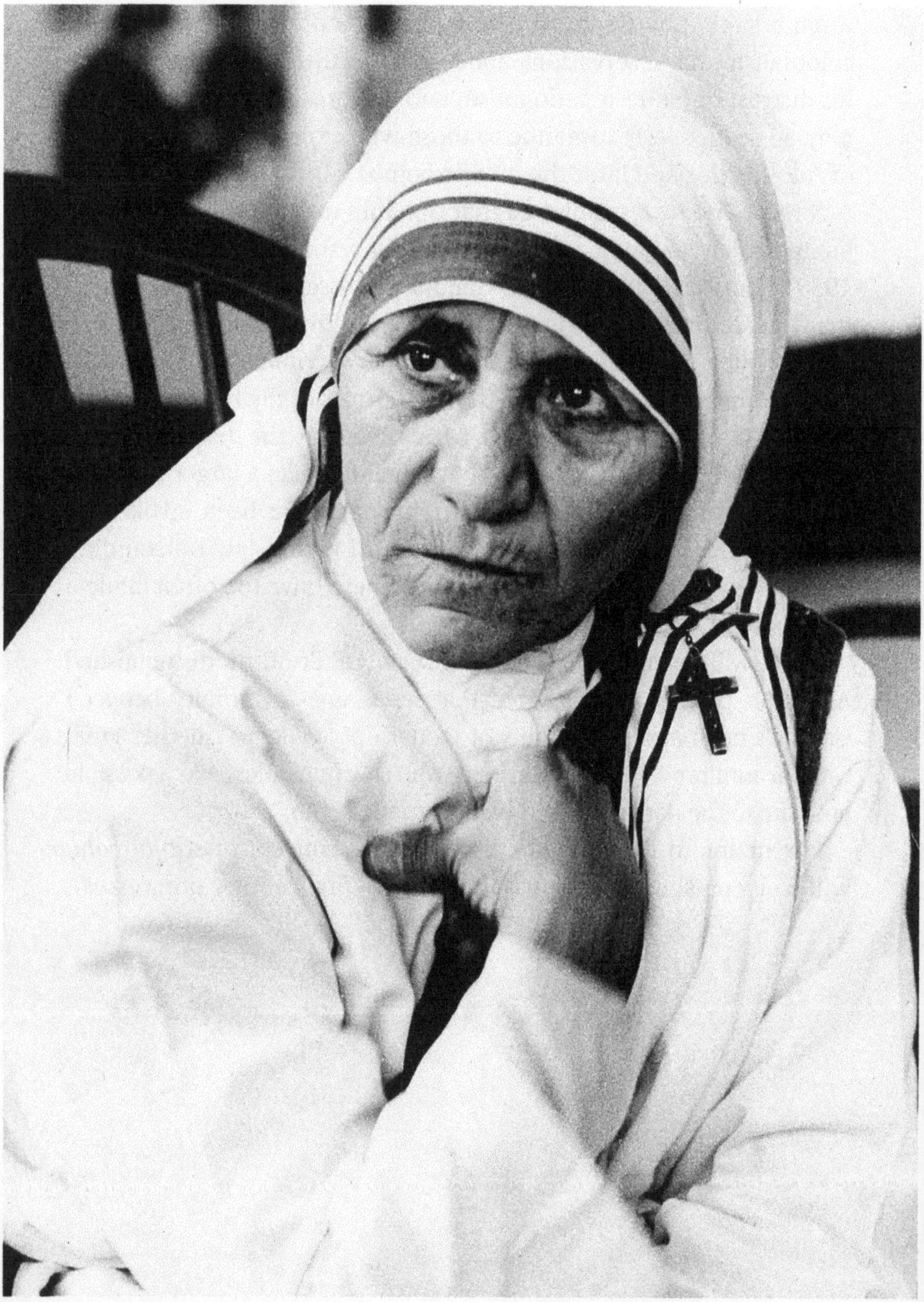

Mother Teresa

Calcutta, India 1980.

'Excuse me,' I asked, interrupting a backpacker who was seated on a low wall munching a samosa. 'Do you know where I can find the Mother House of the Missionaries of Charity?'

'Sure,' she said in an accent that sounded Scandinavian. 'Do you see that big road over there?' She pointed towards a teeming boulevard one hundred metres distant. 'That's AJC Bose Road. If you follow it north for about ten minutes, it'll be right there on your left. Number 54A.'

'Thank you.'

'It's a four-storey building with wooden shutters,' she added. 'You can't miss it. Look for a statue of the Virgin Mary on the corner of the building.'

'You sound familiar with the place.'

'Very,' she replied. 'When I first arrived in Calcutta, about eighteen months ago, I volunteered there. They do great work.'

'I appreciate your help,' I said.

'Good luck,' she replied before taking another bite of her samosa.

I followed her instructions, taking to the footpath next to the boulevard, dodging potholes and building materials strewn across my path and ducking under scaffolding. I wove through the crowds of people busily going about their daily activities or sitting on the sidewalk casually talking and eating. Powerlines crosshatched the sky overhead, and my head reverberated with the cacophony of cars, buses and scooters tooting and blaring at each other and at pedestrians crossing the chaotic road.

A sign marked a narrow, tiled laneway to the entrance at 54A.

I stepped inside and said to a nun who happened by, 'I'm here to meet Mother Teresa. Do you know where I might find her?'

'Is she expecting you?'

'Yes, I have an appointment.'

'Follow me,' she smiled. 'I'll take you to the chapel.'

I followed her through the hall into a large room with benches lining the walls. Its interior was spartan. Hessian mats were strewn on the floor, and the windows were covered with wooden shutters. A table with a white tablecloth served as an altar, and a statue of the Virgin Mary stood next to it. On the wall nearby was a crucifix. I could see through the chapel door people in the courtyard, some sitting in the lotus position in quiet reflection, others meditating.

It was a mild February morning. A slight fog settled on the benches in the courtyard.

'Hello,' I heard a warm, soft voice say.

I twisted around and saw a woman dressed in a white sari and veil bordered with three blue stripes. She was wearing simple brown sandals. There was a crucifix attached to the left side of her sari, below her collarbone. I was surprised by her small stature – she was no more than five feet tall – her face was creased with deep wrinkles that indicated she smiled far more often than she frowned. Her dark, deep-set eyes under heavy brows were her most striking feature. Although her lips were narrow and her face thin, there was nothing austere about her expression.

'Hello,' I said. 'I'm Shoshanna Shank from *The Guardian*.'

'I've been expecting you,' she smiled.

'It's a great pleasure to meet you,' I replied.

She grinned, sat down, and, pointing to a chair opposite, said, 'Please be seated.'

'Thank you. I'd like to start by talking about your family and childhood. But before we get to that, can I ask how you describe yourself?'

Her eyes moved to the ceiling as she considered her response. 'By blood, I am Albanian. By citizenship, Indian. But those are superficial. My essence is that I am a Catholic nun. As to my calling,

I belong to the world. As to my heart, I belong entirely to the Heart of Jesus.'

'I've been told that you don't like talking about your childhood, but our readers are interested in that part of your life.'

She frowned. 'It is unimportant.'

'I promise not to dwell on it.'

Mother Teresa pondered for several moments before speaking. 'I had a very happy upbringing. My mother, my father, and we children would pray together each evening. Prayer is God's greatest gift to the family. It maintains family unity. The Gospel of Matthew says that God is there when people come together in prayer.'

'Thank you for that. Let me check my facts. You were born on the 26th of August 1910, in Skopje, the current capital of Macedonia in Yugoslavia, to Nikola and Dranafile Bojaxhiu?'

She nodded.

'The following day, you were baptised Agnes Gonxha Bojaxhiu. You received your first communion at the age of five and a half and were confirmed in November 1916.'

She nodded once more, and I noticed her eye sockets were dark with age and fatigue.

'You have a sister, Aga, who was born in 1904 and brother, Lazar, who was born in 1907.'

'My parents had five children, but two died,' she said in a soft voice.

'I'm sorry.' Your father, Nikola, was Albanian?'

'He was.'

I decided to take a different tack.

'I met your niece, Agi, in Palermo, and she told me that her father, Lazar, would tell stories about your house being always full of visitors who sang, played games and talked long into the night.'

Her warm eyes went misty. 'I remember as well. My father was the only Catholic member of the Skopje town council. At one time, he ran a pharmacy, then he was a building contractor and eventually traded in luxury goods and foods including oil, sugar, cloth and leather.'

'So would it be correct to describe him as a successful businessman?'

Mother Teresa nodded. 'I suppose so. We lived in a large house with a lovely garden, flowers and fruit trees. It was on the same street as the Church of the Sacred Heart. Whenever my father returned home from a business trip, we children were excited to greet him. He always had presents for us.'

'It sounds like the recipe for a perfect childhood,' I prompted.

'He was a stern disciplinarian,' she replied. 'But he always regaled us with funny accounts of his travels abroad. And he was a generous man who encouraged us to be compassionate to those less fortunate than ourselves. "Never forget whose children you are and from what background you come," he would always say.'

'How did that generosity express itself,' I asked.

'When my father travelled, he left money with my mother so that she could feed anyone in need who came to the door. Sometimes she went out, often accompanied by me, to deliver parcels of food and money to the poor.'

'Your father was prominent in Albanian nationalist politics, I believe.' I consulted my notes. In 1919, he travelled to Belgrade to attend a political dinner. When he returned home some days later, he was haemorrhaging badly and rushed to hospital. He underwent emergency surgery but died the following day.'

'That's true,' she said. 'It was 160 miles to Belgrade. I remember he staggered home in the early evening.'

'Do you know the cause of his death?'

She shrugged. 'That remains unknown. But many have speculated that his political enemies poisoned him. His support for a Greater Albania made him many enemies.'

'I'm very sorry,' I said, realising the inadequacy of my condolences as I expressed them.

Mother Teresa smiled. 'Thank you. His funeral was a significant event. Large crowds gathered, including official delegates from the city council and representatives of other religions. Every jeweller's shop in the city was closed, and the pupils in all the schools received commemorative handkerchiefs.'

'Is that an Albanian custom?'

She nodded. 'The number of handkerchiefs given away is, traditionally, an indication of the wealth of the person who dies.'

'I see,' I said, scribbling a note to that effect. It would provide some local colour to the story. 'What effect did your father's death have on you?'

'I became extremely close to my mother. We were a very Catholic family. My mother was deeply involved in the local church, and she took us to morning mass most days when not working in the house or helping others. I have fond memories of her carrying her rosary beads in her pocket and very often saying the rosary.'

'Is it fair to say that she was more religious than your father?' I asked.

She nodded. 'My mother was also a compassionate woman who instilled in me a deep commitment to charity.'

A particularly loud volley of horn-blowing penetrated the room from the boulevard outside. We paused until the stillness of the chapel was restored.

'My father's death brought an end to our financial security,' Mother Teresa continued. 'My mother was forced to take up sewing and embroidery in order to support us,' she said, her voice expressionless.

'Is it true that, while you were no longer wealthy, your mother opened her house to the city's destitute?'

'Yes,' she smiled. 'My mother taught us that we must never eat a single mouthful unless we are sharing it with others. And when I once asked who the people eating with us were, she said: "Some of them are our relations, but all of them are our people."'

'Was she political like your father?'

'Oh yes. Like my father, she was an Albanian nationalist, too.'

'Agi told me she'd heard from her father that you were a sensible young girl, a little too serious for your age. The sort who never stole a bit of jam. She said you were very tidy and a studious, book-loving girl.'

Mother Teresa paused. 'My father had high expectations for my education. He was very progressive, sending not just his son but also his two daughters to school.'

'And where was this?'

'The convent primary school at Sacred Heart of Jesus and then a state-run secondary school. I played the mandolin, sang in the local Sacred Heart choir and was often asked to sing solo. I also acted in the theatre, danced and wrote poetry.'

'You sound as though you were a very artistic and creative young woman. Can we talk about the role that Farther Franjo Jamrekovic played in your life?'

She smiled in fond reminiscence. 'Father Jamrekovic was our parish priest at the Catholic church, Sacred Heart of Jesus in Skopje. Often he read letters from missionaries in India and Africa to the congregation and explained the life of missionaries.'

'So is it fair to say that he influenced your decision to go to India and dedicate your life to God?'

Mother Teresa nodded. 'Yes, there's no doubt he played a major role in my decision. Our congregation made an annual pilgrimage to the Church of the Black Madonna in Letnicë, and it was during one such trip, at the age of twelve, that I first felt a calling to religious life.'

'And six years later, in 1928, you decided to become a nun.'

Mother Teresa smiled. 'I was eighteen. I set off for Ireland to join the Sisters of Loreto in Dublin at the Institute of the Blessed Virgin Mary. It is an order of nuns with missions in India. I took the name Sister Mary Teresa in honour of the French Saint Thérèse of Lisieux. She was renowned for her piety, goodness and courage in the face of illness and early death.'

'And is it true that you never saw your family again?'

Mother Teresa sighed and bowed her head. 'In 1946, Enver Hoxa came to power. He was a Stalinist, and he turned Albania into a police state – it became impossible to visit.'

'That must have been very difficult,' I ventured.

She shrugged. 'It was a great shock to my mother when I answered the call to be a missionary. She shut herself in her room for twenty-four hours. Finally, she came out and told me, "put your hand in the hand of Jesus and never look back". I left, and that was the last time I saw her. But ever since, I've believed that God doesn't have to judge me. My mother will judge me because I made her suffer so much. So, if I am not faithful to my vocation, my mother will judge me.'

'A very powerful thought,' was all I could say.

'Because my family and I suffered so much from the separation, I make the sisters write once a month to their families.'

She spoke so calmly about these sorrows and trials that it was hard to credit she had been much affected by them, and yet I had heard her speak just as calmly about the cruellest suffering of the poor and abandoned. Perhaps that helped give her perspective on her own misfortunes. 'You left the Institute and travelled to India to work as a teacher in the Order School in Calcutta, is that correct?'

'Yes, and a year later, I travelled to Darjeeling in India for my novitiate. I made my First Profession of Vows in May 1931.'

'Where was your first assignment?'

'In Calcutta, at the Loreto Entally community where I taught at Saint Mary's High School for Girls. It is a school run by the Loreto Sisters and dedicated to teaching girls from the city's poorest Bengali families.'

'Is that where you learned the local languages?'

'Yes, I became fluent in both Bengali and Hindi while teaching geography and history. On the 24th of May 1937, I took my Final Profession of Vows to a life of poverty, chastity and obedience, becoming the spouse of Jesus for all eternity.'

'And that's when you became Mother Teresa, is that correct?'

She nodded. 'Such is the custom for Loreto nuns. We assume the title of Mother upon making our final vows. Of course, I continued to teach at Saint Mary's, and in 1944, became principal.'

'I'm sure that was very rewarding.'

Mother Teresa gazed at me. 'Not at all, if you mean in the sense of personal ambition. My sole commitment was to educate my students and lead them to a life of devotion to Christ. While at Saint Mary's, I would often utter this prayer: "Give me the strength to be ever the light of their lives, so that I may lead them at last to you.'"

'How long were you there ... at Saint Mary's?'

'Seventeen years.'

'What made you leave?'

'I was called by God,' she said with a shrug as if the answer was self-evident.

'Can you be more specific?'

'It was September 1946. I was on a train from Calcutta to Darjeeling in the Himalayan foothills for a religious retreat when God spoke to me. The message was clear. I was to leave the convent and help the poor while living among them. It was not a request or a suggestion. It was an order.'

'What you have described as your "call within a call", I believe.'

Mother Teresa nodded. 'That's correct.'

'And what was the reaction of your order? You had taken a vow of obedience, and you could not leave the convent without official permission.'

'At first, I met with some opposition. But after nearly a year and a half of persuasion, in January 1948, I finally received approval to pursue this new calling.'

'And this involved a change of clothing as well?'

'Yes, when I left the Loreto Convent, I put on the white sari with the blue border, which I've worn ever since.'

'Where did you go?'

'First, I underwent six months of basic medical training with the Medical Mission Sisters of Patna. Then I returned to Calcutta and found temporary lodging with the Little Sisters of the Poor. And that December, just before Christmas, I ventured into the slums for the first time. I visited families, washed some children's sores, cared for an old man lying sick on the road, and nursed a woman dying of hunger and tuberculosis. I started each day in communion with Jesus in the Eucharist and then went out with my rosary beads in hand to find and serve him among the unwanted, the unloved, and the uncared for.'

Her voice was surprisingly deep and resolute for someone of

her small stature. I could well imagine that, by sheer force of personality, she could move easily through the slums of Calcutta – or walk into a boardroom.

'So you were working alone?' I asked.

'Initially,' she replied. 'But after some months, I was joined, one by one, by my former students.'

'I read that at first, you had to beg for your daily meals.'

Mother Teresa nodded. 'That is true. I was used to a life of relative comfort. Now I had no income and no way to obtain food and supplies other than to beg. There were times during the first three or four months when I felt humiliated. Tears would stream down my cheeks, and I was tempted to return to convent life. But I was determined to follow God's guidance. I promised myself that I would learn how to beg, no matter how much abuse and humiliation I endured.'

'Your situation changed in October 1950, when you received permission from the Vatican to establish a new congregation,' I prompted.

She smiled. 'Yes, the Missionaries of Charity, a Roman Catholic religious order of women. It was officially established in the Archdiocese of Calcutta.'

Looking down at my notes, I turned the page. 'With only a handful of members, most of them former teachers or pupils from St Mary's School, you continued your work of service to the poorest of the poor.'

'The Vatican approved our supplementary vow of devotion to the hungry, the naked, the homeless, the crippled, the blind and the lepers, in addition to our vows of poverty, chastity and obedience. We were concerned for all those people who feel unwanted, unloved and uncared for throughout society. People who have become a burden to the society and are shunned by everyone.'

'It sounds like very emotionally demanding work.'

She shrugged. 'Many people were not suited to it. I told each volunteer that a "burning fire" was required for success. We went on to open a hospice for the poor, a home for sufferers of leprosy, and a home for orphans and homeless youth. And a centre for the blind, aged and disabled.'

'You ultimately convinced the Calcutta city government to donate a dilapidated building that you could use as an open-air school and a home for the dying and the destitute.'

She smiled and, after a moment, said, 'God has been very good to us. As the ranks of our congregation swelled and donations poured in, we were able to expand the scope of our charitable activities.'

'Please tell me more about these charitable activities.'

'In 1952, we established a hospice where terminally ill people could die with dignity. And five years later, in 1957, we began to work with the lepers of Calcutta. We established Shanti Nager – the Place of Peace – for lepers in 1965.'

She leaned back in her chair meditatively. 'Over the course of the 1950s and 1960s, we established a leper colony, an orphanage, a nursing home, a family clinic and a string of mobile health clinics. We also began to send our sisters to other parts of India.'

I was writing furiously as she spoke.

'In 1971, I travelled to New York City to open our first American-based house of charity.'

I knew I could research the work of her American charities later, so instead, I said, 'I would like to talk with you about some of your awards, but before I do, may I ask a question that I know our readers will be interested in?'

Mother Teresa nodded, indicating to me to proceed.

'With so many bombs and guns causing havoc around the world, how can we achieve peace?'

She hesitated, her eyebrows drawing together in thought. After a long moment, she said, 'To bring peace, just get together and love one another, bring that joy, that strength of presence of each other into the home. And we will be able to overcome all the evil that is in the world.' Almost as an afterthought, she continued, 'If we really want to love, we must learn how to forgive.'

'Thank you,' I said as I recorded her quote in shorthand. 'You have been honoured with many awards throughout your life. The Indian Padma Shri in 1962 and the inaugural Pope John XXIII Peace Prize in 1971, to name just a few.'

She shifted uneasily in her chair. 'In February 1965, Pope Paul VI bestowed the Decree of Praise on the Missionaries of Charity. But this was not important. What was important was the work we did.'

'And with regard to your work: it was not limited to those with religious vocations. You formed the Co-Workers of Mother Teresa and the Sick and Suffering Co-Workers for people of various faiths and nationalities – all who shared your spirit of prayer, simplicity and sacrifice. I believe this led later to the establishment of the Lay Missionaries of Charity.'

'This was done at the suggestion of others,' said Mother Teresa, as if eager to offload personal credit for her achievements.

'That may well be,' I said, 'but in 1979, you were awarded the Nobel Peace Prize in recognition of your work "in bringing help to suffering humanity". However, you refused the traditional Nobel honour banquet. You requested that the 192,000 US dollars in prize money be given to help the poor in India.'

She smiled and said in a quiet voice, 'I thank God.'

I glanced at my watch. 'I've taken up too much of your time,' I said. 'But before we finish, I'd like to ask you about some of the Catholic Church's more controversial doctrines—'

'In the eyes of some,' she interjected.

'Indeed, in the eyes of some,' I echoed. 'You have been especially criticised for your vocal opposition to contraception and abortion.'

Mother Teresa leaned forward. 'I feel the greatest destroyer of peace today is abortion,' she said, passion evident in her tone.

I nodded, prompting her to continue.

'If a mother can kill her own child ... whether born or unborn ... what is to prevent me from killing you or you killing me? A human life is a human life.'

I remained silent for a few moments before asking my final question. 'Mother Teresa, what would you like your legacy to be?'

'That of a humble servant of God,' she promptly responded. 'Nothing more and nothing less.'

'I think that's an excellent place to conclude our interview.

BERNARD MARIN

Thank you for your time.'

'My pleasure,' she said as she stood up to leave.

Endnote

This fictionalised conversation with Mother Teresa is set in the Mother House of the Missionaries of Charity to celebrate her seventieth year. She is considered one of the greatest humanitarians of the twentieth century.

After several years of poor health, as well as heart, lung and kidney problems, Mother Teresa died on the 5th of September 1997, at the age of eighty-seven. She was honoured with a state funeral by the Government of India. Her body was buried in the Mother House of the Missionaries of Charity. In a short time, her grave became a place of pilgrimage and prayer for people of all faiths and classes.

At the time of her death, the Order of Missionaries of Charity had more than four thousand sisters and hundreds of thousands of lay volunteers. There were six hundred and ten foundations in one hundred and twenty-three countries around the world, including homes for orphaned children, homes for people with HIV, leper colonies and hospices for the dying.

In 2003, the publication of Mother Teresa's private correspondence revealed the crisis of faith she had suffered for most of the last fifty years of her life. She referred to it as 'the darkness' and the 'painful night' of her soul. These feelings began around the time she began her work for the poor and lasted until her death, leading her to seek a more profound union with Jesus. In one despairing letter to a confidante, she wrote of her struggle against emptiness and darkness. She cried out to God for help, asking him to save her from the agony of doubt. 'Where is my faith?' she wrote.

Such revelations are surprising considering Mother Teresa's compassion and dedication to the service of others. Still, history has shown it is not unusual for saints to be tormented about their faith.

In 2002, the Vatican recognised a miracle involving an Indian woman named Monica Besra, who said she was cured of an abdominal tumour through Mother Teresa's intervention on the one-year anniversary of her death in 1998. Mother Teresa was beatified as Blessed Teresa of Calcutta on 19 October 2003 by Pope John Paul II.

On 17 December 2015, Pope Francis issued a decree attributing a second miracle to Mother Teresa. It cleared the way for her to become a saint of the Roman Catholic Church. The second miracle involved the healing of Marcilio Andrino, a Brazilian man in a coma due to a viral brain infection. His wife, family and friends prayed to Mother Teresa and, according to a statement from the Missionaries of Charity, when Marcilio was brought to the operating theatre for surgery, he woke without pain and was cured of his symptoms.

Mother Teresa was canonised as Saint Teresa of Calcutta on 4 September 2016, one day before the nineteenth anniversary of her death. Pope Francis led the canonisation mass, which was held in St Peter's Square at Vatican City. Tens of thousands of Catholics and pilgrims from around the world attended the ceremony to celebrate the woman who was known as 'the Saint of the Gutters'. At the canonisation mass, Pope Francis declared that Blessed Teresa of Calcutta was hereby elevated to sainthood, urging all Catholics to venerate her as such. In his homily, the Pope went on to praise her life of service, describing how she was a generous dispenser of divine mercy who gave of herself to all in need.

Francis told how Saint Teresa dedicated her life to the world's unwanted and discarded. How she prostrated herself to serve the poorest and most afflicted, never losing sight of the essential truth that all people, born and unborn, were created in the image of God. Above all, the Pope urged the faithful to follow her example and practise compassion.

Despite widespread praise for her achievements, Mother Teresa's life and work have not been without controversy. Perhaps her most high-profile critic was the writer Christopher Hitchens, who lambasted her in his book *The Missionary Position: Mother Teresa in Theory and Practice*. There, Hitchens argued that Mother Teresa glorified poverty for her own ends and provided a justification for the preservation of institutions and beliefs that sustained widespread poverty. He went on to claim that Mother Teresa has consoled and supported the rich and powerful, allowing them all manner of indulgence while preaching obedience and resignation to the poor.

In a letter to the editor of *The New York Review of Books* published in December 1996, Hitchens wrote that Mother Teresa told the *Ladies' Home Journal* that her friend Princess Diana would be better off when free of her marriage. As Hitchens told it, when Mother Teresa made this remark, she had only just finished advising the Irish electorate to vote 'no' in a national referendum that proposed the right of civil divorce and remarriage.

Mari Marcel Thekaekara was a volunteer at Shishu Bhavan, Mother Teresa's orphanage for abandoned children. She said Mother Teresa was an autocrat and that nothing happened at the orphanage without her explicit permission. Mother Teresa insisted that the personal letters of her sisters be scrutinised, sometimes by herself, and she forced young sisters to walk miles in the scorching sun, often barefoot, on the burning hot pavement.

Thekaekara also recalled an occasion when her mother insisted that she go with her children to Mother Teresa's chapel to be blessed. Her mother said to Mother Teresa, 'My daughters volunteered at Shishu Bhavan when they were young.' She recalls Mother Teresa's abrupt, rude response, 'When you were a child. But now? You do nothing for the poor now, I suppose?'

Despite these critical accounts of her personality, Mother Teresa has remained the object of widespread veneration throughout the world. Her unwavering commitment to aiding those most in need is admired by many who see her as compassionate, caring and charitable.

In the view of her adherents, Mother Teresa combined profound empathy and a fervent commitment to her cause with incredible organisational and managerial skills. This unique fusion of dedication and ability enabled her to develop a vast and effective international organisation of missionaries to help impoverished citizens across the globe.

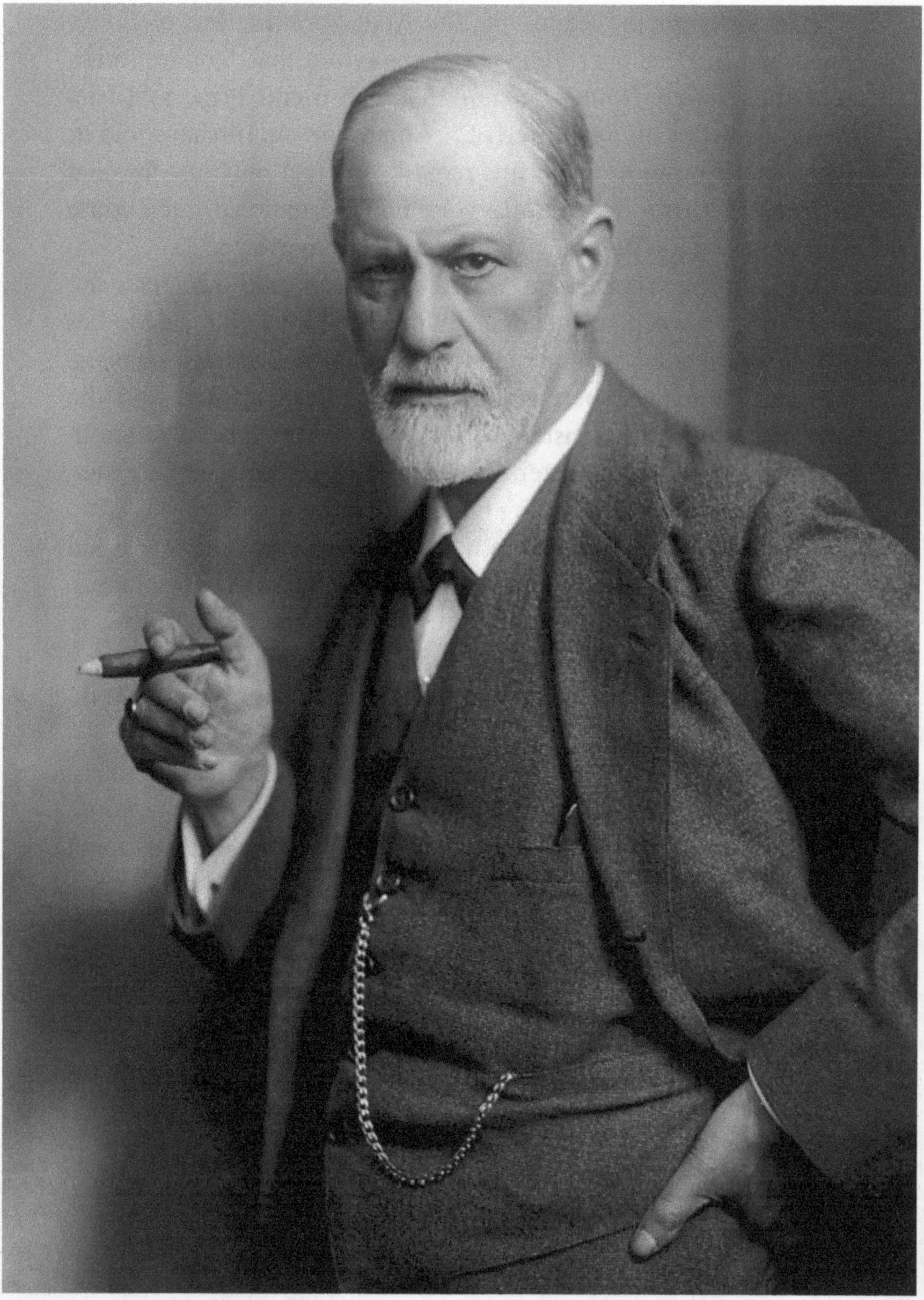

Sigmund Freud

Vienna, 6 May 1926.

The celebrity fuss began on his arrival. The close-trimmed beard framing his face was immediately recognisable from photographs gracing hundreds of books, newspapers and magazines. The eyes of a dozen diners tracked him as the maître d' fawned over Café Prükel's most famous patron.

The maître d' bowed and guided him to the table where I was sitting before shuttling off with the great man's homburg and overcoat in hand.

'Good afternoon, Herr Silberer,' said Sigmund Freud. 'Or should I refer to you by your nom de plume Sil-Vara?'

'Either will do,' I replied, trying to hide my discomfiture behind my best poker face. Within the first thirty seconds of our meeting, he had already turned around the interviewer–interviewee dynamic.

Freud waved his hand in a proprietary gesture that encompassed the dining area. 'I thought our initial meeting in a more informal setting would be best – and this is my favourite establishment.'

I nodded appreciatively towards the cup on the table in front of me. 'I'm never one to pass up the opportunity for a Viennese coffee, so I wholeheartedly approve.'

Freud responded with a smile. 'Excellent. Your editor said that you'll be writing a feature article for the Sunday supplement?'

'Yes, we know our readers would be very interested in your background and how you developed the field of psychoanalysis. We're prepared to allocate the entire supplement page. Twenty-five hundred words.'

'That's a lot?' Freud enquired.

'Put it this way, the average news article run is less than five hundred words. So yes, it's quite substantial.'

Freud gave a purse-lipped nod of acknowledgment. 'Shall we begin?'

I opened the notebook that lay beside the coffee cup. 'I'd like to start with a few biographical details.'

He shrugged as we were interrupted by the arrival of the maître d' with a pot of coffee and plate of apple strudel. 'Will there be anything else, Herr Professor?' he asked.

Freud simply smiled and shook his head, and the maître d' bowed and returned to his station opposite the entrance to the café.

'You were born into a Jewish family in Moravia,' I continued. 'Were your parents religiously observant?'

Freud shook his head. 'My father was born into an orthodox home, and while he was something of a biblical scholar, my mother never maintained a kosher home while I grew up.'

'And you?' I asked.

'I don't subscribe to the tenets of any religion.'

'Although you've written that you identify as a Jew,' I countered.

He shrugged again, this time in acknowledgment. 'That's true. In part, because the world gives me little choice in the matter, but I view the belief in an all-knowing, all-powerful God as irrational. And I consider myself to be a rational man.'

I nodded. 'When you were four years old, your family moved to Leipzig and then Vienna. Why?'

'As you note, I was a small child. But as I was later given to understand, my father's textile business ran into trouble, and we moved to pursue new commercial opportunities.'

'So, your first real memories are of Vienna?'

'No, I remember the Moravian forests where I used to play as a child. I remember the smells ... playing hide and seek with my father among the trees.'

'And Vienna?'

Freud touched his beard as he smiled ruefully. 'I have never truly felt at home in Vienna, despite having lived here most of my life.'

I pressed on. 'You earned a doctorate in medicine from the University of Vienna in 1881?'

He nodded. 'Correct, and my habilitation four years later in 1885. During that time, I worked at the psychiatric clinic of Dr Theodor Meynert.'

'Could you please explain what a habilitation is for the benefit of our American readers? We have an arrangement with the *New York Times* for the republication of our material.'

'Certainly.' Freud smiled. 'It's a post-doctoral academic qualification required to teach at the university level.'

'Then you began to teach at the University of Vienna?' I asked.

'Not immediately. I spent a year in Paris studying under neurologist Jena Charcot. When I returned, I began to teach neuropathology at the medical school. I also opened a private practice specialising in nervous and behavioural disorders.'

'And what motivated you to move from study of the physical brain to emotions and the mind?'

Freud smiled noncommittally. 'I think that's enough for now. We've covered the basics of my biography, and I wanted to meet you before delving into … deeper matters.'

'To see the cut of my jib, so to speak?'

His brow furrowed. 'I beg your pardon?'

I grinned. 'An English turn of phrase that I picked up while living in London. It means to assess someone's character.'

'I see,' Freud replied. 'But in any event, I suggest we meet tomorrow at my apartment and continue our conversation there.'

'That would be wonderful. Thank you.' I turned to beckon a waiter. 'Let me get this.'

'Don't be silly,' said Freud with a dismissive wave. 'You are my guest.' He signalled to the maître d', who nodded and scribbled a notation in a leather-bound notebook.

✦ ✦ ✦

At 08:55 the following morning, I pushed open the large oak door of the imposing five-storey stone apartment block. With its cobbled floor and coffered ceiling, the foyer resembled an arcade. At the far end were two glazed doors, their panes etched with antique female figures, opening onto a rear service courtyard – but I made for the staircase.

As Freud's apartment was on the second floor, I proceeded on foot. I pushed the bell, and after an interval, the door was opened by a woman of late middle age with her brown wavy hair parted on the side and gathered at the back into a braided bun.

'Frau Freud, my name is Geza Silberer. I'm here to meet with your husband.'

Magda Freud bowed her head solemnly. 'He's in the waiting room. Please follow me.'

She led the way through the apartment, past glass cabinets cluttered with Egyptian scarabs, Roman death masks, Etruscan funeral vases, bronze coffins and mummy portraits.

The founder of psychotherapy rose from his seat as I entered.

'I see you found me.'

'Not difficult,' I replied. 'Berggasse No. 19 is one of the most famous addresses in Vienna.'

I glanced around the room, taking in the bookshelf packed with journals next to a glass cabinet crowded with ancient figurines and antiquities. A bust and a wooden statue of a Chinese sage graced a side table. There was a couch against the opposite wall, a rug beneath a square wooden table and two chairs facing the sofa. Paintings and framed certificates hung from the walls.

I turned to face Freud, who was waiting in polite silence.

'Sorry. Are you ready to begin?'

'That's usually my line,' replied Freud dryly, and we laughed together for a few moments before I continued.

'Picking up where we left off, in conjunction with Joseph Breuer, you began to publish studies on the traumatic histories of hysteria patients.'

'That's correct,' he said. 'A discussion of traumatic events leads to what I call "catharsis".'

'By that, you mean a purging of emotion through vicarious experience?'

Freud smiled. 'Yes, I see you've done your homework.'

I nodded, both in affirmation and as a sign he should continue.

'Well, around that same time ... the turn of the century ... I began to analyse myself. I began to examine my dreams as a window into my unconscious.'

'And this was the foundation of modern psychotherapy?'

'I think it was,' Freud replied. 'I became convinced that mental disorders could be treated by investigating the interaction between conscious and unconscious elements of the mind – and by bringing repressed fears and conflicts into the conscious mind.'

I consulted my notes. 'In a letter to Wilhelm Fleiss, you described your self-analysis as "more difficult than any other".'

'In many ways, it was excruciating,' Freud replied with a rueful smile. 'But necessary. Otherwise, I would be a blind man leading the blind.'

I nodded. 'Of course, and in the year 1900, you published your ground-breaking *The Interpretation of Dreams*.'

Freud laughed lightly. 'Not so ground-breaking in the beginning. The initial response was ... underwhelming, let's just say. The first print run of six hundred copies didn't sell out for eight years.'

'Really?' I responded in a tone that reflected my surprise. 'But it's now considered such an authoritative work.'

'That's true,' Freud conceded. 'I've always likened the book to a good bottle of Scotch whisky. It improved with age. Speaking of which ... would you care for a drink?'

'Certainly,' I replied, not wishing to offend my host.

Freud rose and walked behind the heavy oak desk adorned by a row of figurines. He bent over and arose with a bottle of single malt. 'I hope this will do.'

I smiled. 'That will be most acceptable.'

'Do you mind if I smoke?' he asked. 'A glass of whisky without a cigar provides only half the enjoyment.'

'Your home, your rules,' I replied while reaching for the proffered glass. 'But now I'd like to ask about free association. It's a major principle of your therapeutic approach, correct?'

I waited as Freud lit his cigar and took a long first draw.

'I'm convinced that we can learn a tremendous amount about the psyche from the words that a person utters. Even if they seem to be off-topic or even ridiculous, they reveal much to those who know how to analyse them.'

'If I understand correctly, you try to discourage conscious efforts by your patients to cooperate with this process.'

'That's correct,' Freud replied. 'The unconscious of the patient will erect obstacles if the conscious gets involved. It is my view that the most effective therapeutic approach towards mental disorders must focus on the spontaneous interaction between the conscious and unconscious elements of the mind.'

'And it's your view that the prime mover in the forging of our character is childhood sexual desire that is repressed in the conscious mind?'

Freud nodded. 'That's essentially correct.'

'This is quite a revolutionary approach,' I observed. 'What can you tell me about how these ideas were received by your colleagues in the medical community?'

'They were met with substantial resistance and rejection.'

'And your then colleague, Carl Jung?'

'Jung and I felt that these new therapeutic methods were too important to fall victim to egos and petty professional rivalries. I founded the International Psychoanalytic Association with Carl Jung as president ...'

'And this led to another ground-breaking work, your paper entitled *The Ego and the Id*.'

'Yes,' Freud confirmed. 'It was published three years ago. The same year I was diagnosed with cancer of the jaw.' He grimaced. 'A most unpleasant experience.'

'I imagine it was very painful.'

'It was painful, as you say, but I refused to take any pain-killing drugs – even during the many surgeries I endured.'

I grimaced, but he just shrugged. 'As I said at the time, I prefer to think in torment than not to be able to think clearly.'

'Did your determination derive from your previous experimentation with cocaine in psychotherapy?'

Freud sighed. 'I've answered this question at least a dozen times before.'

'I apologise, but this is an issue of considerable controversy. Ernest Jones said—'

'Ah yes, Ernest Jones,' Freud interjected, shaking his head in obvious disgust. 'The Welshman who claimed that I unleashed evil on the world.'

'And?' I prompted.

'And what?' replied Freud, annoyance now evident in his tone. 'Jones was embittered by the fact that his first love ended up in analysis with me after he failed to help her.'

'So perhaps you could clarify matters by discussing the details of your experience with cocaine?'

Freud gazed at the ceiling for a moment and then said, 'My interest was piqued in part by an article about a German soldier who used it to overcome exhaustion on a lengthy route march. But I was also influenced by the sufferings of my friend, Ernst von Fleischl-Marxow. I recommended cocaine as a treatment for his addiction to morphine, which developed after his thumb was amputated.' He broke off suddenly.

I smiled sympathetically. 'I realise this must be a difficult topic in light of Dr Fleischl-Marxow's later death by overdose. But you're surely aware that this matter has been used by your detractors as a weapon to attack your personal and professional integrity.'

Freud shrugged. 'My enemies will do what my enemies will do.'

I resolved to press the point further. 'Your critics have put out a narrative that you were just a young man in a hurry, looking to make a name for himself in medical research. And that cocaine was your vehicle for doing so.'

Freud sighed. 'It is true that for a time, I considered cocaine a wonder drug of sorts.'

I consulted my notes. 'I believe you went so far as to describe it as a "magical substance" that was "far less harmful than alcohol".'

He gave a rueful smile. 'I see that you've read *Über Coca*.'

I nodded. 'I like to be thorough.'

'Too thorough, some might say,' Freud replied in a tone that seemed only partially in jest. 'Let me just say that I personally found that it provided relief from the anxiety and depression that was plaguing me.'

'But you ultimately concluded that harm inflicted by cocaine outweighed any benefits it might confer. What led to this about-face?'

Freud looked down, shaking his head. 'I think we've devoted enough time to this particular subject. What else would you like to discuss?'

'Fair enough,' I conceded. 'I would like to ask about the development of your interest in psychotherapy. After all, you were a qualified doctor and could have chosen any specialty – surgery, for example.'

Freud gazed out of the window for a moment at the bright sky. 'I think that the connection between how an individual perceives life and how the unconscious affects those perceptions was a natural leap for me to make once I started to become interested in neurology. In fact, following my time at the University of Vienna, my early research in neurology was intended to help prove my theories on the unconscious.'

'Can we delve a bit more deeply into your methodology? How did you develop your practice?'

'I asked my patients questions about their dreams and what they remembered about their relationships with their parents and others. Then I documented their experiences of those dreams and our sessions in case studies. I recorded their progress, my diagnosis, and how effective my diagnosis was. There seemed to be several cases that backed up my ideas about unconscious motivations.'

I hesitated a moment and heard myself say, 'Was Dora one such case?'

There was a brief silence.

'As you know, Dora was my patient in 1900,' he said. 'I accepted her accusation that her father's friend had made sexual advances to her.' He paused for several moments before continuing. 'When she told me a couple of her dreams, I diagnosed her loss of voice as hysteria.'

Freud started to get to his feet, seemed to remember something, and sat back down. 'I only treated her for eleven weeks.' His face was suddenly taut as he continued, 'When I told her she was afraid of Herr K, but even more afraid of herself, and of the temptation to yield to him, she became angry and ceased therapy.'

He began to blink rapidly, and I sensed he was particularly troubled by her case.

'But two years later, she returned and told me she had confronted Frau and Herr K, who had confessed, and her symptoms had mostly cleared up.'

'And what was the response when you published that case study?'

Freud sat up straighter. 'Some said it was crass insensitivity to the realities of adolescent female sexuality. Others said it was an immoral use of my medical position. But it wasn't all negative. Ernest Jones was led by the study to become a psychoanalyst. Carl Jung also took up the study enthusiastically.' Freud relit his cigar.

'I want to come back to Carl Jung later, but now can you elaborate on your ideas about unconscious motivations?'

He tilted his head and blew a series of perfect smoke rings that dissipated slowly as they rose towards the ceiling.

'Our motivation comes mainly from the unconscious region of our brain.'

'The id,' I prompted.

Freud nodded. 'Yes, the id. Our physical needs, desires and impulses, our aggression and antisocial impulses, all arise from the id, especially our sexual drives. It is our instinctual self if you like. It acts according to the pleasure principle, which dictates that we seek immediate gratification of our impulses without regard to the consequences. Within the id are the two basic desires, Eros and *Todestrieb*, or what some have called Thanatos.'

I nodded for him to continue.

'Eros is the desire for sex, and *Todestrieb* or Thanatos is our destructive impulse. Everything we do is based on these desires and impulses. If the needs of Eros and Thanatos aren't met, we could do something horribly impulsive. But, if the therapist can help the patient find acceptable outlets, the patient can keep these drives in check.'

I thought for a moment before speaking again. 'So, what is the cork, the ego or the superego?'

Freud smiled. 'That's an interesting way to frame it. Perhaps the ego is the cork. It acts according to the reality principle. It enables an individual to delay gratifying any immediate desire and to function effectively in the real world.'

'And the superego?'

'The superego can be thought of as the conscious self, which punishes misbehaviour with feelings of guilt.'

'So when the bottle bursts, the superego regrets all that broken glass?'

'I see why you became a writer,' he said with a dry chuckle. 'Your talent for metaphor is obvious.'

I nodded my thanks. 'If I can recapitulate ... and please correct me where I get it wrong ... you investigate the unconscious motives, desires and guilt underlying the mental disorders of your patients. Then you try to find safe "release valves" for the destructive and sexual drives, thereby reducing them and helping to cure the patient.'

'Precisely so,' confirmed Freud. 'Because when the unconscious becomes overwhelmed, it sets up defence mechanisms, which include disorders like depression.'

'Can we now turn to you and Jung?'

Freud dropped his head and glanced at me over the top of his glasses, then rubbed the side of his face and said, 'If we must.'

'As I understand it, you were twenty-one years older than Jung,' I said.

'That's right.' Freud got up abruptly and walked to the window, and stood with his back to me. I watched him framed against the light.

'You were colleagues and close friends for about six years?' I continued.

'Yes, we met in Vienna in 1907,' he said as he turned towards me. 'Our first meeting lasted for more than thirteen hours.'

I tried to hide my astonishment. 'What did you talk about?'

He looked at me blankly and did not respond.

As the silence lengthened, I became aware of a sudden heaviness in my chest. I took a deep breath and was relieved to be able to breathe without difficulty, although the heaviness remained.

'Two years after we met, we toured America together,' Freud said, ignoring my question. 'That culminated in the American Psychological Association's conference.'

'Yet by 1913, your relationship had broken down?'

There was another long silence. Then he said in a strained voice, 'He was my heir apparent. I had been the victim of ongoing anti-Semitism, and he was a bright young gentile with charisma. I thought he could take psychoanalysis into places denied to me.'

'You went into great detail about your feelings on the topic of anti-Semitism during another interview you gave to G. S. Viereck.'

Freud frowned. 'I always saw myself as the product of Germanic culture first and foremost. Not only in the sense of language but in an almost spiritual sense, as well. I worshipped the genius of Goethe, Schiller and Beethoven. And I still do, but while I am in the Germanic culture, I no longer feel that I am of the Germanic culture.'

'So now, how do you define yourself?' I pressed.

'Ethnically, you mean?'

I nodded.

Freud emitted a sad sigh. 'I suppose I am a Jew who lives in a German-speaking country. One who has been shaped and moulded by the German language and culture.'

'But you previously expressed the view that religious faith is irrational mythology. Doesn't that include Judaism?'

'I am not a religious Jew – I don't believe in the existence of God – but I am proud of being Jewish, as, no doubt are you,' Freud observed. 'Your colleague, Theodore Herzl, is well aware of the complexities we European Jews face. The thesis that Jews will never know security from persecution without a sovereign state of their own is his reason for founding the Zionist movement, is it not?'

I shrugged. 'You have a point. But let's get back to Carl Jung.'

'All right,' said Freud in the resigned tone of someone about to undertake a distasteful task. 'For several years, Jung was content to champion my ideas, but then things changed.'

'How so?'

He shrugged. 'To me, the human psyche consists of the id, ego and superego. But to Jung, the psyche is made up of the ego, the personal unconscious and the collective unconscious.'

I scribbled furiously in my notebook. 'Can you elaborate on that?'

'Jung believes dreams can have many different meanings according to the dreamer's associations. To me, the content of most dreams is sexual. Repressed and expressed sexuality is the biggest motivating force behind behaviour. But Jung believes psychic energy is a motivator of behaviour and sexuality is only one part of that.'

Freud paused, glancing out the window for a moment before turning back to me.

'As I previously told you, I believe religion is escapist nonsense, but to Jung, it is a necessary part of an individual. He believes in the paranormal: mythology, kabbalah, Buddhism, Hinduism, alchemy ...' Freud's tone was scornful as he numbered those belief systems on his fingers. 'I'm a sceptic. I've described occultism as "the black tide of mud". I have no time for it.'

I waited for him to continue. When he did not, I broke the increasingly awkward silence. 'I believe you fainted in Jung's presence?'

He gazed at me, and I noticed his lips quivered. 'That's because he harboured death wishes towards me.'

'I've heard homosexual feelings referred to when your relationship with Jung has been discussed ...'

He was silent for a moment and then said, 'Jung acknowledged the same feelings, but he was unable to tolerate intimacy between men because of his own early sexual trauma inflicted by an older man whom he had liked and trusted. So, he had to break away. Any collaboration between us eventually became impossible.'

There was a sudden squall of rain against the glass – a sun shower – and when I looked out the window, I noticed a rainbow arching over the city.

'Where do you think you stand in the history of psychology?' I asked, hoping to move to safer ground.

He gave me a nod and a smile. 'I think it's fair to say I am the undisputed founder of psychoanalysis as a method of curing mental illness.'

'Some have compared you to Christopher Columbus, who sailed into the unknown and discovered a continent. You too explored the unknown and discovered previously unknown features of the human mind.'

'And yet some have also tried to discredit me and claim that my methods are unscientific.'

'Does that concern you?'

He thought for a moment, the deep lines around his mouth betraying some discomfort.

'How do you feel your research holds up today?' I added.

'I believe in the truth of my ideas.'

'Which of them do you consider most important?'

'The work I'm most proud of is the analysis of myself. To look at myself as a conscientious observer and discover the motives for my own actions was one of the hardest things I had to do in my life. But it was necessary to look at my own mind as carefully as I look at others. How else could I claim to have an insight into the human mind?'

I noticed that he had become wan, and he periodically grimaced as if in pain. Then I realised that his speech was becoming less clear. I remembered that the malignancy of the upper jaw diagnosed three years earlier had necessitated an operation in which a prosthesis was fitted to allow him to speak.

As if reading my mind, he blurted, 'I detest my mechanical jaw; it's embarrassing, and the struggle with the mechanism consumes too much precious strength.'

'Will you be all right for a bit more? I promise not to go on too long.'

Freud nodded.

I flashed a grateful smile. 'With the exception of the University of Vienna, you have been lauded and honoured around the world. Does it upset you that your own alma mater has failed to bestow recognition on one of its most notable alumni?'

He shook his head. 'The University of Vienna is under no obligation to support me or my work.'

'Does that mean you are indifferent to public fame and professional renown?'

He smiled wryly. 'Let me put it this way; I am far more concerned about the future of my children than the future of my own name and reputation once I am dead. I hope that their lives will not be too difficult, although I can do nothing to ensure this. My family history has taught me that life is always a struggle.'

Freud lapsed into silent introspection, staring through me rather than at me. It was as if he were engaged in some kind of interior dialogue. After several long moments, he continued.

'Despite my years, I still enjoy life,' he murmured, 'nature, my family, the seasons, a good meal. I have had intellectual companionship ... of a sort, and I have learned to accept life humbly and with good cheer. What more can I ask?'

'Do you believe death is the end of everything, or that the personality survives death?' I asked.

'This question doesn't interest me. Everything that lives must die.'

'But wouldn't you like to be reborn, perhaps in some other being? Does mortality not trouble you?'

He gazed at me intently. 'Truly, no. I have not the slightest wish to be reincarnated in any form whatsoever. All human behaviour is driven by selfish urges and desires, so my next life would differ very little from this one. I'm perfectly content to know that this tiresome business of living will end one day.'

'Your equanimity at the prospect of your own mortality is most impressive,' I said.

'Don't misunderstand me,' said Freud. 'I am not an ascetic. I still enjoy life's little pleasures – my children, my garden, what relief from pain I am granted – but there is no reason to prolong life.'

With a wry smile, he stood up, turned and walked to the window. Indicating the garden, he said, 'I am far more interested in the blossom on that tree than in anything that may happen to me after I am dead.'

He turned, walked slowly back to his chair and sat down, awaiting my next question.

I immediately obliged. 'Some would say that life has always been a puzzle, but psychoanalysis has made that puzzle far more complicated.'

He shook his head. 'I disagree. Psychoanalysis simplifies the puzzle of life. Analysis leads to a fresh synthesis; it identifies impulses from the tangle and winds them on the correct bobbin. And, if this doesn't stretch the metaphor too far, it produces a thread that can lead a man safely out of the labyrinth of his unconscious mind.'

I smiled. 'An apt metaphor.'

Freud met my smile with one of his own that was brimming with renewed enthusiasm. 'This is a new science, and we are still only just at the beginning,' he said, his face alight. 'To mix my metaphors, I have dug into the mind and found monuments, but in the future other analysts may find entire islands.'

'Time will tell,' I said, looking at my watch. I realised we'd been together for more than three hours. 'Speaking of time, it's time for me to take the tram back home,' I said. 'Thank you for agreeing to talk with me – I really appreciate it.' I stood up.

'It's been my pleasure,' Freud said as he walked me to the door.

As he opened it, I felt the cool air on my face.

'I am not a pessimist,' he said abruptly. 'Not while I can enjoy and be grateful for my children, my wife, and my garden.' He shook my hand. 'See these flowers,' he said, indicating a vase on the hall table, 'they are drawn towards the light, but they have no complexes. Don't you love flowers? Such beauty. They make me happy.'

I nodded, thanked him once more, and we parted.

As I left Freud's house, it began to rain. I turned up my collar and hurried towards Schlickgasse. I had much to contemplate.

Endnote

This imaginary conversation with Sigmund Freud is set in 1926. It uses translations of Freud's own remarks, or close interpretations of them, to remain faithful to what he actually said. At that time, Freud's prestige in the intellectual community was enormous. Some considered his psychoanalytical theories dangerous, while others thought them unscientific. His private life was also the source of considerable rumour and speculation.

Much of this controversy revolved around Freud's relationship with Minna Bernays, the younger sister of his wife, Martha. Minna became an integral part of the Freud family after coming to live with Sigmund and Martha in 1898, their tenth year of marriage. Minna often holidayed with Freud while her sister remained at home with the children. It has been established that a hotel register, during one of those vacations, read 'Dr. Sigm Freud u frau' and had them occupying a double room.

Further muddying the waters was Carl Jung, who stated in a later interview that Minna told him of the sexual relationship between herself and Freud. Yet in-depth analysis of Minna's correspondence with Freud has found no indication that their affection was anything other than platonic. This is one of those conundrums surrounding Freud's life that, at this point, must go unresolved.

Freud's seventieth birthday was publicly celebrated in Vienna. Austrian radio transmitted an appreciation of his work, and social democrat Mayor Karl Seitz congratulated him personally. Schoolchildren presented him with an award of 30,000 marks raised from public contributions. From Otto Rank, Freud was given a luxury edition of Friedrich Nietzsche's works. Despite scientific differences with Rank, Freud took this Nietzsche edition with him into exile in London. The *Almanach der Psychoanalyse* of the International Psychoanalytical Press was published for the first time in the year after Otto Rank retired as director of the Press, and, in 1928, Freud published two texts in it on humour and fetishism. Also, among the many celebrations, the Jewish B'nai B'rith movement held a festive meeting. It issued a special edition of its newsletter to honour Freud.

Over the last sixteen years of his life, Freud would have thirty-three surgical procedures on his jaw. It was only towards the end that he consented to take aspirin to address the pain.

In 1933, the Nazis had publicly burned some of Freud's books because he was Jewish. In 1938, his youngest daughter, Anna Freud, was arrested and interrogated by the Gestapo. In June of that year, Freud moved to London with his wife and Anna to escape the Nazis. There he continued to see patients up to a month before his death in London on 23 September 1939, at the age of eighty-three. Consoling herself after Freud's death, Martha would say, 'In the fifty-three years of our marriage, there was not a single angry word between us.'

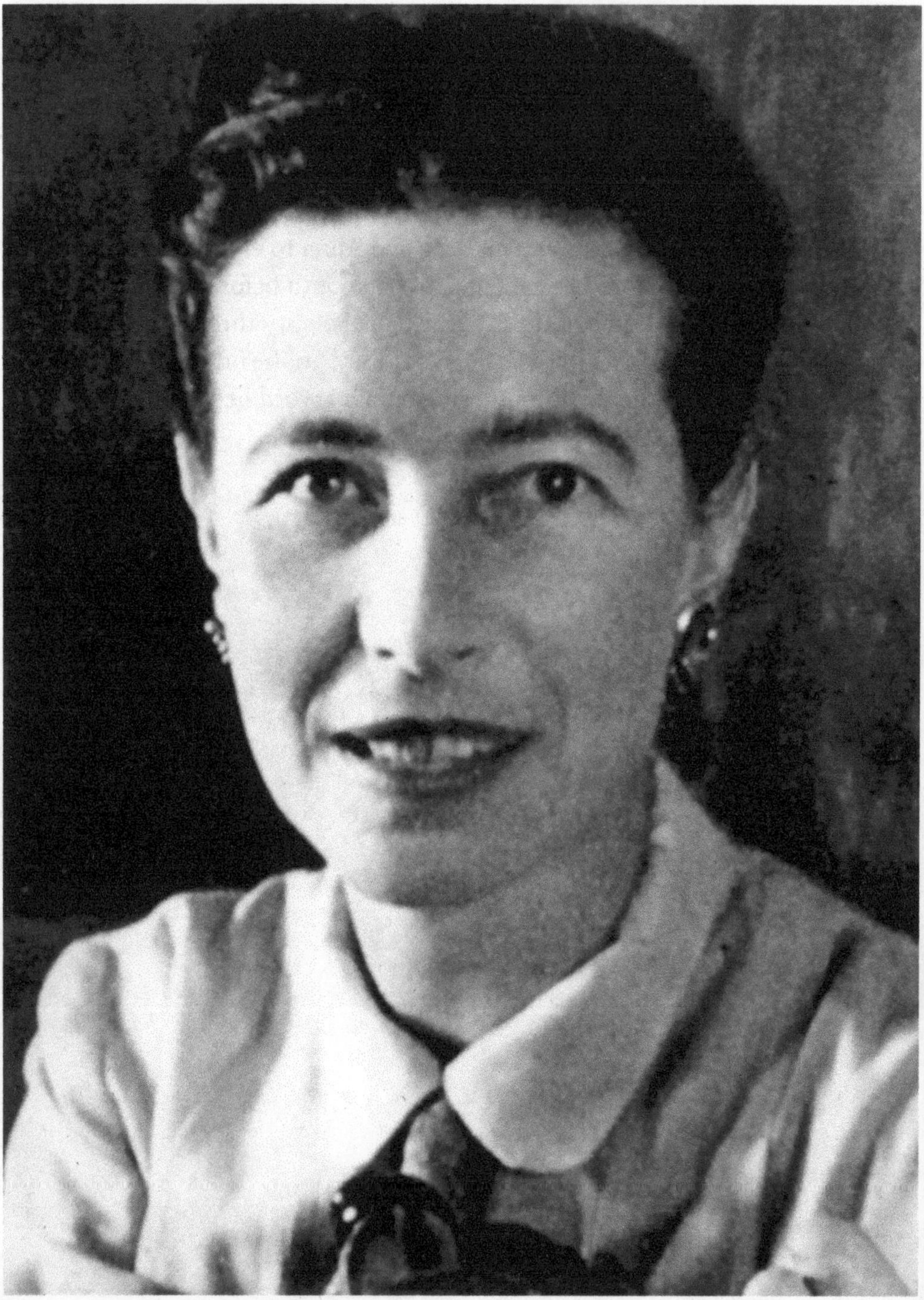

Simone de Beauvoir

Paris, France, 9 January 1968.

'Let's meet at Café de Flore,' de Beauvoir suggested. Do you know it?'

'Isn't that where Ernest Hemingway used to eat?'

'Among many others,' she replied. 'You'll find it at the corner of Rue Saint-Benoît and the Boulevard Saint-Germain. Would 11 o'clock tomorrow be convenient? That way, we can continue on through a working lunch.'

'I look forward to it. See you then.' My hand trembled as I replaced the telephone in its cradle.

My nervousness persisted the following day as I made my way up the stairs from the depths of the Saint-Germain-des-Prés Metro. As I emerged into the sunlight, I saw the café across the street. Its trademark flowerboxes, which would be bursting with riotous colour in spring, were thick with greenery above white canvas awnings that proclaimed the establishment's name.

I crossed the boulevard and walked through the maze of alfresco tables into the café's Art Deco interior. The Café de Flore was the epicentre of Parisian artistic and intellectual life. The list of luminary patrons encompassed nations and genres alike. Guillaume Apollinaire, Jean-Paul Sartre, Andre Breton, Louis Aragon, Paul Éluard, Albert Camus, Marguerite Duras and Maurice Merleau-Ponty were all counted among their number. Apart from Hemingway, other notable expats had spent time on the café's red moleskin seats: Truman Capote, Lawrence Durrell and, of course, Picasso.

Parisian writers and artists have always frequented cafés, not only for the social life but often to find somewhere warmer and more pleasant than their tiny, unheated apartments. In 1939, Boubal, the manager, had installed a larger and more powerful coal-fired heater to warm the café, which would have made it an attractive place to work.

I climbed the stairs and stopped, scanning the room. An elegant middle-aged woman looked towards me expectantly from a table in the far corner. She was wearing a turban, a black cashmere crew-neck jumper and a tweed skirt. She held herself erect and perused me with an assessing gaze.

'You must be Miss Huntington,' said de Beauvoir in fluent French-accented English with an air of noblesse oblige.

'Je suis en effet. Je suis ravi de faire votre connaissance,' I replied in no less fluent French.

'So should we continue in English or French?' she asked.

'*Celui que vous préférez*,' I replied without hesitation.

'Very well then, I choose English,' de Beauvoir said. She gestured with a regal wave. 'You know, this used to be my office. The floor was taken up almost entirely by existentialists silently writing, and Boubal allowed me, and others, to go all day without consuming very much. He even set up a special phone line for Sartre. But please sit down.'

'That's very interesting,' I said, cloaking my unease behind what I hoped was a convincing smile. I extended my hand. 'Thank you for taking the time to speak with me.'

Her handshake was warm and strong, and her voice was deep and slightly husky. 'My pleasure. I hope you don't mind, but Sartre will join us later. He is meeting me here at noon for lunch.'

A wave of anxiety swept over me, and all I could manage was a polite nod.

'When we spoke on the phone, you said you are with the *Times Literary Supplement,* is that so?'

'Yes. Ever since you wrote *The Second Sex,* our readers have been very interested in you and in women's issues.'

'Well, before we begin, I must compliment you on your fluency in French,' said de Beauvoir, her smile that of a teacher bestowing praise on a favoured student.

I blushed. 'Thank you. My parents are partial owners of a vineyard in the Dordogne. So, all my school holidays were spent outside Bergerac. I also read Modern Languages at Cambridge. My Part II Tripos were on Molière's *Tartuffe*.'

De Beauvoir's mouth curled in a polite smile. 'So, let's begin. Where would you like to start?'

I took my notebook from my satchel. 'At the beginning, if we may, with your childhood.'

She shrugged as we were interrupted by the unbidden arrival of the maître d' with a shot glass filled with amber liquid.

'Johnny Walker Black?' I said as the whisky was placed on the table in front of her.

De Beauvoir grinned. 'He knows me too well,' she said. 'But you appear to have done some background research. Johnny Walker is indeed my favourite whisky. But what about you? Would you like anything?'

I shook my head. 'It's a bit early for me.'

'Tea with tarte Tatin? Or maybe a croissant?'

'Tarte Tatin and tea, thank you,' I said, nodding towards the maître d'.

'Will that be all?' he asked in the barely disguised tone of contempt that was the trademark of so many waiters at finer Paris establishments.

De Beauvoir nodded her head regally, and he retreated to the stairs.

'So, you were born on ... let me see ... 9 January 1908 in Paris to Georges Bertrand de Beauvoir and Francoise Brasseur ...'

'And I have a sister, Hélène, two and a half years younger. I'm told that as a young child, I was jealous of her, but not for long.'

Hadn't many of us felt the same emotions when usurped by a younger brother or sister, I thought.

De Beauvoir smiled. 'I recall my childhood differently. In my memory, I was always proud of being the elder sister; I felt myself to be much more interesting than an infant bundled up in a cradle. As far as I was concerned, I had a little sister; that doll-like creature didn't have me. Besides, I also had Louise.'

'Louise?'

'My nanny. I felt secure with Louise, always. She used to dress me in the mornings and undress me at night – and she slept in the same room as me. Every morning she would curl my hair and sometimes remark on how dark it was, how pretty. When she had finished, we would gaze with satisfaction at my blue eyes and my face framed with ringlets. She was a calm young woman who never raised her voice and never scolded me without good reason.'

A waiter arrived with my tea and tart, and de Beauvoir paused until he departed.

'In the evening, Louise used to sit beside me on the bed, showing me pictures and telling me stories. Oh, and sometimes she took Hélène and me to the fair – we enjoyed ourselves immensely on those days.'

'In doing my research for this interview, I was told that you were a happy, well-behaved little girl, albeit somewhat opinionated.'

She ignored my attempt to steer her towards the origins of her intellectual life. She said instead, 'My happiness reached its height during the two and half months we spent every summer in the country. My mother was more relaxed there than in Paris, and my father devoted more time to me then as well.' She smiled to herself. 'We usually spent a few weeks at La Grillière near Limoges. With so many servants at our disposal, I found the castle suited me well. I used to spend most of my days on the croquet lawn with my sister and cousin, and the rest of the time, I would read.'

'Would it be fair to describe your childhood as one of privileged affluence?'

'I suppose,' she said, shifting her weight on the chair, as if in an unconscious expression of discomfort over a depiction of the bourgeois existence she had spent her life railing against. 'Meyrignac was our country house, of course, not the castle. On rainy days, we stayed inside, but when the weather was fine, I would go for a walk in the gardens. But my chief pleasure was to rise early in the morning and observe the awakening of nature. With a book in my hand, I would steal out of the sleeping house and quietly unlatch the garden gate and venture out into the surrounding woods and fields.'

'But weren't your parents worried about you?'

'They were mostly unaware. At home in Paris, I saw very little of my father. He would leave home every morning for the Law Courts carrying a briefcase stuffed with dossiers under his arm. When he came back in the evening, he would bring Mama a bunch of Parma violets, and they would laugh and kiss. But we children were largely ignored.'

'Meant to be seen but not heard. Or so goes the saying in English,' I suggested.

'Precisely.'

'Your father studied law and worked as a legal secretary, I believe?'

De Beauvoir smiled as if in fond reminiscence. 'I treasured the times when Papa would play with me. He would sometimes astonish me with magic tricks, pulling francs from behind my ear. I loved it whenever he made a fuss of me.'

De Beauvoir settled back in her chair. 'My father loved literature, and he was an atheist.' Her face darkened. 'But he was also a conservative, a man with aristocratic pretensions whose politics were decidedly right-wing.'

My hand flew over the page as I tried to record her exact words in my barely adequate shorthand. 'And your mother?'

'Mama was more distant than Papa, but she inspired the most tender feelings in me when I was young. I would sit on her knee and cover her skin with kisses. I still remember her skin… so fresh and youthful.'

'She came from a wealthy bourgeois family and brought a significant dowry, did she not?'

De Beauvoir nodded. 'Yes, we were affluent. Our apartment had a renaissance dining room, silk hangings over the stained-glass doors, velvet curtains in Papa's study and red carpet throughout.' She paused for a long moment and then smiled mirthlessly. 'Her fortune was lost in the wake of the First World War.'

I murmured a sympathetic 'hmm' and waited for her to continue.

De Beauvoir shook her head, her lips pursed in a scornful

grimace and her tone contemptuous. 'But as I grew older, my view began to change. My mother was a deeply religious woman, thanks to her upbringing. So, at first, she turned our poverty into a virtue. As soon as I could walk, Mama took me to church and showed me portraits of the child Jesus, of God the Father, of the Virgin, and of the angels,' – she numbered them off on her fingers – whether of wax, plaster or paint.'

She looked up at me with a wry smile. 'But at the age of fourteen, I had a crisis of faith and decided there was no God, and I've remained an atheist ever since.'

'What prompted your crisis of faith?' I asked.

'Since the age of seven, I'd been making my confession to Abbé Martin twice a month. I was very pious. I received Holy Communion three times a week, and between classes, I would slip into the school chapel and offer my lengthy prayers.'

De Beauvoir paused.

'And then?' I prompted.

She grinned as if savouring a delicious memory. 'Then one day the Abbé said, 'It has come to my ears that my little Simone has changed. That she is disobedient and noisy, that she answers back when she is reprimanded. These are grave sins, and from now on, you must be on your guard against these things.' I gazed back in horror at this imposter who I'd been told was a representative of God on Earth. With a burning face, I left the confessional, determined never to set foot in it again.'

'What did you do?' I asked. 'And what caused you to react so strongly to such a run-of-the-mill Catholic rebuke?'

She shrugged. 'I suppose it was bound to happen. I was too much of an extremist to be able to live under the eye of God.' She was quiet for a long time and then said, 'I felt great relief at finding myself in agreement with those liberal spirits I admired.'

'Which spirits in particular?'

'Most notably Voltaire,' she replied. 'His contempt for religion was inspirational to me when I was forging my own worldview.'

'Did your rejection of religion cause tension between you and your mother?'

'That and her bourgeois orientation became a source of great conflict between us,' she said frankly. 'My embrace of atheism was followed by my decision to pursue and teach philosophy ... Speaking of spirits ...' She glanced at the waiter with a raised index finger. He nodded and before long returned with another shot of Johnny Walker.

'And you, Madame?' he enquired.

'Nothing for me, thanks,' I said, conscious that I needed to keep my wits about me.

I took another mouthful of tart, washing it down with tea while de Beauvoir savoured the first sip of her second whisky.

I forged on. 'Your mother was very devout, and your father was a non-believer. Did that cause tension in the home as you grew up? How did this clash of different views affect you?'

De Beauvoir smiled. 'I think it is the reason I became an intellectual.'

'Could you elaborate?'

'Well, you see, my childhood was in an atmosphere of endless disputation – I was not only able to cope with it, but I found it stimulating.' Her eyes were bright.

I consulted my notes. 'At about the time you became an adolescent, or not long after, the boot and shoe factory where your father worked began to fail. Your father went into financial advertising, I believe, but he was ... shall we say, less than successful?'

'Worse than that. We had to move to a different house, much smaller and far less comfortable than the previous one. The carpets were threadbare, there was no bathroom, only a wash place without running water; every day, my father had to empty the heavy slop pail that stood under the washstand. There was no central heating; in winter, the apartment was icy cold, and the room I shared with my sister was too tiny to sit in. My mother claimed she had decided to do without domestic help, but frankly, we could not afford it. Worst of all, I found it painful to never be on my own.' Then, quite suddenly, she looked down and fell silent. 'It was a brutal awakening for me,' she said at last in a subdued voice.

Before I could pose another question, she went on. 'Poverty was hard for Mama to bear; her nerves were always on edge, and my father lost his sweet temper. They shouted at each other over the merest trifles. Papa would grumble about the hard time we were having. Whenever my mother asked for housekeeping money, he made a violent scene. He started going out in the evenings much more than previously and spent Sundays at the races – whilst Mama was left alone.'

'So he became a lesser man in your eyes?'

Giving me a sidelong look, she said sardonically, 'He would complain particularly about the sacrifice his daughters imposed on him: my sister and I had a feeling we were making unwonted demands upon his charity. I resented him for that.'

'And where did your intellectual zeal come from?'

'I always loved learning – I was an intellectually curious child. And my mother was very willing to answer my questions until I began to challenge her religious faith. She helped me with my homework and my lessons. When I started going to school, my father was interested in my progress and my successes. From an early age, he gave me edited selections from the great works of literature and encouraged me to read and write.'

'You began your education at the Institut Adeline Désir, a private Catholic school for girls,' I said, again consulting my notes.

'Yes,' she said promptly, 'I remained there until the age of seventeen. I went on to study at the Institut Catholique, Institut Sainte-Marie and the Sorbonne.'

'In 1929, you took second place to Jean-Paul Sartre in the highly competitive *agrégation* exam for those seeking a career in teaching.'

Her smile betrayed the faintest hint of smugness. 'Yes. He had failed at his first attempt, and this was his second try. At twenty-one, I was the youngest student ever to pass the exam in philosophy, and thus became the youngest philosophy teacher in France.'

'Quite an achievement,' I said. 'Did you always want to be a writer?'

De Beauvoir sighed. 'I didn't feel that I was a born writer, but at the age of fifteen, when I was asked what I wanted to do later in life, I wrote in a friend's album, "to be a famous author". I'd set my heart on that profession to the exclusion of everything else, and so

I pursued my studies with vigour. My schoolwork and reading were the great passions of my life.'

'Did you never consider the conventional roles for a woman?' I asked cautiously.

De Beauvoir, clasping her hands on the table, leaned forward. 'I never wanted to be a mother or a wife.'

'Not marriage? Did you never consider it?'

She shrugged. 'Only once when I was young. To my cousin, Jacques Champigneulle. He would always greet me with a brilliant smile whenever I went to his apartment, and I suppose his kindness warmed my heart. Jacques was good looking, with a boyish beauty. Yet he never aroused in me the faintest sexual desire. At times he was everything to me; at other times, absolutely nothing at all. In retrospect, I can see that there were many differences between us.'

She examined me for a few moments with her deep blue eyes. There was nothing of the coquette about her when she mentioned sexual desire. She was a striking woman – her face beautifully proportioned – and her manner was friendly but somewhat formal and a little distant.

'Despite my hesitations,' de Beauvoir continued, 'I always retained a deep affection for him. He was charming, and he had conquered more than one female heart. But his intellect soon ceased to dazzle me, and his attractiveness diminished as a result.'

She went on quietly. 'After that, I never again entertained the possibility of marriage, preferring to live the life of an intellectual – I can't remember considering pregnancy and childbirth, nor did I associate them with my own future. I was averse to marriage and maternity.'

'Since we have been talking about relationships, perhaps now is the time to talk a little about Sartre?'

She smiled, and there was a light in her eyes suddenly.

'Where do you want to start?' she asked. 'At the beginning?'

I smiled. 'Why not?'

'We first met in his room at university during a study session to speak about Leibniz. Then later, on Bastille Day, Sartre, Maheu – or Herbaud, as I called him – and I had dinner in an Alsatian restaurant and sat on the lawn in the Cité Universitaire and watched the fireworks. Herbaud had told me that Sartre had wanted to make my acquaintance. Later Sartre took us to rue Montparnasse, where we drank cocktails until two o'clock in the morning. I thought he was very amusing, even though at the time I was involved with Herbaud.'

Her voice was buoyant, and her face had come alive as she talked of Sartre.

'Soon after our oral exams, we were rarely apart, except to sleep. We went to the Sorbonne together to sit our written exams, we drank at the Balzac, and at the second-hand bookstore by the Seine, he bought me copies of *Pardaillan* and *Fantômas*. In the evenings, he would take me to see cowboy films, and we would talk for hours sitting in pavement cafés or drinking cocktails at the Falstaff.'

After rattling off this list, she was silent for a moment, looking about at the other patrons or perhaps hoping to catch the eye of the waiter. Her glass, I noticed, was empty again.

'So you were seen at all the Latin Quarter's trendy establishments,' I said with a smile that she returned.

'For my part, I was beginning to feel that time not spent in Sartre's company was time wasted. I remember him saying to me that he would take me under his wing and that I should try to preserve what was best in me: my love of personal freedom, my passion for life, my curiosity, my determination to be a writer.'

'So were you his protégé or his competitor?' I asked.

She pondered for a moment, chin on palm. 'Day after day, I set myself up against Sartre in our discussions, but I was simply not in his class. It was the first time in my life that I felt intellectually inferior.'

'But aren't you short-changing yourself? During my research for this interview, I was told that one of your professors said you were the real philosopher. Yet you have always insisted that while Sartre was a true philosopher, you were only someone who dabbles in philosophy.'

She moved further back in her chair and said, 'Jean-Paul's work was much more important than mine. He was much more creative. So naturally, I bowed to this and put his work before my own.'

My incredulity must have shown because de Beauvoir pressed home the point.

'He was, and is, highly intelligent, and he makes me laugh. He's a very generous man, too, preferring to spend money on others rather than himself. We are both ambitious, we both love cocktails, and we both love to talk. Apart from a few minor differences, I've found a great resemblance between his attitudes and mine.'

'Does that commonality of view extend to politics?' I asked.

'Most certainly,' she declared with a hint of indignation. 'In 1960, we signed Manifesto 121, supporting the right to refuse military service in Algeria, which was fighting for its independence from France, as you know. Our militancy placed our lives in danger.'

Leaning forward again, her elbows on the table, she said, 'Last year, we were put on a list of boycotted authors because of our support for Israel.' Her voice was now strident.

'That boycott was in Algeria, I understand, not France.'

She shrugged and changed the subject. 'When the Russians suppressed the Hungarian revolution in 1956, we broke off relations with the Communist Party. We have always gone our own way. In short, on most issues, Sartre and I think as one. It's as simple as that.'

'Except when it comes to marriage,' I observed. 'Isn't it true that Sartre proposed to you?'

She tilted her head. 'I see you've done your homework.' She inspected her nails for a moment. 'I turned down his offer because I knew he didn't really want it. And I decided our love did not require it. We had intense conversations and a lifelong unity of intellect, opinions and ambitions. Marriage was redundant.'

'But that provided you with no security. What about children? You have no regrets?'

De Beauvoir snorted. 'Security? Truly? From the moment we met, he and I have been the closest of companions. We do not live in the same apartment, but we are always near each other. We see each other daily, spend our annual six-week vacation in Rome together and are completely open about our other liaisons – our relationship is central to both our lives.' Her voice was deep and confident.

'By liaisons, you mean other lovers,' I said, more as a statement than a question.

De Beauvoir smiled. Her face looked brighter and younger, but I thought there was a tinge of sadness in her eyes.

'It was Sartre who set the terms of our relationship. He said the love between us was essential, but we both should be free to experience other love affairs that are contingent, and it has provided us both with a range of emotional experiences.'

The morning sun, breaking through the clouds, shone on the edge of the table.

'I believe you made a pact: not only would you never lie to one another, but neither of you would conceal anything from the other.'

She nodded.

'You have had fewer love affairs, I believe, but Sartre has taken full advantage of this arrangement. How has each of you dealt with jealousy, I wonder?'

She sighed. It was as if she were engaged in an interior dialogue with herself. Then she smiled slightly and said, 'I was distressed to discover I sometimes felt jealous. But Sartre said that jealousy is the enemy of freedom: it controls you, and you should be controlling it.'

She was silent again, then she shook her head slowly and came back from wherever she had been.

'What were the benefits of your pact with Sartre then?' I asked, not wishing to press too hard on a subject she may have found painful.

'Well, it was an affront to conventional standards of domesticity, to begin with, and that appealed to me. My life to that point had been a struggle to escape from the culture of my family. My mother had been educated in a convent; my father was a conservative Paris lawyer…'

I managed a half-smile, watching the waiter approach once more.

'I knew Sartre would never be faithful, but neither would he harm me. Ever since I met Sartre, I have never been lonely.' She looked at me steadily. 'The only thing I dread is that he will die before I do.'

She made a convincing case, but I was not so sure that the reality would have been as easy as she seemed to imply.

She paused while the waiter returned with another shot before saying, 'Who cares if our relationship is not a passionate and enduring romance? We have a great and liberating friendship, which has been the one undoubted success of my life. Sartre is a warm, lively man in every part of his life, but not in bed, and our sexual relations were virtually over by the end of the war.'

Until this point, I'd been able to keep my feelings in diplomatic check. But de Beauvoir's matter-of-fact recounting of Sartre's career as a roué and her rationalisations of his sexual rakishness was more than I could bear. My facade of journalistic objectivity cracked.

'So you turned a blind eye to his philandering and even played the role of procuress for him,' I blurted. 'You were completely subservient to him,' I ventured.

De Beauvoir's mouth opened in an 'O' of shocked surprise. But only for the barest of moments. Her air of aplomb almost immediately reasserted itself. 'My dear, whatever do you mean?' she asked in a tone of condescension.

I glared into the deep blue pools of her eyes. 'I mean Bianca Bienenfeld. Remember her?'

'Oh that,' de Beauvoir replied dismissively.

'Yes, that. The young girl ... your student ... who you introduced to Jean-Paul Sartre. After he was done, you dropped her. And you knew she was Jewish but did nothing to help her when the Germans won in 1940. Did you know most of her family were deported to Auschwitz?'

De Beauvoir remained silent for several moments, observing me with the cool gaze of a vivisectionist in a biology lab. 'Mademoiselle Huntington, given that most of your allegations pertain to the behaviour of Sartre, I suggest you wait with your ... bill of indictment until he arrives, and you can pose your questions directly to him. But if you persist, this interview will be over.'

I hesitated. After all the logistical work that had gone into arranging the interview, my editors would have my head if it were truncated because I pushed too hard. I shrugged my assent.

'Without delving into the substance of your allegations, I wonder why this is so important to you? Your indignation is obvious. You'd be a very poor poker player,' she said with a tight smile.

I sat silently as my mind raced through the options that faced me. How much should I tell her? She'd already displayed an arrogant indifference bordering on the sociopathic. Wouldn't giving up more information place me at a greater disadvantage?

But in the end, I couldn't help myself. Like the mesmerised subject of a hypnotist, I felt compelled to speak. 'I was exploited by an older man. Sexually … while at Cambridge.'

'Ah,' de Beauvoir said with a knowing nod. 'A don, I presume?'

My eyebrows arched in surprise. 'How did you guess?'

She laughed cruelly. 'Darling, you may view your story as the greatest tragedy since Tristan and Isolde, but it's really nothing special. The sexual conquest of an ingénue by a prominent older man is the oldest tale in human history.'

'But …' I sputtered before de Beauvoir cut me off.

'After Sartre joins us, you'll be able to ask the man himself. But I think you were about to ask about my extracurricular love life?'

Sitting back in my chair, I buried myself in my notes as I struggled to regain my composure. 'You were romantically involved with the American novelist, Nelson Algren, soon after the war ended,' I offered after several agonising moments.

She smiled smoothly as if no harsh words had been exchanged between us. 'We were together from 1947 to 1951.'

'The author of *The Man with the Golden Arm*,' I said while I considered my next question.

'It's a great read,' I added, glancing at my watch. Eleven-thirty. Another half-hour to burn before Sartre joined us. If he was punctual.

'I agree. His tenderness and friendship were so precious to me that I can still feel warm and happy and grateful when I think of him.'

'But it ended,' I observed.

She nodded. 'When our relationship finished, I wrote him a letter and told him, "I have lost your love, and it was painful, but I shall not lose you. You gave me so much that you could never take it back."' Her voice trailed off into rueful silence.

I pressed on. 'And Claude Lanzmann?'

Her face went from glum to gloating. 'He was twenty-six and Sartre's secretary when we first met – I was forty-four.'

De Beauvoir paused as she produced a cigarette from her purse and lit it, exhaling loudly and watching the tobacco smoke swirl towards the ceiling. 'He was my first absolute love,' she sighed, 'the love one never encounters or, only once. I adored him with all my body and soul ... and in many ways, he was my destiny, my eternity, my life.'

'How long were you together?'

'We lived together from 1952 until 1959. In the morning, we got up, dressed and worked – we didn't speak until lunchtime. Then in the afternoons, I would go and write with Sartre.'

'And Lanzmann didn't mind this arrangement?' I asked.

'Of course not,' she protested, but then her face darkened. 'To be totally frank, it was I who struggled when I discovered that he'd had an affair that he did not tell me about.'

'You mean Lanzmann?'

De Beauvoir nodded. 'That was not how things worked with Sartre. We shared everything; we had no secrets.'

She examined her cigarette, which had been reduced to a column of grey ash that she held upright while carefully guiding it to the ashtray.

'I was told that you found greater sexual bliss with Lanzmann than you did with Nelson Algren?'

Her expression became stony. 'You are digging too deep.'

I paused for a moment to focus my thoughts. 'All right, I'll ask this: do you think you would have given up your affairs if you could have had Sartre for yourself?'

She looked at me in silence for a moment, her eyes hooded, then she gave me an icy smile and did not respond. She took out another cigarette and lit it, drawing the smoke deep into her lungs.

'Aren't you quoted as saying that "homosexuality is as limiting as heterosexuality"?'

De Beauvoir grimaced. 'So people have said, and yet I have no recollection of saying such a thing. But I do believe that human sexuality is fluid. I've never liked placing people in arbitrary categories.'

I decided a change of topic was called for.

'Let's talk about your writing. Who do you regard as your greatest literary inspirations?'

She cleared her throat. 'Hemingway without question. I also admire the writing of Kafka, Proust and Joyce.'

'Ah yes, the greats of modernism,' I said. 'I'm more inclined towards Shakespeare and Webster myself.'

'Webster? As in Noah Webster of dictionary fame?'

'No, no, John Webster,' I said. 'He was the seventeenth-century playwright who penned *The Duchess of Malfi*.'

'I'm not familiar with it,' said de Beauvoir.

I smiled, savouring the momentary reversal of the intellectual dynamic. 'It's an extraordinary work. Webster's phrasing is absolutely sublime. He's surely the equal of Shakespeare at his best. Some have said even better.'

De Beauvoir's head canted forward in a purse-lipped nod. 'Sounds impressive. I'll have to seek it out.'

'I'm sure you'll enjoy it. But back to your oeuvre. *The Second Sex* was first published in Paris in 1949. It earned you both notoriety and admiration. It was a ground-breaking, risqué book that became a runaway success, selling over 20,000 copies in its first week. Since then, the book has been widely translated and has become a landmark in the history of feminism. What prompted you to write it?'

'In 1946, I was working on the *Ethics of Ambiguity*. When that was finished, I began to think about writing something more autobiographical. After a discussion with Sartre, I decided this involved thinking through what it meant to be a woman. I'd been told from an early age that I "thought like a man". As if men had a monopoly on intellectual capacity,' she huffed. 'This project of exploring myself fused into the broader project of *The Second Sex*.'

'The book shattered many taboos, attracting praise and criticism alike. Particularly controversial was your negative portrayal of marriage, your advocacy of contraception and your endorsement of abortion. Not to mention the references to women taking young lovers.'

De Beauvoir shrugged, the curl of her lips clearly conveying her contempt. 'The outrage of the small-minded has never bothered me. The truth is the conservative bourgeoisie views women's liberation as a danger because it corrodes the moral underpinnings of the social system that has benefited them materially.'

'You mean the Marxist infrastructure–superstructure dynamic?'

She nodded. 'And Gramsci's theory of cultural hegemony. I merely entered sex into the same equation. Men's sexual desire and desire for posterity have subordinated women rather than liberated them.'

'Just as master and slave are also linked by a reciprocal economic need that does not free the slave.'

'Indeed, and is that the relationship we want?'

I paused, steeling my nerves for another question that delved beyond social nicety. 'All well and good. But I still can't get past the fact that you allowed Sartre's sexual desires and needs to dictate the shape of your relationship. Isn't there a fundamental contradiction … a hypocrisy even … between what you wrote and how you lived?'

De Beauvoir fixed me with a frigid glare. 'I told you these were matters for Jean-Paul. What is it the Americans say … "three strikes and you're out"?' You have had two. One more, and I walk away.'

'Very well,' I said grudgingly.

She forged on, expounding in a long-winded manner as if oblivious to my discontent. 'Woman is not born, she is made, she becomes a woman,' she said. 'No biological, psychological or economic fate determines the figure that the female presents in society; it is civilisation as a whole that moulds her.'

De Beauvoir raised her eyes to the ceiling as if communing with a feminist deity. 'Some, who like to keep things simple, say the woman is a womb, an ovary, but they are wrong. It is certainly true that the whole organism is directed towards the perpetuation of the species – but she is much more than her anatomy.'

'What about the traditional female functions of wife and mother?' I challenged. 'Shouldn't they be afforded greater respect and recognition?'

'What utter nonsense!' she growled. 'Throughout history, men have always been the wielders of power, physical and economic. From earliest times, they've ensured that women occupy a subordinate position and state of dependence.'

'All undeniable,' I replied. 'But how much of this subservience was caused by the brutal realities of pre-industrial life? Short life expectancies, the perils of childbirth and massively high child-mortality rates? War, famine and pestilence?'

'Pah,' said de Beauvoir. 'The subjugation of women served men's economic interests and their moral ambitions. Even today, some men feel threatened by women's competition. We mustn't allow ourselves to be conditioned exclusively to male desire.'

'But again, how do you reconcile—' I halted, mid-sentence, in response to de Beauvoir's ferocious glower. Sartre was due any minute, and I didn't want to squander the opportunity to put some questions to him.

She took up her glass, realised it was empty and set it down again. 'I became a feminist because I decided it was necessary to fight for the situation of women. Recently, I have become even more aware of women's lack of power.'

Yeah... all right, I thought. 'So how important do you think *The Second Sex* is today?' I asked, in a conscious shift to safer ground.

'*The Second Sex* retains its relevance, despite the changes that have occurred in women's position since its publication.'

'You have said that today, almost twenty years after *The Second Sex* was published, there hasn't been the change you hoped for in the condition of women. How optimistic are you about the future?'

She eyed me intently and said, 'I am certain the changes women are struggling for will, in the long run, be achieved.'

'Before we finish, can we talk about melancholia?'

She nodded.

'Many of the protagonists of your novels are quite ... troubled. They suffer from depression and alcoholism. Some of them use hard drugs. Is this merely a literary device to heighten the tension in your fiction, or is there something autobiographical about these character depictions?'

De Beauvoir hesitated. 'Let's just say that large quantities of alcohol and I are not unacquainted.'

'And melancholia?'

Her face darkened as she reached for and lit another cigarette. 'I've been known to burst into tears on occasion.'

'Any thoughts as to why that might be?'

Her shoulders heaved in one of her now familiar dismissive shrugs. 'Perhaps my mother's hostility? Once I rejected religion, she became very adversarial.'

She paused to flick the ash off her cigarette into the brimming ashtray. 'I suppose my father's indifference also played a part. Once I became an adolescent, I felt he preferred my prettier sister. After I began to show interest in philosophy, our estrangement deepened. He was a bourgeois conservative who thought intellectuals were all leftist agitators.'

'Rather true in your case,' I observed. 'And Sartre?'

'In the autumn of 1933, Sartre went to Berlin,' she said. 'In his absence, I grew depressed. I had no husband, no children, no home – not that I wanted or desired those things.'

'Of course,' I murmured, hoping that an affirmation would prolong her confessional revelations.

'Think of it this way,' de Beauvoir continued. 'I was twenty-six years old. An age where you think you might begin to amass some measure of accomplishment in life. Then I learned from Sartre that he had fallen in love with the wife of his colleague.'

'You must have been crushed.'

'Not at all,' declared de Beauvoir, shaking her head with vigour. 'From the outset, Sartre had warned me that he was liable to embark on such adventures. I had accepted the principle, and I had no difficulty in accepting the fact.'

But the sadness in her eyes betrayed her protestations. She continued, her voice now sombre with dark recollection. 'When Sartre returned from Berlin, I was nearly thirty. I drank too much, and he blamed my depression on alcohol.'

'He did?'

She nodded, and a thin sigh escaped her lips. The lines on her forehead had deepened. 'The loss of sexual passion causes depression in many of my characters, and this is made even worse by the loss of youth and beauty and the thought of death.'

'Oscar Wilde suffered from that same anxiety,' I noted.

'Yes,' she replied. 'But I didn't have access to a magic portrait like Dorian Gray.'

Suddenly, there was Sartre at the top of the stairs. A short, stocky man in round glasses, he was dressed in oversized clothes, loose-fitting blue trousers, a floppy beige cardigan and a wrinkled open-necked shirt.

I rose shakily to my feet and waited behind the table as he walked towards us. The moment of truth.

De Beauvoir followed my gaze and said when he reached us, 'Jean-Paul, this is Miss Huntington, from the *Times Literary Supplement*. She's doing a story on me but has some questions for you as well.'

'Oh?' murmured Sartre as he offered his hand in greeting.

His palm was damp and soft.

'I'd like to ask you about Bianca Bienenfeld.'

A startled look flashed across Sartre's face as he exchanged glances with de Beauvoir.

'Why is this private matter of any interest to you?' Sartre asked.

'Madame de Beauvoir mentions Bianca by name in *La Force de l'âge*. I was intrigued and made some enquiries,' I replied calmly, determined that his hostility would not force me off balance. 'I met with her, and she told me everything.'

'And Miss Huntington had an unhappy *affaire de cœur* with one of her professors at Cambridge,' announced de Beauvoir in the tone of an informant revealing a state secret.

Sartre nodded at her and then turned to face me. 'I don't know what you've heard or what you think you know, but ....'

'I know Bianca's version of your love affair before the war. Now I'd like to hear yours.'

'And you intend to write this in your article?' asked Sartre, his mouth now set in a smirk I found infuriating.'

'That's a decision for my editors. But I think it's a relevant part of the story.'

'How old are you?' Sartre asked rhetorically. 'Late twenties, early thirties? Your head filled with the spirit of sexual liberation?

Well, let me explain the facts of life to you. If you include these … allegations in your article, I will call every intellectual voice in France to my defence. Your editor, Arthur Crook, will be inundated by letters, telephone calls and telegrams from senior journalists and immortals of *l'Académie française*. Your Prime Minister, Mister Wilson, will receive a call from the Élysée Palace stating that your article threatens the honour of France. And your article will never see the light of day.'

'But that would never happen in Engla—'

Sartre cut me off with an impatient wave of the hand. 'It's time for you to grow up and understand the way the world really works. Forget the Magna Carta and Milton's *Areopagetica*. You imagine you will expose us with this story. But if you persist with this foolishness, you will destroy your career. That I promise you.'

Shaken by Sartre's threats, I could think of nothing more to say. I gathered my things without a word and left the café, hailing a taxi to the Gare du Nord for the first leg of my trip home to London.

An hour later, I was ensconced in the first-class carriage of the 1:35 to Calais. I was oblivious to the snowy fields of Picardy that were slipping by the carriage window.

Would Arthur Crook have my back when push came to shove? It's true he agreed that I should raise the Bianca Bienenfeld matter with de Beauvoir when I first proposed the interview idea at our editorial meeting the previous month. That was the easy part. Far harder would be proceeding with publication in the face of the political pressure Jean-Paul Sartre threatened to exert.

The more I thought about it, the more I reluctantly concluded that Sartre was right. As much as it infuriated me, every instinct told me that indeed he was. The Americans had a saying that you can't fight city hall, and there's no way I'd be able to prevail against the juggernaut someone of Sartre's stature could send down on me and my editor. The prospect of being righteous but hungry had little appeal. In the end, I would opt for self-preservation over martyrdom.

Perhaps one day, the whole truth would come to light. Perhaps one day, the world would see that these luminaries of French intellectual life had feet of clay. However, this revelation would not come from my pen. It rankled, but I'd just have to learn to live with it.

Endnote

This imaginary conversation with Simone de Beauvoir is set in 1968 on her sixtieth birthday. It relies on de Beauvoir's own remarks, or close interpretations of them, to remain true to what she said. During her lifetime, de Beauvoir was regarded as a pioneering feminist icon. Still, her image was severely tarnished by revelations of sexual predation that came to public knowledge with the posthumous publication of her letters in 1990.

Many of de Beauvoir's admirers were shocked by the hypocritical inconsistency between her public persona and her private life with Jean-Paul Sartre. Sartre demanded tolerance for his philandering as a non-negotiable condition of their relationship. De Beauvoir's attempts to rationalise his sexual liaisons through feminist rhetoric are considered by many to be hypocritical and unconvincing.

The enabling role de Beauvoir played in Sartre's sexual abuse of underage girls was even more questionable. In 1993, Bianca Lamblin (née Bienenfeld) wrote a book detailing the sequence of events leading to, and including, her seduction by her university professor, de Beauvoir. When de Beauvoir tired of the teenager, she passed her on to Sartre. Bienenfeld waited until both Sartre, and de Beauvoir were dead before she wrote her book and set the record straight.

When de Beauvoir died in 1986, the President of France, Jacques Chirac, was reported in *The New York Times* (15 April 1986) as saying that her 'unquestionable talent made her a writer who deserves her place in French literature. In the name of the Government, I salute her memory in respect.' Four years later, her letters were released, and her work and life were thrown into question.

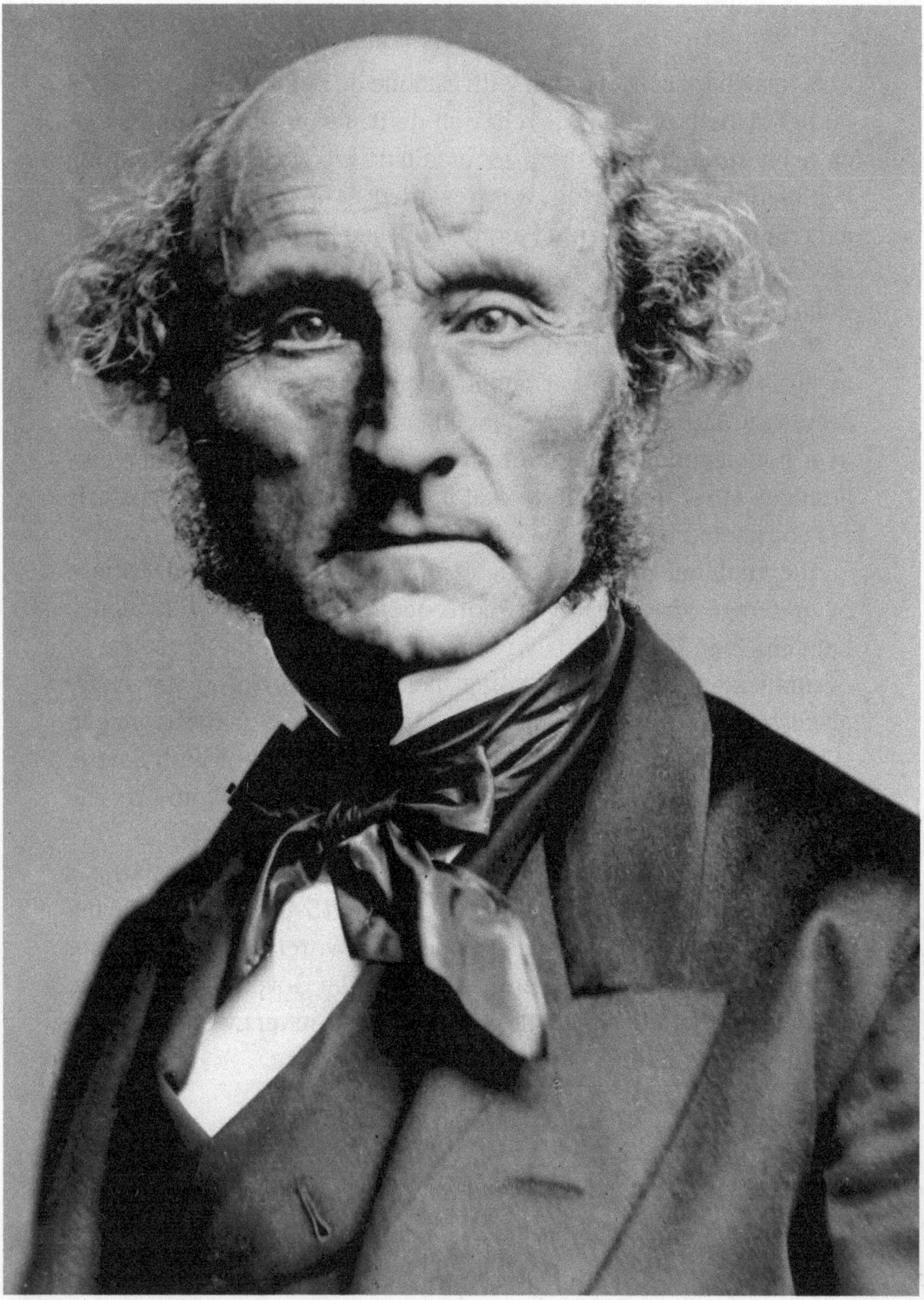

John Stuart Mill

Westminster, London, 20 May 1868.

It was a warm, dry July day when I arrived at the Palace of Westminster. I stepped off the omnibus at Bridge Street, taking care to avoid the steaming pile of ordure freshly deposited on the pavement by the team of horses pulling the carriage. Turning left at Big Ben, I walked towards the entrance to Parliament House. Finding my way to the members' lobby, I walked past the members' letter boards, statues of prime ministers and then through the arch. I could see the Commons were in session when I looked through the Judas window.

Being early for my interview, I walked up the stairs to the public gallery that faced the Speaker's chair. Once seated, I could look down to see Prime Minister Disraeli sitting opposite William Gladstone, the Leader of the Opposition. My eyes scanned the Conservative benches for a distinctive countenance, the thin, severe mouth and narrow nose, that small trademark lump on the forehead over the left eyebrow. It was John Stuart Mill, just as stiff, stern and proper as I remembered him from the time I first heard him speak. I looked down at his bald pate, the grey, curly hair at the back and sides trailing off into leg-of-mutton whiskers. Head down, he was reading a document and seemed deep in thought.

'Order! Order!' the Speaker cried and struck his gavel.

The sound jolted Mill, who raised his head and scanned the public gallery. He caught my eye, expressionless, and pointed to the door.

I stood and set off down the stairs.

After we had introduced ourselves and shaken hands, he opened an adjacent door and said, 'Let's go into this meeting room.'

'*The Westminster Review* kindly asked me to interview you; they intend to celebrate your birthday in their next edition,' I said.

'Flattering but unnecessary,' he rejoined.

'May I wish you many returns of the day, sir.'

He smiled briefly and asked, 'Will you send me a copy before you submit it for publication, please?'

'I'm sure we shall, but I will have to speak with my editor,' I told him.

The meeting room was small, clean and neat. One wall was lined from floor to ceiling with a bookcase full of leather-bound English law reports. The ceiling was high and vaulted. A large window opposite the door was bright with sunlight, warming the room and dispensing a faint scent of beeswax polish from the furniture. I could see Westminster on the other side of St Margaret Street. There was a steel engraving of London Bridge on the wall above the wooden panelling. We settled ourselves into leather chairs at each side of a table.

Mill was not particularly tall, but he was so thin that it accentuated the impression of his height. His gaze was direct, his eyes clear, but I noticed he was afflicted by a tic above his left eye. He had a noble brow, high cheekbones and a straight nose, his narrow lips set in a determined line. Formally dressed in a dark frock coat with a silk necktie arranged in a flat bow, he had encased his long thin legs in wide trousers, perhaps to disguise his bony shanks.

I was about to interview the most influential English-speaking philosopher of the century, the author of *On Liberty*, among countless essays and other books. I felt a slight sense of apprehension.

'Right. Well, let's begin,' he prompted.

I pulled out my notebook and turned to the list of questions I'd prepared. I could feel the perspiration on the palms of my hands.

After a moment's thought, I began. 'Much has already been written about *On Liberty*, your controversial views on women, slavery and your election to Parliament, so with your consent, I thought we might leave those matters for now. Can we discuss your father first of all, and your upbringing and education, and perhaps then your health... and, of course, Mrs Mill,' I gulped, my nerves no doubt obvious.

He emitted a huff of amusement and nodded.

'You were born in London on 20 May 1806 and are the eldest son of James Mill.'

He nodded.

'And your father?'

'Was a man of considerable intellectual ability. Sir John Stuart, Baron of the Exchequer in Scotland, recognised my father's gifts and paid for him to go to the University of Edinburgh. He completed his studies and was ordained a minister in the Church of Scotland, but ultimately rejected religious belief.'

I was surprised that James Mill had strayed so radically from the path set out for him in life, but there would be time enough to ponder that after the interview.

'He worked as a private tutor for various families in Scotland,' Mill continued, 'and ended up taking residence in London. In 1819, he obtained an appointment with the East India Company.'

He paused for a moment before forging on. 'While working there, he wrote about politics and religion for a number of different periodicals and managed to offend both the conservatives and the budding Romantics.'

Mill paused again, a slight smile gracing his face.

'And his major works ....' I flipped over a few pages in my notebook, 'included *The History of British India* in three volumes, *Elements of Political Economy, Analysis of the Phenomena of the Human Mind* – two volumes, and for the *Encyclopedia Britannica, Essays on Government, Jurisprudence, Liberty of the Press, Prisons and Prison Discipline, Colonies, Law of Nations and Education*.'

'Yes, my father had extraordinary mental energy and a great breadth of interests, extraordinary determination and application as well, of course. He was quite prolific. It took him about ten or twelve years to write the *History of British India*.'

'And your mother?'

'My parents married in the year my father began work on his *History*. They had a large family, and much of his time was employed educating me, his eldest son,' Mill said.

He stood abruptly, pushed back his chair and walked to the

window. For a time, he gazed out over the River Thames before returning to his seat.

'You never attended school or university?' I enquired.

For a long moment, he stared at me, and I once again noticed that spasmodic twitching above his eye.

'My father supervised my education meticulously,' he said. 'His mentor, Jeremy Bentham, the father of English utilitarianism, also took a great interest in my education. I was … a … project of sorts. They intended that I would be the complete utilitarian – a perfectly rational man.'

I glanced up from my notes, thinking what a joyless boyhood he had just described, but he continued, his tone measured. 'My father was studious himself and a hard taskmaster. He refused to waste time, and he applied this rule stringently to my education. As my teacher, he demanded the utmost of me. Unfortunately, his temper was irritable and, spending so much of our time together, I bore the brunt of it, whereas my brothers and sisters were spared.'

Mill stared long and hard at the window, and I wondered whether he might be envisioning some long-ago scene.

He ultimately turned back to me. 'His younger children loved him tenderly,' he said, 'and I… I was loyally devoted to my father… naturally.'

After this somewhat faint praise, there again was a long pause, which I felt I had to fill. 'I believe, sir, that you learnt Greek from the age of three?'

'Yes, *Aesop's Fables* was the first Greek book that I read, followed by *The Anabasis*. When I was eight, I began to study Latin and the Greek poets – *The Iliad, The Odyssey* and many others.'

For a few moments, I recalled my own enjoyment of *The Iliad*, although I'd read Cowper's translation in English.

'I read Plato when I was nine,' Mill continued, interrupting my reverie. 'I can remember preparing my Greek lessons at the same table where my father was writing his *History of British India*. He was an impatient man, but even so, he insisted that I interrupt his work whenever I didn't understand the meaning of a word.'

Secretly I quailed at the thought of working at my lessons within such an inflexible regime. 'Had you no toys, no children's books?' I enquired.

'My father had no interest in playthings, but occasionally a friend or relative would give me a gift. I received *Robinson Crusoe* as a boy, which was a delight, and my father borrowed the *Arabian Nights* and *Don Quixote* and several other books of that sort for me.'

I found myself pitying the young John Mill as the adult continued to describe his childhood.

'Between 1810 and 1813, we were living in Newington Green. My father's health required daily exercise, and much of my learning came during our morning walks.'

I smiled. That was a far more pleasant image, the father and son walking and conversing.

'Each morning, we walked before breakfast, and he insisted I give him an account of what I had read the day before. I got into the habit of making notes on slips of paper so I could explain to him what I'd been reading.' Mill placed a thin, veined hand on the table. 'In our talks, my father would expound on his ideas about civilisation, government, morality and mental cultivation.'

He stared at his hands for several moments, his face pensive.

'My father always demanded that I restate, in my own words, what he had said, which is an excellent way to ensure full understanding. I found the same thing occurred when I was required to teach my younger brothers and sisters Latin after I turned seven.'

I was scribbling furiously as he spoke, but part of my mind recoiled from the thought that not only had he worked so hard at his own learning, he also had to teach his siblings from the age of seven!

'My father insisted that I read books about men of energy, men of resource and men who struggled against the odds and overcame them.'

There was a long silence, during which he sat very still, then he seemed to collect his thoughts. 'Shall I ring for tea?'

'Thank you,' I replied. He went to the door and was gone long enough for me to catch up on my notes.

'Tea is a passion,' he said as he re-entered the room, followed not long after by a maid carrying a tray laden with tea things and a plate of biscuits. She bobbed a curtsy and left as Mill settled down to pour our tea.

After we were both furnished with tea and a biscuit, Mill continued as if there had been no interruption. 'From the age of eight to twelve, I was taught geometry, algebra and calculus, but having allowed his knowledge of these to fade with time, my father soon left me to my own devices, demanding I solve difficult problems for which I was totally unprepared.'

I smiled in commiseration. 'I, too, found mathematics trying, and that was despite the benefit of several good teachers. Perhaps mathematics requires a certain kind of intelligence,' I hazarded. I fell silent, fearing I might have overstepped the mark.

But Mill took a sip of tea and forged on with the story of his boyhood. 'When I was eleven and twelve, I wrote a history of the Roman government,' he said. 'I also wrote verse at my father's insistence. I had little ability and less enthusiasm for the task. He made me read Shakespeare, although he had no great admiration for his work. Nor did he admire many poets other than Milton, Goldsmith, oh, and Thomas Gray's poem "The Bard". Of our contemporary poets, we read not one line, and it was not until I was a man that I read and delighted in the romances of Walter Scott.'

'I loved *Ivanhoe*,' I said.

Mill smiled, nodding in agreement. 'My father urged me to write verse because he said many things are better expressed in rhyme than in prose. The verses I wrote were rubbish, of course, but the practice improved my expression.'

The sound of a child crying came faintly through the window, and I glanced out to see a nanny wheeling her small charge briskly along the street in a perambulator. Mill seemed unaware and continued without pause.

'I devoured chemistry, and at the age of twelve, I sat the exams for university entrance.'

Twelve, I thought, *what were my pastimes at twelve*? Certainly, I'd had no thought of university.

'From that age, my father's instruction was focused on logic. He taught me how to dissect an argument. He made me read Plato and Demosthenes aloud, losing his temper with every deviation from proper elocution. His own elocution was excellent but had he demonstrated the rules he sought to impart, I may have learned them sooner.'

There was no reproach in his tone, rather a faint wistfulness as he continued his personal story. 'My father's *History of British India* was published at that time, and it also contributed to my education. I read the manuscript to him while he corrected the proofs. Its criticisms of society, institutions and acts of government stimulated and guided me and were of fundamental importance to my subsequent progress – it was a remarkable book.'

'Had your father spent long in India?' I asked.

'No, not at all,' said Mill. 'He never set foot in India. He spent his entire career at the Company's London headquarters.'

'It's quite remarkable,' I said, 'that such a comprehensive study could be compiled entirely from written records without any firsthand experience.'

'Well, he was a talented—'

Unexpectedly, the door opened. 'I do beg your pardon,' a man said as he stepped into the room. 'I didn't realise this room was occupied.' He turned and closed the door behind him.

Mill continued as if there had been no interruption. His powers of concentration were remarkable.

'—man. The following year, in 1819, my father took a job at the London head office of the East India Company. In that same year, he took me through a complete course of political economy.'

Political economy at the age of thirteen, I thought, astounded.

'Each morning on our walks, he would explain a portion of the subject matter and demand that I give him a written account of our conversation the following morning. Often, he would make me rewrite it, again and again. He used my notes to write his *Elements of Political Economy*, which encouraged me to take a strong interest in the subject, which I found I enjoyed.'

Listening to him, I wondered whether anything simple, intimate or human had ever passed between father and son when they conversed. I had the impression that James Mill would have repressed anything he regarded as frivolous, and the thought of that eager boy, so much in his father's company yet so alone, saddened me. But I had not the courage to broach this issue, so I said only, 'Your achievements at such an early age were remarkable.'

'On the contrary,' he replied, 'I do not consider myself quick of apprehension – what I achieved could be done by anyone of average capacity. If I've accomplished anything, I owe it to my father. He gave me the advantage of a quarter of a century over my contemporaries.' Then he hesitated for a moment and said, 'Most boys have knowledge drilled into them; my father encouraged me to think for myself.'

Hmm, perhaps, I thought, *as long as you thought about the subjects he considered important.*

'Did you have much to do with other boys during your youth?'

He shook his head. 'My father was determined that I should escape the corrupting influence of boys my own age and avoid the contagion of vulgar modes of thought and feeling. He was prepared for me to pay the price of that lack of companionship – the absence of those things that boys learn for themselves when they are free to roam.'

Mill paused. 'I had no friends, and my amusements were mainly books.'

I found my feelings towards Mr James Mill hardening into something resembling abhorrence. How could he possibly know the price his son would have to pay for growing up friendless, without one true companion? I recalled my own boyhood and gave thanks that my father's ambitions for me had been of a more conventional kind.

'No holidays were allowed,' he continued, 'because my father believed the habit of work should not be disrupted or a taste for idleness acquired. He believed I had ample leisure time in every day to amuse myself.'

'Can you summarise what manner of man your father was?' I asked, struggling to repress a note of asperity in my voice.

'Energetic,' Mill replied. 'He reproved me for my mental slackness in matters of daily life. The children of energetic parents often grow up unenergetic, you know, because they lean on their parents.'

Mill hesitated a moment. 'My father regarded conceit as evil. I was not allowed to flatter myself in comparison with other boys. From my own conversations with him, he ensured I remained humble.'

'And were you?' I asked. 'Humble, I mean.'

'Growing up, I was not aware that any of my achievements were unusual for my age. I do not think that I was conceited. I talked of matters beyond my age, was argumentative, and I didn't always treat my elders with the respect they thought due, so many people regarded me as disagreeable and conceited.'

I glanced at him, not quite believing he could be disrespectful.

'My father taught me that the standard of comparison was not what other people did, but what I could achieve for myself.'

'And your religious education?' I enquired.

'I considered contemporary religion just as irrelevant to me as ancient religion. That was how I was brought up. The beliefs of English people were no more persuasive than those of the Ancient Greeks. My father analysed religion with as much rigour as he analysed anything else. As a result, I grew up thinking that religion was just another area of intellectual enquiry and of no particular relevance to me.'

Although I was an infrequent churchgoer, I nevertheless found this wholesale dismissal of Christian belief quite shocking and could think of no rejoinder. Fortunately, Mill needed none.

'My father had no such advantage. Before he rejected religion, he had been brought up Presbyterian,' Mill said. 'He found it impossible to believe that a world so full of evil was the work of an author with infinite power and perfect goodness.'

I found it hard to fault his logic. If God is omnipotent, omniscient and good, then, in the face of evil in the world, we believers are reduced to saying God works in mysterious ways. I looked up from my notebook and indicated by a gesture that he should continue.

'My father believed religion was dangerous because it sets up devotional feelings and beliefs that are fictitious,' said Mill. 'He felt that these beliefs are accepted as substitutes for genuine virtues and that this is not good for mankind. He concluded that it is the duty of all rational persons to convince others that the current beliefs in religion are not only false but harmful. That by speaking out, we might abolish all vulgar prejudices.'

There was a momentary silence before he continued. 'Socrates was a great influence on my father. His moral convictions of justice, truthfulness, perseverance, regard for the public good, estimation of persons according to their merits, a life of exertion and aversion to self-indulgence were all acquired from Socrates. Like my father, I had a deep respect for Socrates and the writings of Plato.'

I looked up, relieved to be on safer ground, but I had not finished with Mr Mill senior. 'Can you summarise the effect your father had on you?'

'In summary, I can say the effect my father produced on my character was determined by the manner of man he was – stoic and restrained in his behaviour and a firm believer in utilitarianism.'

'The greatest good for the greatest number of people,' I said.

'Just so. He rated intellectual enjoyment above all others and had contempt for feelings and passionate emotions.'

'He sounds rather cold-hearted,' I ventured.

'Perhaps.' Mill took out his handkerchief from his jacket pocket, wiped his nose and put the handkerchief away. When he again spoke, it was on a slightly different topic.

'Because I spent a lot of time with my father in his study, I had the good fortune to meet many of his closest friends.'

I looked across at him, my interest piqued.

'I saw much of Mr Jeremy Bentham and Mr John Austin, the father of legal positivism. In 1820, Mr Bentham's brother, General Sir Samuel Bentham, invited me to stay with him and his family in the south of France. My six-month visit extended to almost twelve months.'

Mill smiled to himself, perhaps recalling the impressions he gained from a country that had become almost a second home. 'His family consisted of one son, who became an eminent botanist, and three daughters, the youngest of whom was two years my senior. I accompanied them on an excursion to the Pyrenees, where we stayed at Bagnères de Bigorre, and made an ascent of the Pic du Midi de Bigorre.'

'I believe the Pyrenees are very beautiful,' I offered.

'You have not visited that part of France?'

'Alas, no,' I replied.

'Ah, you must; everyone must. Pau, the Bagnères de Luchon ... we stayed at Bayonne, I remember, a very pretty town. The beautiful mountain route of Castres and St Pons, from Toulouse to Montpellier, near the foot of the singular mountain of St Loup, is unforgettable. It was my introduction to mountain scenery, and it made a deep impression on me; in fact, it fired my passion for nature.'

I gave thanks for shorthand as I scrawled the list of French names in my notebook.

Mill continued, 'During my residence in France, I acquired a familiar knowledge of the French language and acquaintance with French literature.'

When I glanced up, I noticed that his expression now appeared livelier. 'The mountain scenery made a profound and lasting impression on me, as did the open friendliness of the people. I came away with my mind broadened so that I no longer judged universal questions merely by an English standard.'

'A broadening of horizons, one might say?' I asked.

'Both literally and figuratively, one might say,' acknowledged Mill.

'In July 1821, I returned to England and resumed my education. My father gave me *Traités de Législation Civile et Pénal*, which outlined Mr Bentham's principal thoughts on politics. The book was a turning point for me.'

'I'm not familiar with that work,' I confessed.

Mill smiled. 'It's the translation of Mr Bentham's writings into French by Pierre Dumont.'

'That you read in French?'

Mill nodded. 'I first read Bentham in 1821, and from then on, my entire happiness was tied up with being a reformer. The idea of being engaged with others in the struggle to reform the world was all-consuming.'

As he spoke, I could not help but wonder whether his solitary childhood made the appeal of working with, and for, others so appealing, but he said nothing further on the subject.

As the silence lengthened, I decided that a prompt might be required to get the conversation back on track. 'At the age of seventeen, you became a clerk at the East India Company, administering Indian affairs from its headquarters in London ... for the next thirty-five years.'

'I see you've done your research,' he replied but did not elaborate further on his employment. Instead, he said, 'At that age, I took a lively interest in many things, architecture, botany, zoology, even music. I practised the piano when I could, I enjoyed walking, and I was engaged in editing a five-volume edition of Bentham's *Rationale of Judicial Evidence*.'

What formidable energy, I mused, silently comparing Mill's achievements to the meagre output of my own boyhood.

'Back then, you were a popular writer, on the radical edge of journalism, if I may say so. You were a leading contributor to Mr Bentham's *Westminster Review*, and you formed and were actively involved in several clubs promoting and debating ideas. All in addition to your full-time work with the East India office. It's an impressive list for someone still four years shy of his maturity.'

He smiled rather sadly and replied, 'That may be true, but in the autumn of 1826, I sank into a slough of despondency. I was overtaken by one of those dull moods in which nothing was pleasurable anymore.' Mill sat and stared silently down at his hands before continuing.

'The whole foundation on which my life was constructed fell apart. My desire to improve the world seemed to lack meaning, and I felt there was nothing left to live for. Initially, I hoped the cloud would dissipate, but it didn't. It seemed to grow thicker and thicker by the month.' He sat back in his chair, shaking his head for several moments.

'I'm sorry to hear that,' I said, realising as they escaped my lips how hollow my words must have sounded.

Mill went on. 'In vain, I sought relief with my favourite books. I felt my distress was not respectable, and there was nothing in it to attract sympathy from others. So, I didn't feel as though I could make my feelings comprehensible to my friends.' A thin sigh escaped his lips. 'The more I dwelt on my plight, the more helpless I felt.'

'That must have been very distressing,' I mumbled.

Mill again shrugged. 'Even though I gave several speeches at the debating society, I frequently asked myself if I should continue living and concluded that I could not bear another year of this distress. I was convinced that the exclusive cultivation of analysis had destroyed in me the capacity for any of the pleasures of human desire. I knew that certain feelings would make me happy, and yet that did not give me the feeling.'

'So, how did you resolve your feelings?' I asked.

'Books,' he said. 'By chance, I was reading *Marmontel's Memoirs* and was moved to tears by the passage describing his father's death.'

I looked at him curiously.

'I suddenly remembered and realised the pleasure that can be found in books. My burden grew lighter, and the dark cloud began to lift.'

'That must have been a great solace,' I said, wondering if it was more than a coincidence that it was the fictional death of a father serving as a catalyst for this change.

'Yes! My burden grew lighter. The thought that all feeling was dead within me was gone. I no longer felt hopeless. No longer a rock.'

His voice exuded greater energy as he went on. 'Before long, I again started to take pleasure in the simple things in life, sunshine, books, conversation, public affairs, and to feel that I could begin to exert myself for my opinions and for the public good.'

In doing my research for this interview, I had learned that eight years after the events Mr Mill was describing, in 1836, during his father's final, prolonged illness, he suffered another mental and physical breakdown. I pondered for a few moments and decided to broach the issue. I concluded that there could be little harm since he had spoken so frankly just now. 'I believe you suffered another ... ah ... bout of ill health some years later?'

'My father's final illness coincided with a period of severe ill health. I spent some time recuperating in Brighton, but it was only after I returned to France that my health improved. It was then that I came to realise I am only content when my mind is fixed on some object other than my own happiness. Only when I could focus on the happiness of others, or on the improvement of mankind, even on art or a similar pursuit, would I know fulfilment. This has now become the basis of my philosophy of life. I also came to understand that my internal culture is of prime necessity to my wellbeing and that poetry, beauty, art and the contemplation of nature are important instruments of my human culture.'

As he spoke of the consolations he had found in his life, of which I was certain his father would have strongly disapproved, the sadness lifted from his face.

'The stimulation of our sensibilities through the appreciation of the arts and nature is a wonderful thing,' I said.

'As a child, I took great pleasure in Mozart. Later, I enjoyed the delicious melodies of Weber's *Oberon* – these memories also helped me recover.'

'And poetry?' I asked, remembering something a mutual acquaintance had mentioned.

'The poetry of Wordsworth, which I read in 1828, with its love of rural objects and natural scenery, was also instrumental in helping me through this gloomy period, which lasted for two years and was a decisive turning point in my life. I also came to realise that my father's view on logic was fundamentally flawed, which motivated me, in part, to write my *System of Logic*.'

I nodded encouragement for him to continue.

'I also realised that the concept of utilitarianism ignores internal culture. In a way, *On Liberty* stands as a rebuttal to my father.'

He looked directly into my eyes without a hint of embarrassment. For my part, I did not know what to reply, remembering that Mill had grown up without the benefit of the fifth commandment – honour thy father and thy mother.

He went on. 'It is here that I provide an alternate view on society. One that takes account of an individual's intellectual culture, reason and truth, as well as their internal culture – feelings, passions, impulses, natural inclinations and personal idiosyncrasies.'

I scribbled furiously, hoping that when I reread my notes, I would be able to understand more of what Mill was saying. I decided to shift the interview to more domestic matters. 'Can we talk for a moment about Mrs Mill and married life?'

Mill stood up from the table and walked to the window. It was a warm, sunny day. The sky was blue, and the tops of the trees in the courtyard outside Westminster were a fresh green. He stood for some moments gazing out at the Abbey. Then he turned and walked back to the table and nodded for me to continue.

'I believe you met your future wife, Mrs Harriet Taylor, when you were twenty-five? She would have been a couple of years younger, I believe.'

'Yes,' he said and stared into space for a moment or two. 'She was a beautiful woman. A great wit, with an air of natural distinction.'

'Were you so taken with her at your first meeting?'

Mill smiled. 'Oh yes. I could immediately see that here was a woman of deep feeling and intelligence,' he said, with a rising warmth. 'A romantic, intuitive woman with passionate opinions. Her views on love, marriage, divorce and the status of women were liberal, some would say extreme, and she was a great orator.'

'Something of a bohemian perhaps?' I ventured.

'Perhaps. She felt a burning indignation at anything brutal or tyrannical and scorned whatever was mean and cowardly. She was a woman of high moral standing, with a thirst for justice.' Then, as though afraid he'd painted too a harsh a portrait of his wife, he said, 'She was also generous, modest, simple, sincere and unselfish. Harriet wrote poetry; she was a woman with a fiery but tender soul …' his voice faded, mid-sentence.

During the hiatus that followed, I gazed through the window, noting how the sun flickering through the trees outside the Abbey cast dappled light onto the lawn.

As Mill continued to speak, I was pulled back into awareness.

'I benefited from her intellect, and I learnt more from her teaching than from all other sources put together,' he continued. 'When I lost my utilitarian community … in 1829 … I felt a great sense of loneliness, but Harriet was a true companion. From the moment we met, she was both a friend and a colleague in every sense. In fact, I have often received praise that I only partially deserved.' He smiled in fond reminiscence. 'Truth be told, my writings were not the work of one mind but the fusion of two.'

He gazed at me as if expecting to detect an expression of surprise on my part. But his paeans of praise for his lady wife's virtues made his acknowledgment of collaboration entirely logical.

Then once again, I noticed that nervous tic above his eyebrow. Was this an indication that an awkward topic was about to be broached?

'Harriet was married at a very early age to an honourable man,' said Mill. 'A pharmacist with liberal opinions and a good education, but he lacked the intellectual or artistic taste that would have made him an ideal companion for her. They had three children.'

He paused for a moment, rubbing the side of his face. 'He was an affectionate friend, and she held him in high esteem.'

Mill volunteered no more information, and I inferred that was my cue for a change of subject. I glanced down at my notebook and considered my next question. Friends of Mill had told me that he and Mrs Taylor were seen everywhere together and that she had courted him so successfully that he fell desperately in love. I did not doubt the latter part was true. Clearly, Mill loved his wife deeply and continued to hold her in exceptionally high regard.

Rather than acknowledge that I listened to gossip, I said, 'Your father disapproved of your liaison with Mrs Taylor, I believe?'

'Yes. But at that early stage, and as I explained to him myself, my feelings towards her were no different to those I would feel towards an equally able man.'

A lengthy silence ensued, but Mill made no move to fill it, so I decided to change the subject. Before I could speak, Mill continued as if he, too, had heard the gossip.

'Harriet lived mostly with her young daughter in a quiet part of the country and was only occasionally in town with her husband. I visited her in both places, and I am greatly indebted to her strength of character, which enabled her to disregard the false interpretations put on my visits while she was living apart from Mr Taylor and on our trips together.'

I looked up; my puzzlement was readily apparent on my face. Contrary to what Mill claimed, it was evident from the accounts of those who knew the two of them that their relationship was intimate from the very start. And what was anyone to think if a man and a woman travelled together?

'I understand the Taylors finally separated,' I said.

'Yes, Harriet went to Paris and invited me to spend six weeks with her. Then she allowed her husband to come to Paris and, ultimately, she decided it was not necessary to make a choice, as convention would usually dictate.' Mill pursed his lips, moved further back in his chair and folded his arms as if daring me to object.

'She and her husband entertained guests at their home some days, and you and the then Mrs Taylor on other days?' I asked.

'That's right,' he said, tapping his fingers against the table.

'A rather unorthodox arrangement,' was all I could say.

I had heard from my most intemperate source that when Mill and Harriet were pining for each other, they would meet in secret at the London Zoo. My source had said that her poor husband's tacit acquiescence had been punctuated by occasional feeble protests.

'I understand that by the mid-forties, you had broken off relations with some family and friends?'

Mill nodded. 'That's right. Harriet had suffered more than I from the tawdry gossip that circulated about us. It became insufferable.'

'But you did eventually marry?'

'Yes. In July 1849, Mr Taylor died. Harriet lamented his passing. He was a good man.'

After a lengthy pause, he continued. 'Harriet observed a respectable period of mourning, and then she and I married in April 1851. We were married for seven and a half years. It was the happiest period of my life,' he said, his voice cracking.

'And did the formalising of your relationship enable the repair of old bonds?'

Mill shook his head. 'My mother and sister were tardy in paying their respects to my wife.'

'And your old friends?'

'Relationships were difficult, so we lived in increasing isolation in Blackheath. But we had each other, and that was enough,' he said, the spirit of defiance clear in his voice.

I looked up, hoping he would continue.

'We seldom dined out, and when we entertained, it was mainly visitors from abroad.'

Mill looked across at the window where a pigeon had landed on the ledge and was busy coo-cooing.

Then his mood suddenly darkened once more. 'Our ill health increased our sense of isolation. I was convinced that our time together would be brief and resented any intrusions into our lives.'

That proved to be true as far as his wife's health was concerned, I knew. Yet here he was, well into advanced years and showing no signs of ill health. Perhaps death was a greater fear for him than for Christians like the rest of us.

'Harriet and I travelled abroad to convalesce, but regardless of whether we were abroad or at home, we withdrew from the literary, social and political circles that we had previously frequented.'

'Why was that?'

Mill straightened his shoulders, moved back in his chair and crossed his arms. 'Society tends to be insipid. Serious discussion is considered a mark of ill-breeding, and the English lack the facility of the French for agreeable conversation about trifles. A person of high intellect should never go into pedestrian society for fear of being harmed and reduced by it.'

Goodness me, I thought such earnestness and condescension. No wonder their friends abandoned them.

But I kept such thoughts to myself as I consulted my notes.

'Sadly, Mrs Mill died suddenly ... in November 1858?' I said.

Discretion being the better part of valour, I didn't mention that I had heard it suggested by some that her death may have been from syphilis, contracted from her first husband.

Mill sat quietly, the only sign of emotion a rapid blinking as he struggled for composure. 'Words cannot express my loss,' he said eventually, 'but because I know that she would have wished it, I have endeavoured to make the best of what life I have left, with what diminished strength I can derive from thoughts of her.'

Outside, the light was radiant, and the sky a sharp, clear blue. I had a powerful urge to be out in the fresh air and sunlight and away from this suffering man and his severe opinions.

For a long time, Mill sat in silence, then he said, 'Nearly all my writings were as much her work as mine. Our thoughts were completely in harmony.'

'*Systems of Logic* was published in 1843, was it not?' I said, again consulting my notes.

'Indeed. We had known each other for over a decade by then, but Harriet's role in that work was not significant. Two years later, I began writing *Principles of Political Economy* and had it ready for publication in 1847. Here she played a much greater role.'

'The book was well-received, as I recall.'

'Yes,' Mill confirmed. 'By 1852, it was in its third edition.'

I pulled my chair closer to the table. 'In 1856, you and your wife began to write *On Liberty*.'

'Indeed. The more I thought about it, the more I considered a book on liberty an absolute necessity. I originally wrote a short essay on the topic, but I felt it required greater attention. In October 1858, I retired from the East India office after thirty-five years of service. Mrs Taylor and I immediately left for the south of France. We had intended to work on the book together, but Harriet's unexpected death at Avignon from a sudden attack of pulmonary congestion forestalled this.'

There was something very touching about the way he spoke – there was such genuine tenderness and love for his lost wife. Warmth radiated from him.

'After the funeral, I had a marble monument constructed for her in Avignon, and I bought a cottage overlooking the graveyard where she was buried. Her daughter and I spend several months of each year there.'

'Had you been worried about her health?'

He pulled out his handkerchief and dabbed at his eye, a kind of heavy sadness settling over him. 'The fear of her death always made me anxious. We discussed the matter, and I promised her that if she should die before me, I would continue our work as best I could.'

'I've read the dedication in *On Liberty*,' I said and quickly consulted my notes once more. '"To the beloved and deplored memory of her who was the inspirer and, in part, the author of all that is best in my writings, the friend and wife whose exalted sense of truth and right was my strongest incitement, and whose approbation was my chief reward, I dedicate this volume ..." and it continues'. I looked up into the eyes of John Stuart Mill and detected the glassy sheen of tears.

'Harriet had the opportunity to review much of the manuscript, but there were important sections she didn't live to revise. The end work is no doubt the poorer for her absence. The single truth of the manuscript had been expressed by Harriet long before its publication in an unpublished essay written early in our acquaintance.'

As he spoke, his hand began to tremble. Mill tucked it under his arm and then continued. 'The whole mode of thinking of the book belonged to Harriet, the boldness of speculation, her ability to get to the heart of every problem and her instinct for always seizing the essential idea; all this was instrumental in the text.'

'The idea of a free marketplace of ideas?' I asked.

'Precisely,' Mill answered. 'Those sections that were scientific or abstract were mostly mine, but the properly human element came from her. I am not fit to write on anything but the outskirts of the great questions of feeling and life without her to prompt me. She was a genius of the highest order.'

'Forgive me for speaking plainly, Mr Mill, but I notice that while you are very modest about your own abilities, you are never modest about those of your wife. In fact, you are forever singing her praises. Few men acknowledge the abilities of the fairer sex at all, apart from those few areas in which ladies are required to excel. Can you explain what makes you so different from other fellows? Perhaps your mother?'

Mill shifted awkwardly in his chair. 'My mother was incapable of intellectual thought. She was more concerned with keeping house and caring for her large family. To be frank, my father made a mistake in marrying so young. Still, my mother was a pretty young woman apparently, and my father ... well, you can imagine.'

He and I exchanged nods of unspoken comprehension.

'Had she been that rare thing in England,' Mill said, 'a really warm-hearted mother, both my father's life and mine would have been very different. But in reality, she was little more than a kind-hearted drudge.'

I tried to hide my shock that the man who so passionately promoted female suffrage and had written *On the Subjection of Women*, which at this moment was being prepared for publication, could hold such views about his own mother.

'I am curious, sir,' I said, 'about the origins of your passionate support for female suffrage and for women's rights. You are mocked for your views in the press, *Punch* ridicules you in cartoons, and yet you do not waver.'

'My views on the emancipation of women were formed early. I recall I was still a youth when I disagreed with my father's views in his 'Essay on Government' that women's interests are the same as men's and, therefore, they should be excluded from suffrage. I strongly rejected that view.

'At first, many took my views on women to be a personal whim, but I was elected to parliament having expressed my opinions plainly, and those opinions have since made great progress.'

I had a half-formed notion that Mill may have been driven into the arms of the fairer sex by his harsh and demanding father, but his rejection of his mother poked a large hole in that theory. Perhaps the truth was more obvious, that he had been swayed by his wife into adopting such an outré idea.

'And so, sir, may I enquire as to the basis of your beliefs in women's emancipation if those beliefs have not grown from the influence of women? Or have you perhaps in this, too, been influenced by your wife?'

Mill shook his head. 'Many before you have thought so, but my strong convictions were not learnt from Harriet. On the contrary, it is likely that the strength of my beliefs may have been the cause of Harriet's interest in me. I believed as I have already indicated, that complete equality in all legal, political, social and domestic relations ought to exist between men and women. These convictions were among my earliest reflections on political subjects.'

'What was your wife's role in crystallising these ideas?' I asked.

'Before we met, my opinion on this topic was little more than an abstract principle. I could see no reason why women should be held in legal subjection to men. Certainly, women's interests require as much protection as those of men. Still, without an equal voice in making the laws by which we are all bound, they are unlikely to obtain it.'

'So your beliefs in this regard evolved entirely independent of your wife?'

Mill nodded. 'Without knowing Harriet, I should doubtless have arrived at my present opinions. But without her input, I should not have fully understood how the consequences of women's inferior position are entangled with all the evils of existing society and with all the difficulties of human improvement. I am painfully aware of how greatly my little treatise falls short of what it would have been if Harriet had lived to express all her thoughts on this question and to revise and improve my imperfect statement of the case.'

Confronted by such a cogent argument so forcefully delivered, I decided to retreat to safer ground.

'Returning to *On Liberty*,' I said, hurriedly scrawling the last of my notes. 'How important do you believe it to be?'

'I suspect it will survive longer than anything else that I have written because the conjunction of Harriet's mind with mine has rendered it a kind of philosophical textbook with a single truth,' he said.

'Single truth?' I asked.

'The fundamental principle is that the sole end for which mankind is justified, individually or collectively, in interfering with the liberty of action of any of their number, is self-protection.'

I inscribed this in longhand, verbatim, nodding for Mill to continue.

'Further, the only purpose for which power can be rightfully exercised over any member of a civilised community, against his will, is to prevent harm to others.'

'Can we talk about liberty and truth?' I asked, pleased with the lofty turn our conversation had taken. 'It seems to me that liberty, not truth, is paramount in making your case for freedom of discussion.'

He smiled briefly. 'Quite correct. The need for competing opinions, even erroneous opinions, is of fundamental importance in order for the truth to emerge from discussion.'

'And what, for you, is harm?'

After a moment, he said, 'If free speech leads directly to imminent violence or physical harm, it may be constrained under the harm principle. An example of harm would be assaulting someone or otherwise causing them injury.'

'So, unless the speaker is about to run you through, you must let him speak?' I joked.

'That's right!' He propped his chin on his hand and said, 'Verbal offence is something that hurts our feelings. This is less serious and should not be prevented because what may hurt one person's feelings may not hurt another's. It's entirely subjective.'

'But ...'

Cutting me short, he said, 'If a person is drunk and his behaviour offends the finer sensibilities, then that is an offence but not a physical harm. If, however, the drunk person assaults someone when drunk, then that is an objective physical harm.'

My head canted in a nod of concession. His point seemed reasonable, although I knew many people who would have regarded drunkenness itself as a crime.

'But the issue is sometimes harder to grasp when it relates to ideas,' Mill expounded. 'So, to write an essay about the sufferings of the poor at the hands of the rich should be allowed, but to express the same views to a mob gathering outside the house of a wealthy employer is likely to lead to physical harm.'

'I see. Now, the book has been highly praised, but it has also had its critics.'

Mill nodded and said, 'The reason I was prompted to write *On Liberty* was because the majority, public opinion, presumes to tell men what to think, what to read, how to dress, how to behave. In short, the majority sets itself up as the judge of what is right and wrong, and that is fatal to individuality.'

His rising passion for the topic was revealed by his voice growing louder with each word. 'I considered it important to adopt a doctrine of liberty that could prevent England from becoming another China, a land with talent, wisdom and fine customs that has, nevertheless, become stagnant for thousands of years. The Chinese made their people too much alike, and I fear that public opinion will do the same to England.'

Referring to my notes, I asked, 'But wasn't it this view of social tyranny that H. T. Buckle, James Fitzjames Stephen and others challenged? Other reviewers, such as those writing for *The National Review*, found different causes for disagreement. Yet despite the critical response, Charles Kingsley, Thomas Hardy, Frederic Harrison and many others have argued that *On Liberty* produced a profound impression on contemporary thought.'

Leaning back in his chair, Mill said with a wry smile, 'It is gratifying that so many people have read it, agree or not, and I think it's fair to say that *On Liberty* became a sort of gospel for many politicians. Out of respect for my late wife, I have made no alteration or addition to it, nor shall I ever.'

I now noticed that Mill seemed tired; his eyes had a slightly sunken look and his cheeks were pale.

'We've been together for two hours,' I said, glancing at my pocket watch. 'Before we finish, there are one or two more things I'd like to raise. Can we leave On Liberty and talk for a moment about the American Civil War and slavery?'

'The two are related, you know,' said Mill with a triumphant smile breaking through his fatigue.

'Yes, of course,' I conceded. 'But three years have passed since the Union victory, and the United States has amended its constitution to outlaw slavery. So I'd like to hear your thoughts.'

'Very well,' Mill said. 'In my view, the slave states were attempting to extend their territory and their abominable practices to new parts of the United States. I considered the war was destined to be a turning point for humanity, either for good or evil. So I could not remain indifferent to this struggle.'

'Please elaborate,' I prompted.

'Confederate success meant victory for the evil of slavery that, in turn, would give courage to the enemies of progress and human decency.' Mill became more animated as he spoke. 'Slavery was the most anti-social form of tyranny of man over man. Those abolitionists – Garrison, Wendell Phillips and John Brown – should be extolled and admired for their fight against the most flagrant of violations of the free principles of their constitution.'

'Many Englishmen saw things differently,' I challenged.

Mill rubbed the side of his face once more, settled back in his chair and said, 'Initially, the upper and middle classes of England, in their naiveté and ignorance, believed the American war to be a dispute about tariffs. That was both immoral and wrong.'

A mild breeze blew through the window, freshening the air. I thought it an opportune time to shift topics once again.

'In 1865, by popular request, you published cheap People's Editions of *Principles of Political Economy*, *On Liberty* and *Representative Government*.'

Mill nodded, 'I gave up my royalties to enable the price to be reduced. I did this even though it was a considerable financial sacrifice. To the credit of my publisher, they fixed this arrangement for a certain number of years, after which the copyright reverted to me.'

'May we talk briefly about your political career?' I asked, then without pausing, said, 'You were elected to the House of Commons in 1865 to represent Westminster, but I'm told that initially, you had reservations.'

'Correct,' he said. 'I was not convinced that I could advance the public good more by sitting in parliament than from the position of writer.'

'So, what prompted you to change your stand?'

'A group of electors sought me out,' he said. 'One of the unforeseen consequences of my election to parliament was that I became known in many quarters where I had never been heard of before, and this increased my readership.'

'You made several controversial speeches.'

Mill gave me a questioning look.

'Women's suffrage, for example.'

'It was called for ... very much overdue. And time has proven me right.' Leaning forward, elbows on the table, he continued. 'I intend to publish a work titled *The Subjection of Women*. To help advance the cause of women's suffrage is by far the most important, perhaps the only really important public service I have performed as a member of parliament.'

'And you spoke in favour of proportional representation, I think?'

'I had come to regard representative government as the best form of a popular constitution. In 1860 and 1861, I wrote a tract called *Considerations on Representative Government*.'

'Do you think you will be re-elected?' I asked bluntly.

Mill smiled. 'I doubt it.'

'Do you have plans for that eventuality?'

Mill folded his arms. 'I look forward to returning to private life. I will alternate between my residences in London and the south of France. I will write, and no doubt I will make speeches.' He smiled faintly.

'Perhaps we might finish there,' I said.

'I need to get back into the chamber in any case,' he said as he stood.

'Thank you for your time, sir. As I said earlier, I'll check with my editor about sending you a draft of the interview before it's published.'

'Thank you,' he said.

Endnote

This imaginary conversation with John Stuart Mill is set in 1868, on his sixty-second birthday. It uses Mill's own remarks or close interpretations of them (many taken from his autobiography, which was published in 1873, soon after his death) to remain true to what he said.

When Mill died, his working-class admirers helped raise a statue of him on the Thames Embankment. Mill asked to be interred in the remote French town of Avignon. Five people came to his burial. This was the one place he wanted to be, with Harriet, in the tiny cemetery where he could rest beside the love of his life.

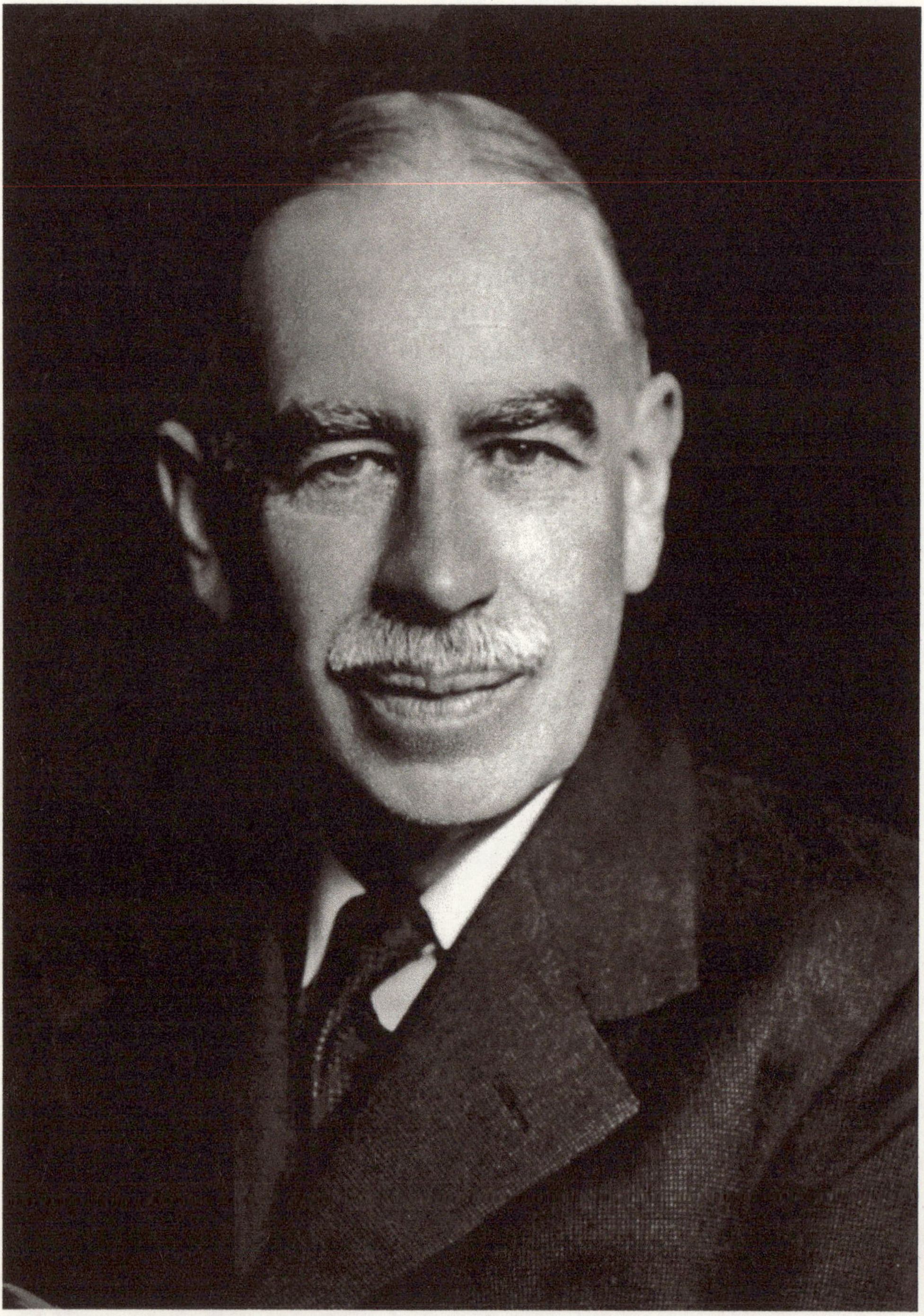

John Maynard Keynes

Cambridge, United Kingdom, 5 June 1943.

'I'm afraid use of the library is for members only,' said a female voice behind me as I perused a leather-bound copy of Carlyle's *Decline and Fall of the Roman Empire*.

I turned and was greeted by a middle-aged woman who looked like a librarian from central casting, thick eyeglasses hanging from a chain around her neck and dark hair drawn back into a low chignon. It was the same woman I had noticed out of the corner of my eye when entering the library. She had climbed down from her perch halfway up one of those library ladders attached to a brass bar that ran the length of the ceiling-high shelves.

'I'm sorry,' I said. 'There was nobody at the desk when I came in. But I'm here to see Dr Keynes.'

Her expression softened into a facsimile of a smile. 'That's different,' she said, indicating a door in the corner.

I nodded politely. 'Thank you very much.' I approached the doorway and knocked before entering. John Maynard Keynes was sitting near the window, a copy of *The Financial Times* in his hands. Rather than his trademark three-piece suit and tie, he was dressed more informally, with a tan jacket and ochre jumper worn over a white dress shirt. He closed the newspaper and rose from his seat, holding out his hand. 'Are we acquainted?' he asked. 'You look familiar.'

'We met several times. But it was many years ago.'

Keynes nodded and indicated a seat opposite his own. 'I see. And where did these meetings transpire?'

I flushed. 'We had a ... dalliance. In Hyde Park ... initially.'

'Ah-ha,' Keynes replied, his mouth curling in a conspiratorial smile. 'And ... how have you been?'

'Fine. After Winchester, I went up to Cambridge. In 1912.'

He gave a nod of approval. 'And what did you read?'

'Law. But my first year as an articled clerk quickly convinced me that a solicitor's life was not for me. So, I moved into journalism.'

'And how has that worked out for you?'

I smiled. 'Quite well, actually. I began at *The Times* and, in 1925, I moved over to the BBC where I've been ever since.'

'And the war?'

I shrugged, pointing to my eyeglasses. 'I tried to enlist but was turned away. Bad eyesight. The army doctor who performed my physical told me, "I wouldn't want you standing behind me with a rifle." But I think I'm here to interview you.'

'Quite right,' replied Keynes. 'Please proceed.'

'I'd like to begin with a focus on your early years.'

'Didn't we talk about that in Hyde Park?' he quipped with an impish smile.

'We were engaged in ... other pursuits at the time,' I said, meeting his eye with what I hoped was an adequate poker face. 'But to the matter at hand, I hoped you might discuss your family ... your childhood.'

'Right. My father was an economics don at Cambridge.'

'And your mother?'

He sat up straight in his chair, his expression now animated. 'Florence Keynes ... née Brown ... was one of the first female graduates of Cambridge. She became the mayor of Cambridge city and president of the National Council of Women of Great Britain.'

I nodded. 'A formidable figure.'

Keynes smiled. 'Indeed. She and I were visiting Paris together when I discovered the glories of impressionist art. Three years later ... in 1908 ... I began my collection. Ten years after that, I persuaded the Chancellor of the Exchequer to allocate £20,000 to buy paintings for the National Gallery when the private collection of Degas was auctioned after his death.'

'Wow.'

'Wow, indeed,' Keynes replied. Gallery director Charles Holmes and I were able to pick up thirteen paintings and eleven drawings by some of the greatest French nineteenth-century masters. I couldn't convince him to bid on any of Cézanne's works for the gallery, but I was able to acquire a small Cézanne still life for myself. Not to mention a Degas, a Delacroix and an Ingres.' He smiled proudly.

'All very impressive,' I said in a dual-purpose tone meant to camouflage my ignorance of fine art while showing diplomatic deference to his passion. 'But I thought we might focus on your economic theories.'

'But that's the point,' replied Keynes, his finger wagging with the enthusiasm of a master preaching gospel to a disciple. 'Economists are the trustees, not of civilisation, but of the possibility of civilisation. We work to ensure that the basic needs of humanity are met so that higher-order things like fine art can be created.'

'You mean like that theory Professor Maslow published earlier this year?'

Keynes nodded. 'Precisely. People who are living at subsistence level don't have the time, energy or education to engage in higher intellectual pursuits.'

I nodded, my hand moving quickly across the page of my notebook. 'What more can you tell me about your childhood?'

Keynes shrugged. 'At age five, I began at St Faith's Preparatory School...'

'That would be 1892?' I interjected.

'That sounds about right.'

'And you did well?'

On the surface, his smile conveyed a degree of modesty. But a glimmer of pride lurking beneath remained discernible. 'My maths teacher said I did "brilliant work", and the headmaster wrote that I was "head and shoulders above all the other boys in the school."'

'So you were quite the prodigy,' I prompted. 'Enough to win a scholarship to Eton in 1897.'

Keynes nodded.

I consulted my notes again. 'And in your first year, you came first in Classics, and the following year you won the Junior

Mathematics Prize.'

'I have a bit of a flair for maths.'

'Something of an understatement,' I observed.

Keynes shrugged again, so I forged on.

'In 1901, you were elected to Eton's debating society. In the following year, you were placed first in the Higher Certificate Examination – first in mathematics, history and for an English essay.'

His mouth expanded into a grin. 'As you noted, you're in the presence of a prodigy.'

I smiled politely, not sure to what extent he was joking.

'Your school reports also noted your leadership abilities. I think one of your teachers described you as a "natural leader to whom his classmates defer".' I looked up from my notes expectantly, hoping to prompt an insightful response. I was disappointed.

'I suppose that's one way of putting it,' he said.

I returned to my notes. 'In 1902, at the age of nineteen, you began your long association with King's College. How did you enjoy your time as an undergraduate?'

The smile gracing Keynes' face transformed into one of fond reminiscence. 'I loved it. I was a frequent speaker at the college debating society. I enjoyed horseriding and played tennis and golf for the college.'

'And your social and intellectual life?'

'Rich ... very rich! Back then, we stayed up well into the night to discuss and debate the issues of the day.'

'In May 1904, you graduated with first-class honours in mathematics?'

Keynes nodded. 'And that same year, I was elected Secretary of the Union and President of the University Liberal Club.'

'All impressive,' I replied. 'After your studies at Cambridge, you took a paid position lecturing there in January 1909, I believe.'

'Yes, and in March that year, I was also made a Fellow of King's College.'

'I think I'm right in saying that two years after that, you were appointed to their Estates Committee, and in 1912 you were elected to the college governing council. You also began to edit the *Economic*

Journal. You were busy indeed.'

'Kept me out of trouble. Sort of.' He gave that now-familiar provocative grin.

I struggled to remain deadpan as I sought refuge in my notes. 'Let me ask you about your passion for the arts, if I may,' I went on. 'And Bloomsbury.'

'Of course. What would you like to know?'

'Theatre was one of your earliest loves, and it has remained so all your life. Where did this interest come from?'

'My parents. They introduced me to the theatre when I was a young boy,' he said.

'I saw a photo of you acting in *The Rivals* in 1903 at university.'

His eyes sparkled. 'I think I was twenty at the time. I looked rather splendid if I remember correctly.'

I laughed. 'Your interest in the arts was not solely limited to the theatre. You've taken an active interest in the ballet. Did you also have aspirations in that regard?'

Keynes exhaled. 'Alas, I was ruled too tall for the corps. It turns out that being six-foot-six entails certain disadvantages.'

'I'm sure. Now moving on, I believe you've amassed a substantial art and book collection?'

'Indeed.' Keynes replied. 'I believe the arts are essential. As I mentioned before, they enrich people's lives. They encourage them to think, feel and live more fully.' He paused. 'The arts are a fundamental expression of a civilised society – an enlightened government should affirm public interest in making a better society, not least through the support of the arts.'

'You've always had an interest in literature as well?'

'Yes, but drama is my true passion,' Keynes declared. 'It distressed me that Cambridge lacked a first-class theatre. As First Bursar of King's College, I released land for the construction of a decent theatre, which was long overdue.'

I nodded. 'And I read that you funded much of the construction personally?'

'That's right. It was called the Cambridge Arts Theatre and, as its founding member, I was perfectly placed to support it.'

'Back then, it was called the Council for the Encouragement of Music and the Arts, wasn't it?'

'That's correct,' he said in a tone of proprietary pride. 'The theatre opened in February 1936, with a gala performance by Vic-Wells Company, featuring Robert Helpmann and Margot Fonteyn.'

'Very impressive,' I said.

'Yes, indeed,' he continued with obvious enthusiasm. The theatre was paid for by a share scheme at the cost of £15,000. I supervised the scheme, but we only raised a little over £2000, so I underwrote the rest.'

I scribbled in haste. 'And what about the broader benefits of the arts?'

Keynes lifted his finger. 'Vital! Vital! Particularly for sustaining morale now that we're at war. Also, the arts are an important part of the economy.'

'Let's talk about some of the broader issues relating to quality of life. I believe you have said people should enjoy shorter working hours and longer holidays.'

Keynes nodded. 'Surely the aim of work is to provide for our leisure, is it not? In one or two generations, people will no longer have to work most of the time to produce goods. Then their main problem will be how to occupy their free time.'

I grinned. 'You have my vote!'

He laughed politely, clearly having heard the same joke many times before.

'So, what prompted your interest in Bloomsbury?'

Keynes sat up in his chair and looked directly into my eyes. 'Well, you know I was at Cambridge with Roger Fry and Desmond McCarthy and, well, one thing led to another. Without question, Bloomsbury and the people I came to know there enriched my life immensely.'

'You were one of the group's core members, I believe.'

'Yes. As you probably know, in 1905, a number of writers, artists and intellectuals who lived and worked in Bloomsbury in London began to meet at the home of artist Vanessa Bell and her sister Virginia Woolf.'

'The author?'

Keynes looked at me with the asperity of a teacher encountering a question from a student who should know better. 'Of course, Virginia Woolf, the author. Who else?'

I blushed as he flashed a brief smile of apology.

'Sorry. Sometimes my passions get the better of me. We became known as the Bloomsbury Group. We rebelled against the bourgeois conventions, restraints and double standards of our parents and Victorian life. We wanted to be free to develop our own ideas and ways of life.'

'But you attracted your share of criticism as well,' I observed.

'Pah,' he replied, hand sweeping across his torso in a gesture of dismissal. 'Our campaign in support of women's suffrage caused controversy. I came under a lot of criticism because I took up the cause for contraception.'

'Ah, yes, the Marie Stopes Society?'

'Just so.'

I smiled, relieved to be once again in this extraordinary man's good graces.

'In 1923, early in my relationship with my wife, I became vice-president of the Society for Contraception.' His mien now became serious. 'Twenty years ago, the restrictions on contraceptives, the woeful absence of sex education, the marriage and divorce laws that were so unfair to women, belonged in the dark ages.' He shook his head in disgust. 'And little has changed since, quite frankly. Women are discriminated against at work; they are not paid for their labour … it's a disgrace. And legal sanctions against homosexuality are also an outrage.'

I blanched and looked down, my eyes boring through the notebook on the desk in front of me.

Keynes continued his rant, oblivious to my discomfort. 'As chairman of the *New Statesman* in 1938, I supported advertisements that enabled men to make contact with one another: "Man not interested in the fair sex" or "seeking holiday companion", that kind of thing. But it didn't go down very well.' He paused, arching his eyebrows while subjecting me to a long, silent, probing gaze.

'I'd like to ask you about the last war.' But my attempt to regain the initiative was parried immediately by Keynes. 'Before we get to that, I'm interested to know whether you've found someone with whom to share your life?'

'Writing is my life.'

'But life without love is like a runner without legs,' he said.

'Mr Keynes, I work very hard. The war has left us understaffed, so I spend seven or eight hours a day at my typewriter churning out copy.' I paused and took a deep breath before going on. 'Then I drag myself home at night and go straight to bed.'

'But it's important to have someone to share your life, my friend. Knowing there is someone who cares is much more important than work.'

'You may well be right, but we're here to talk about you, and I was asking about the war.'

Keynes sighed. 'I was a conscientious objector, as were others in the Bloomsbury Group, and before you ask, yes, we were criticised for our stance. Because many of us came from upper-middle-class professional families and were sexually promiscuous, we were seen as self-indulgent libertines, as elitists who thought of themselves as an intellectual aristocracy.'

'Some of your critics said the Bloomsbury Group took themselves far more seriously than their work objectively deserved.'

Keynes didn't rise to my bait and replied with equanimity. 'I hope our achievements are not overshadowed by our backgrounds and lifestyle. I think it's fair to say ... objectively speaking ... that the most important writers and artists of the twentieth century are, or were, members of Bloomsbury.'

'No doubt the novels and essays of Virginia Woolf are widely read and important,' I said, in an attempt to rectify my previous faux pas.

Keynes simply nodded. 'E. M. Forster is one of England's most influential writers, and Lytton Strachey's *Eminent Victorians* and *Elizabeth and Essex* are simply brilliant biographical masterpieces.'

'What about Duncan Grant and Vanessa Bell?'

'Fine artists, who are well regarded by the likes of Pablo Picasso, Jean Cocteau and Erik Satie when he was alive.'

I smiled. 'I'm reminded of Bertrand Russell's comment that "every time I argued with Keynes, I felt that I took my life in my hands and I seldom emerged without feeling something of a fool". Were you such a formidable opponent?'

He shrugged.

'Your colleague, Sir Kenneth Clark, remarked that, while kind in many ways, you have a penchant for "humiliating people in a cruel way".' I looked up from my notes to gauge Keynes' response. He simply shrugged again.

I forged on. 'At the risk of treading on sensitive ground, Sir Kenneth thinks that perhaps it was your illness that heightened your impatience with … more pedestrian intellects. That the awareness of your own mortality might have made you a bit more acerbic towards others?'

Keynes snorted. 'Ken should stick to running the National Gallery and leave psychotherapy to the professionals.'

He paused, and his demeanour softened. 'There I go, doing precisely that for which I stand condemned.'

'I'm sorry if I delved too deeply,' I said. 'But if you're willing, I'm sure my readers would like to hear more about your health.'

'My health issues materialised early,' he said. 'I only began at St Faith's at age eight-and-a-half because I was so often sick.'

'And now?'

'Now I just have to be careful. My doctor has laid out protocols to prevent me from straining my heart. But the work … it's so overwhelming,' Keynes said. 'I serve on the Court of Directors of the Bank of England, and I'm a senior adviser to His Majesty's Treasury.'

'Yes, your workload is heavy. What does your doctor think?'

'He's less than pleased,' replied Keynes. 'But some things are more important than a single individual. We're working towards a system of international economic coordination that will prevent another depression and the disaster of Versailles.'

I nodded. 'You left the peace conference in protest at the harshness of its terms on Germany, did you not? I believe you even described it as a "Carthaginian peace".'

'I wrote that phrase in 1919 for my book *The Economic Consequences of the Peace*. And we're now reaping the whirlwind of that punitive wind we sowed after the last war. It was so stupid and so predictable,' Keynes said, shaking his head in frustrated regret.

I smiled with all the cheer I could muster. 'Perhaps we should turn to a lighter topic. I'd like to hear more about that art collection you mentioned previously.'

His face brightened.

'I'm told that most of your closest friends are artists, writers, or critics of art and literature.'

He settled back in his chair and laughed. 'Those who do, and those who opine on what those others do.'

I smiled.

'Friends have helped me acquire the works of international masters such as Cézanne, Matisse, Picasso, Renoir and many more, and of course, I have bought art regularly from friends such as Vanessa Bell, Duncan Grant, Roger Fry as well as the work of other English painters.'

'Quite a collection then.'

'I like to think I've put together a reasonable collection,' he said, his tone betraying a taint of wariness.

'And in addition, you're supporting the artistic community,' I said.

'Precisely,' said Keynes, his passion suddenly rekindled. 'As I've said elsewhere, a patron of the arts performs an invaluable function. Without patrons, art cannot easily flourish. That is why I supported my friends and other English painters, such as William Roberts, Walter Sickert and Ivon Hitchens, by buying their work.'

'You also assisted them with direct financial aid, I believe?'

'In 1909, I subscribed to the Contemporary Arts Society, which was launched to buy paintings by contemporary British artists,' he said, flashing a smile. 'I won't deny that I was always very happy to return from a trip and find Cézanne in my bedroom and Sickert over my piano.'

A shaft of sunlight struck the brass light on the table, making it gleam and illuminating the creases on the green leather tabletop.

'And the London Artists Association?'

'Yes, at the instigation of Roger Fry, in 1925, I set up the London

Artists Association to assist young artists with their financial affairs. The association organised exhibitions and had the backing of financial guarantors. This enabled artists to show their work at minimal cost while being guaranteed a small income if the work failed to sell.'

'As I understand it, guarantors were given the option to purchase exhibited work at pre-arranged prices,' I said.

'That's correct, the first exhibition was held in 1926. Although the association only survived for eight years, many artists such as Ivon Hutchins, Henry Moore, William Roberts, Paul Nash and William Coldstream benefited from their membership.' He gave a smile of satisfaction.

Light rain was falling once more, and the rich, dank scent mixed with the musty book smell of the library; I was glad to be inside.

'You were also a serious book collector, I believe?'

He cleared his throat and said, 'Before we talk about my book collection, may I ask if you had difficulty accepting your own ... tastes. All off the record, of course.'

I felt my throat tighten, and I glanced around to make sure we could not be overheard. 'As you know, when we met, I was very confused and upset.'

Keynes reached over and placed a consoling hand on my forearm. 'Go on,' he said.

'I felt sorry for myself, I suppose. Back then, I lived in a daze. And when I wasn't in a daze, I felt irritated and unclean. At night I couldn't sleep. I would lie in bed and cry – all the anxieties and fears that I was holding onto would erupt in the darkness.'

I paused, trying to control the tears that were already pricking my eyes. 'I spent so long trying to deny who l was. I scourged myself ... literally. I tried with women, but it never worked. The spark was simply never there, and then I finally accepted myself. I just wanted to be happy, but I didn't know how.'

Keynes gave an avuncular nod.

'Being with you calmed me and reassured me,' I said. 'Everything seemed natural and normal. But apart from that brief time, things didn't look up for me until long after you and I separated. At first, rather than confronting my ... proclivities, I pushed them aside and hoped they would go away.'

'We can't change the essence of who we are,' said Keynes with a rueful sigh. 'Lord knows I tried as well ... and failed.'

I nodded my agreement. 'Eventually, I came to realise that I needed to confide in someone. A real friend to talk things through. That wasn't easy; I was scared. But after I worked up the courage to speak with this particular friend, it brought me some peace. He was an older man too.'

Keynes smiled. 'I'm glad you were able to find a confidant. Have you had any great loves?'

I shrugged. 'A few. I've had a couple of relationships that lasted for a while. But now I'm alone once more.'

'One day, when the time is right,' he said.

'Perhaps,' I replied, staring at my notebook before looking up. 'But we seem to have got a bit off track. We were about to discuss your book collection.'

'Yes, of course. Mea culpa. My collection focuses on the intellectual history of Western Europe, especially literature, philosophy and science. It includes incunabula and original manuscripts written by Isaac Newton.'

'How marvellous,' I said, 'I wish I could see even part of it.'

His eyes twinkled. 'Yes, it is rather marvellous,' he said. 'I've been very fortunate.'

I glanced down at my notes to hide my disappointment that no invitation had been extended. 'Last year, you were appointed chairman of the Council for the Encouragement of Music and the Arts?'

'Yes. It was set up to maintain standards in music, drama and the visual arts during wartime and to foster public participation. I think this is very important for morale in a time of war.'

'And the ballet ...?'

His face clouded. 'The future of ballet in Great Britain became uncertain after the death of Diaghilev in 1929. In 1930, Lydia and I were on the first committee of the Camargo Society. Lydia was in charge of choreography, and I was treasurer. We wanted to sponsor regular programs of ballet in London to fill the void left by the financial crisis.'

Keynes tugged at his earlobe as he spoke. 'I managed to keep the society solvent until it ceased active production in 1934 when its assets were turned over to become the Royal Ballet.'

'You mentioned your wife, Lydia Lopokova?'

'What would you like to know?' he asked, his voice now wary.

'Well, for a start, how did you first meet her?'

'Two months before the end of the first war, I went to Ballets Russes and saw her on stage. I immediately became an admirer and returned many times, visiting her backstage after her performances.'

'She was a very accomplished ballerina,' I acknowledged.

'She danced with Nijinsky,' he said, in a voice full of pride. She joined the ballet in 1910.'

'I believe you told Vanessa Bell that you were "very much in love".'

'Someone's been talking out of turn,' he said. 'Loppy was perfect in every way, so in August 1925, we married and, as a wedding present, I took her to see her family in Russia.'

'And Duncan Grant was best man at your wedding?' I tried to keep my tone neutral.

'That's right. 'We've remained close friends,' he said.

'Wasn't that somewhat awkward? In light of your past ...' I paused, not quite knowing how to frame the question politely.

Keynes smiled at my obvious discomfort. 'You mean our dalliance?' I nodded.

He gave a dismissive wave. 'I've never allowed such matters to inhibit my friendships. But you're not here to discuss my private life, are you? So, I suggest we move on to other matters. Economic policy, perhaps?'

'Of course,' I replied, feeling chastened. 'Did you always enjoy economics?'

'In the autumn of 1905, I attended economic lectures by Marshall at Cambridge. Marshall wrote to my father, encouraging me to take up a career in economics. And in the same year, I think, I wrote to Lytton Strachey about how much I enjoy economics and that I even might have some talent at it.'

'No doubt about that! But what about the First World War and your time in Treasury? You don't seem to think much of politicians.'

Keynes' contempt was obvious. 'In my experience, many of them are awful, stupid and inhuman, with minds and opinions as deplorable as their characters. It was unbearable seeing our youth going to be slaughtered in the trenches. A horrible nightmare.'

'I agree with you,' I said. 'And what was your role at Treasury?'

'It involved developing the system of applied war loans. In August 1914, the gold reserves of the Bank of England were limited, and the banks feared that the declaration of war would trigger a run. So, I suggested Treasury should encourage people to lend money to finance the war effort by issuing interest-bearing paper banknotes.'

'And when America came into the war, the US Treasury adopted a similar practice, I think.'

'That's right, the US Government issued so-called Liberty Bonds.'

'UK debt rose sharply during the war, of course ....'

'That's right. Our national debt increased from £650 million in 1914 to £7.4 billion in 1919, and Britain was forced to borrow heavily from America. I helped negotiate terms for Britain with her creditors.'

I consulted my notes. 'Towards the end of the war, you were appointed Companion of the Order of the Bath on the King's Birthday Honours list for your wartime work.'

He simply smiled and fiddled with his spectacles.

'But then I read you had sympathy for the Russian Revolution. Can you enlighten me?'

Keynes shrugged. 'I don't deny the contradiction. Although what frightens me personally is the prospect of impoverishment.'

'Perhaps that explains your commitment to preserving the market economy by making it more ... egalitarian?'

'The market economy can only survive if it earns the support of the public by raising living standards,' he said as if speaking to an auditorium of undergraduates.

'Moving on to the end of the war, in your capacity as a member of the British delegation to negotiate the Treaty of Versailles, you and Treasury began to consider the financial compensation Germany should pay other countries for the war.'

'That's correct,' he replied. 'We concluded that the struggling German economy could pay only £2000 million in reparations. An independent committee estimated that the cost of the war effort was £24,000 million and Germany should pay £1200 million per year, interest and principal until the capital was paid off.'

'But your proposals were rejected by the French.'

Keynes shifted in his seat. 'The French were implacable in their quest for vengeance ... for their pound of flesh and more. So I resigned and went home to write *The Economic Consequences of Peace*.'

I thumbed through my notebook. 'You said... let me find the quote... "If we aim deliberately at the impoverishment of Central Europe, vengeance... will not limp."'

'The Treaty was a deliberate recipe to bankrupt Germany. It was obvious that the burden of impossibly high reparations would breed political resentment with disastrous consequences.'

'You came under a lot of criticism when the book was published, I believe.'

Keynes smiled. 'It wasn't the first time my views were attacked and probably won't be the last. In this case, many people were critical because they believed German criminality should be punished. The terrible casualties we suffered during the war bred vindictiveness in the hearts of some.'

'In January 1922, you published your second work on German reparations, *A Revision of a Treaty*.'

'Yes, I documented the events that had transpired since the war and made a further argument for a reduction in payments by Germany. I foresaw that the imposition of draconian terms on Germany would sow the seeds of another war.' Keynes gave a doleful shrug. 'I derive no pleasure from being correct. This current war is a global catastrophe. Even worse than the first.'

I consulted my list of questions and realised that my time must be running out. I pressed on.

'In the mid-1920s, you criticised Britain's decision to return the gold standard to the pre-1914 level. Why?'

'Because the artificially high value of sterling made life difficult for British exporters,' Keynes explained. 'As it turned out, the return to the gold standard in 1925 was widely blamed for the prolonged deflation and high unemployment we experienced for the rest of that decade. And then, after the onset of the Depression, in September 1931, the government abandoned the gold standard and devalued sterling by 20 per cent.'

'So, in October 1929, Wall Street and other stock markets crash, heralding the Great Depression, and you argue that the correct course of action is to encourage spending and discourage saving. That ran counter to the prevailing wisdom of classical economics, which said thrift is required in hard times.'

'The engine that drives enterprise is not thrift but profit,' Keynes declared. 'The "classical" response was to rely on free markets to balance the budget – through tax increases and cutting government spending.'

'So you attacked Ramsay MacDonald's 1931 austerity budget, particularly the wage cuts for schoolteachers,' I said.

'I also criticised Macdonald's tax increases and his reduction in infrastructure and home-building programs. I was concerned that this would cause both deflation and unemployment to worsen. I argued that the government should do the opposite. And, in 1933, I continued to argue that the government should borrow money and undertake large-scale public works to stimulate the economy.'

'Apart from President Roosevelt and his New Deal, yours was a lone voice.'

Keynes smiled. 'I don't believe the final chapter has yet been written about my economic views.'

'In terms of those views, how important is your book, *The General Theory of Employment, Interest and Money*, in spreading your message? Do you believe your ideas are radically new?'

'That depends on your definition of "radical",' Keynes replied. 'But I think it's fair to say that my book will change economic theory and the way the world thinks about economic problems. The difficulty lies in not so much developing new ideas as in escaping from the old ones. When somebody persuades me I am wrong, I will change my mind.'

'I've heard that quoted,' I acknowledged. 'And you've found that not everyone is so … flexible?'

Keynes shrugged. 'Facts are what facts are.'

'In June last year, you were awarded a hereditary peerage, elevating you to a seat in the House of Lords.'

His face broke into a wry grin. 'That's right. You now have the honour of addressing Lord Baron Keynes of Tilton in the County of Sussex.'

I chuckled.

'But far more important is my place in the House of Lords, where I sit with the Liberal Party,' Keynes said while stealing a glance at his watch.

I picked up his cue. 'Right,' I said, 'it's getting late, and we've been talking for quite a while. I should be on my way. Thank you for your time, sir, I very much appreciate … ' But my voice dwindled into silence mid-sentence.

'What is it?' he asked.

'Nothing,' I mumbled.

He looked me square in the eye and said, 'Out with it.'

Still, I said nothing.

'Come on, we're old friends,' Keynes said with that same wry smile.

I felt my face grow hot and decided to throw caution to the wind.

'Well, there is something I'm curious about.'

'What's that?' he asked.

'I've always wanted to know why you ended our … relationship so abruptly.' I couldn't keep the bitterness from my voice.

The smile on Keynes' face was not unkind. 'How long have you been carrying this?'

I said nothing for several moments.

'Over the years, the thought comes and goes.'

He paused, looked at me and rubbed the side of his face. 'I didn't wish to hurt your feelings.'

I shook my head. 'Don't misunderstand; I'm not accusing you of anything. But it's something I never understood. It's been a mystery to me. I thought we were good together.'

He looked dolefully into my eyes. 'I made a mistake. Back then, I was young and didn't know any better,' he said bluntly. 'To be frank, I thought mainly of myself. I'm sorry.'

BERNARD MARIN

'I appreciate your honesty.'

He stood up and offered his hand, and then I took my leave. I felt the warmth and texture of his skin long after I'd left the library.

Endnote

This imaginary conversation with John Maynard Keynes is set in 1943 on the occasion of his sixtieth birthday. It relies on Keynes' own remarks, or close interpretations of them, to remain faithful to what he actually said.

During his lifetime Keynes was regarded as one of the most influential economists of the twentieth century. Regarded as the founder of macroeconomics, he created a revolution in economic thinking with his unconventional approach. His economic principles challenged classical economics and emphasised the importance of state intervention to control the 'boom' and 'bust' phases of an economy.

In 1927, while continuing his academic and bursarial duties at King's College, Keynes developed the first draft of his groundbreaking text, *The General Theory of Employment, Interest and Money*, which, after substantial work, was finally published in February 1936. He argued that full employment could be maintained only with the help of government spending, believing that unemployment occurs when people don't spend enough money. Lower spending results in demand falling further. This vicious cycle leads to job losses and a further drop in spending. Keynes' solution to the problem was for governments to borrow money and boost demand by pushing money into the economy. Once the economy recovered and began to expand, governments could pay back the loan and return to surplus.

At the time, proponents of classical theory argued that full employment could be reached by making wages sufficiently low that markets would eventually return to equilibrium '… in the long run'. Keynes responded by saying, 'In the long run, we are all dead.' This seemed to be typical of Keynes' trenchant wit.

Keynes was well respected, even by his detractors. Austrian economist Friedrich Hayek's economic theory was very different from Keynes'. Still, on Keynes' death, Hayek remarked: 'He was the one really great man I ever knew, and for whom I had unbounded admiration. The world will be a very much … poorer place without him.'

In the 1970s, Keynes' work was challenged by the stagflation of the decade and classical economists and monetarists, such as Milton Friedman, criticised his economic models.

In 1999, *Time* magazine listed Keynes among the 'Most Important People of the Century', and *The Economist* described him as 'Britain's Most Famous 20th Century Economist'.

Keynesian thought remains an important topic of debate to this day. The economic turmoil caused by the global economic crisis of 2007 led to a resurgence of interest in Keynes and his ideas. The debate between the Keynesian model of economics embraced by Bush and Obama (which favours bailouts and other government interventions to try to stabilise the market), and classical economic theory (which regards government intervention as detrimental and favours letting the market sort itself out with minimal government interference and regulation), is more heated than ever before.

Keynes had always wanted to be independently wealthy, but the path to riches was a rollercoaster for him. In August 1919, he had opened a trading account and begun speculating in the currency market. Trading on high margins, he initially made large profits. Less than a year later, he had lost a fortune and, in order to fund his losses, he was given £5000 by a financier and obtained a £1500 advance against future sales of *The Economic Consequences of Peace*, in which he predicted the catastrophic effects of the heavy war reparations on Germany.

By July 1920, he was back in the currency market, this time speculating successfully. Four years later, in December 1924, his assets had grown from near penury in 1920 to almost £60,000. He was, finally, a wealthy man by the standards of the day.

In 1937, Keynes suffered a life-threatening thrombosis of the coronary artery and moved to Ruthin Castle in Wales to rest. He was forced, perhaps for the first time in his life, to do little work. The following year, Keynes was fifty-five years old. Although continuing to suffer poor health, he resumed his work in Cambridge.

In July 1944, Keynes suffered a heart attack while in the US – he travelled there six times, including four times during the war. In December 1945, Keynes returned to Britain – his health having worsened due to fatigue. He suffered a slight heart attack in February 1946 while visiting the ballet at Covent Garden. In March, he suffered a severe heart attack on the train to Washington in the US, where he had gone for the inaugural meeting of the International Monetary Fund. On 21 April 1946, he died at home. He was survived by his wife, parents, brother and sister.

In his will, Keynes instructed his executors, Geoffrey Keynes (his brother) and Richard F. Kahn, to divide his papers into two parts – personal and economic. Geoffrey Keynes was to take responsibility for the former, and Kahn the latter. The will further directed that Geoffrey deposit his share in King's College library and that, on his death, ownership pass to the College.

Those personal papers included a detailed account of Keynes' many sexual encounters and incriminating correspondence with his lovers. Letters to and from Lytton Strachey and Duncan Grant were particularly amorous. In accordance with the terms of his Will, this catalogue of his paramours was released into the Keynes archive at King's College in 1982.

Source of photographs:

Wikimedia Commons – John Stuart Mill, original photo, London Stereoscopic and Photographic Company, c. 1870; Albert Einstein; Marie Curie, Tekniska museet; Sigmund Freud, by Max Halberstadt; Mahatma Gandhi. Alamy: Simone de Beauvoir; John Maynard Keynes; Mother Teresa.

About the Author

BERNARD MARIN AM was born in 1950 and graduated from the Prahran College of Advanced Education in Melbourne in 1970. He established his accounting practice in 1981 and currently works with the staff and partners of the practice as a consultant. Bernard lives in Melbourne with his wife, Wendy.

Shawline Publishing Group Pty Ltd
www.shawlinepublishing.com.au